Ed,

Happy

Black Sheep's Meadow

A. J. Mayers

A J Mayers

This is a work of fiction. Names, characters, businesses, organizations, places, events, and incidents are the product of the author's imagination or are used fictitiously. Any resemblance to actual persons, living or dead, or actual events is entirely coincidental.

Copyright © 2014 by A.J. Mayers

Edited by Mary Lou Lopez

Cover art by Dexter Brown

www.aj-mayers.com

ISBN 978-1-304-42679-6

This story is for my Aunt Frances and Aunt Patricia. Thanks for being my home away from home and inspiring my own strength through yours.

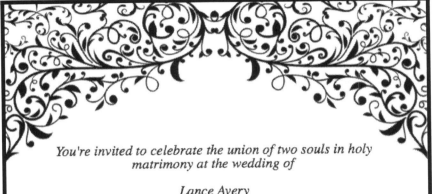

You're invited to celebrate the union of two souls in holy
matrimony at the wedding of

Lance Avery
and
Amy Aberdeen

Please join us in a celebration of their vows, and a
wonderful evening of merriment and marriage.

We request the honor of your presence at their marriage
on Saturday, the seventeenth of June two thousand and
fourteen at six o' clock in the evening

St. Austin Church
619 Lone Star Lane
Austin, Texas

Reception to follow.

Chapter One

A man wearing a black hoodie walked up the steps and into a cabin located in the Texas hill country. He pulled out a brass key from his black jeans pocket and quietly inserted it into the lock. At first, the door creaked when he pushed it open, so he decided to push slowly so it would not resound throughout the quiet cabin. There was a light on upstairs. Someone was home, and the man did not want the person upstairs to know he had intruded.

He closed the door behind him and twisted the lock. He pulled off his leather boots and set them by the side of the door. He placed the keys back in his pocket and tiptoed in the direction of the kitchen. It looked as if someone had recently finished dinner. The dishwasher in the cabin was running, which muffled some of the sounds of his movements in the kitchen.

The man kept on walking through the kitchen, which was very modern and updated for the twenty-first century, even though the cabin itself was built in the seventies. He walked into the living room and saw a piano. There were music sheets left on top of the piano, and they were scattered as if someone had been playing and did not bother to tidy up.

He passed the piano and headed over to the staircase, which was carpeted. He carefully walked up the stairs, yet a few of them creaked as he stepped on them. He would stop after every creak to ensure he had not been heard. His heart began to race. He thought that the sound of his heart pounding against his ribcage would echo throughout the hall. He heard shuffling upstairs. Someone was pacing back and forth. He heard the sound of a woman's voice talking, but there was no sound of anyone else responding to her conversation. It appeared that she was on the phone. There was laughter, and she sounded very happy.

The man clenched his hands and put them back in his pocket. He crept up slowly to the top of the staircase and arrived at the second floor. He could see a light shining through the room where the woman was. The door was ajar and the light lit up the dark hallway. Her voice was much clearer.

"I'm nervous and excited for our wedding tomorrow. I'm glad that alterations were completed for the dress. That was a nightmare. So many things went wrong with the planning, I almost felt like the universe was against us marrying," the woman said to someone on her cell phone.

The man's heart continued to beat. He looked through the door and saw the woman. She was in her lingerie. It was pink and lacey. She was a beautiful woman with wavy strawberry blonde hair, and bright blue eyes. She was not wearing make-up, yet she had a natural beauty. She was very thin and her body looked as though she spent time at the gym.

The man smiled mischievously, and his eyes took in every inch of her soft porcelain skin. Then a dark thought struck him. He had a flashback to his childhood.

A fourteen-year-old boy asked his mother if he could shop at a department store on his own. She nodded her head while on her cell phone with a friend, and gestured for him to be on his way.

The boy left the make-up store his mother was at and walked into a clothing department store. He went to the men's section and browsed through the shirt section.

"Can I help you?" a male attendant asked the boy.

"I'm just browsing. Back to school shopping," the boy answered.

"Ah," the man said. "What school?"

"Lady River High School," the boy replied.

"What's your name?" the attendant asked.

"My name is Lance," the boy responded.

"Hello Lance, my name is Marvin," the sales clerk said.

Marvin extended his hand for Lance to shake. Marvin held Lance's hand for a bit longer than seemed normal. Lance pulled his hand away awkwardly and Marvin smiled and stared into Lance's blue eyes.

"You have great eyes," Marvin said. "Are you at the mall alone?"

"My mom is at another store," Lance replied. "I'm alone here."

Marvin smiled and his eyes opened with what appeared to be excitement.

"Would you like me to help you find some great clothes that will make you look cool in school? Freshman in high school I'm guessing?" Marvin asked.

"Yes, it is my freshman year," Lance said. "Sure you can help me. Nothing too expensive though."

Marvin grabbed Lance by his arm and led him to another section in the men's department. He started to pull out various shirts without even asking what Lance's size was.

"Do you need to know my size?" Lance asked.

"I think I can figure out what your size is," Marvin said. "I've done this for a almost ten years. I started working for the company at twenty."

"So you are thirty now?" Lance asked.

"Ah, they teach you math in school then?" Marvin teased. "But let's not talk about my age. I'm very young...like you."

Lance smiled awkwardly and followed Marvin around as he showed him their jean collection.

"What kind of fit do you like?" Marvin asked. "Not baggy. That would be trashy. How about slim? You have a nice build."

"Um, ok," Lance replied.

"Perfect," Marvin said, and he snapped his fingers. "Now that we have jeans, how about underwear? Do you wear boxers or briefs?"

"Um, boxers," Lance replied nervously.

"Let's do boxer briefs," Marvin replied. "They are all the rage. They fit snug and keep everything nice and together."

Lance felt his face go read in embarrassment.

"No need to be shy," Marvin said. "I wear boxer briefs too. It's nice to have something that will keep my parts safe and sound."

Marvin winked at Lance and then grabbed his arm again and led him to the dressing room.

"Ok it's time to try on your clothes. I think you should try on these pair of shorts," Marvin said while handing Lance a pair of athletic shorts. "And...I want to see how they fit on you. No need to be shy. We're all men here."

Lance went into the dressing room and tried on his pair of shorts. He looked at himself in front of the mirror and smiled. He did like the way they looked on him.

"Show me," Marvin said.

Lance timidly opened the dressing room and Marvin walked in and closed it behind him.

"You look amazing," Marvin said turning slightly red. "Would you like to get my employee discount? It's fifty percent off. I can get it on all your clothes here. These are name brands. You will look really great."

"Um, I mean if you want," Lance said feeling his heart beat nervously. "That's, er, very nice of you."

"Good," Marvin smiled, and he put his hand on Lance's shoulders and began to gently massage them. "In return, maybe you can do me a favor?"

Lance came back to reality. He felt goose bumps run up and down his spine as he peeked into the room where the woman was lounging around in her underwear. He felt aroused by her presence and the excitement of her not knowing he was looking at her almost naked. He had sexual thoughts charge through his mind of running into that room and cutting off her underwear with the pair of scissors he saw on her nightstand.

Lance focused his thoughts on his motives for the night and what he wanted. He crept back away and walked down the steps to the living room. The timing was perfect because he heard the door to the woman's bedroom fully open, and the hallway lights were turned on shortly after.

"I'm going to tidy up the kitchen a bit," the woman said into her cell phone. "My parents are going to use the cabin next weekend and I want it to be clean. You know how OCD they are."

The woman appeared in the kitchen wearing a pink robe. She smelled like roses. Her scent permeated the air. Lance took a whiff of it and felt his blood rushing through his veins. His pheromones were tickling his senses and giving him powerful urges.

The kitchen opened up into the living room, which offered places to hide. Lance ducked behind the couch and watched as the woman took out the dishes from the dishwasher and placed them back in their respective cabinets.

"I'm so tired Jill," she said to the person she was on the phone with. "I need my beauty rest for the big day tomorrow. Are you ready to be my lovely maid of honor?"

Suddenly the woman screamed and dropped a plate on the ground. It shattered into hundreds of pieces on the tile floor.

"Oh my God!" she yelled into the phone.

Lance stood up and was about to say something when the woman began to laugh.

"I'm so dumb," the woman said on the phone. "I'm sorry if I scared you. I just thought I saw someone in the bushes outside looking into the window in front of me and staring at me. I think I imagined it."

Lance's heart began to race again. He kept debating in his mind on how he was going to approach her. He wanted to feel her body. He wanted to put his hands all over her soft skin. He wanted to smell her hair. He wanted to take the robe off her.

"I'm going to let you go, Jill," the woman said. "I'll see you bright and early at the salon. Kisses."

The woman ended her call and set it on the kitchen counter. She opened a closet and pulled out an old broom and dustpan. She began to sweep up the pieces of the broken plate.

Lance stood up. She had her back to him. He pulled out the chair in front of the piano and reached for the music sheets. It was the music for the *Wedding March*. Lance smiled and his heart began to race. He had made up his mind on what he wanted to do with the woman; he was going to take a risk. He opened the piano and placed his hands on the correct keys and began to play the song.

The woman turned around so quickly and dropped the broom. She was about to yell, but when she saw Lance her jaw dropped. The fear in her eyes escaped her and turned quickly into shock.

"LANCE!" she yelled. "What the hell are you doing here?"

Lance took off his hoodie. He had blue eyes and jet-black hair. His face was clean-shaven, and slightly freckled. He was twenty-nine years old.

"Hi Amy," Lance said. "I'm sorry for the surprise, sweetie."

"You can't see me the night before!" Amy snapped. "It's bad luck! You're not supposed to see me until I walk down the aisle tomorrow."

Lance ignored her and kept playing the song. He then turned to her and winked.

"Walk down to me now, honey," he said. "And feel free to take off your bath robe."

"You're so stupid," Amy said and her look of anger turned into a happy smile.

"You know you want to laugh," Lance teased.

"I'm mad at you," Amy said, but she began to laugh. "You scared the shit out of me."

"I love you," Lance said.

"Stop playing the *Wedding March*, silly," Amy said, and she walked over to Lance and sat next to him. She gently pushed off his hands. "Save that for tomorrow."

They exchanged in a long passionate kiss. Lance put his hands on the ties of her robe, but Amy slapped them off.

"You should go," Amy said. "We're getting married tomorrow. This can wait until tomorrow night."

"You have me all hot and bothered," Lance said.

"That's your fault for coming here unannounced and scaring the crap out of me," Amy said.

"Looks like you did not need me to scare you," Lance said pointing at the broken pieces of glass on the floor.

"I imagined something in the bushes and it scared me," Amy admitted.

"I can see that," Lance teased.

"Promise me you won't see me until I walk down the aisle?" Amy insisted. "You need to leave now, and I don't want to see you until then. Is that ok?"

"Fine," Lance said, and he kissed Amy on the lips. "I love you. I'm the luckiest guy in the world. I can't wait to marry you."

"Me too," Amy said. "Now get the hell out of my parents' cabin and let me have my last night alone."

"Ok," Lance sighed, and he put his copy of the cabin key on the kitchen table. "See you tomorrow."

"Bye," Amy smiled.

Lance walked out of the front of the cabin and closed the door behind him. Amy reached for the broom and continued to clean the broken pieces of glass on the floor.

By mid-afternoon the next day, the Texas heat had reached a sweltering point. The wedding was being held at St. Austin Church. Amy was fanning her freshly done make-up in the church holding room where she was waiting with her bridesmaids and maid of honor.

"This Texas summer heat is horrendous," Amy said to her maid of honor Jill.

Jill had short, platinum blonde hair and bright green eyes. She was wearing her pink bridesmaid dress and matching high heels.

"You chose to have your wedding in June," Jill said. "I blame you for these hot flashes I'm having."

"Actually, Lance picked the date. Thanks for being a trooper," Amy said. "Has anyone seen my mother?"

"I haven't," Jill replied.

Amy picked up her cell phone from the sofa in the holding room. She found "mom" in her contacts and pressed the iPhone's screen to initiate a call.

"Mom, where are you?" Amy asked impatiently.

"I'll be over to your room soon dear," her mother said.

In another room in the chapel, Amy's mother, Grace, was speaking to Lance's best man Edward.

"You haven't seen or heard from him at all?" Grace asked angrily. "And you are just telling us *now*?"

"Lance's family did not want to cause a panic," Edward said.

Edward was in a black tuxedo. He had dark brown short hair, olive skin, and brown eyes. He was sweating heavily under the stress of their missing groom.

"They've been trying his phone," Edward continued. "It keeps ringing and ringing. He's not even answering any text messages."

"Can you call Lance's parents and get them on the phone for me?" Grace asked. "This wedding cost my husband and I an arm and a leg. The ceremony is starting in twenty minutes!"

Grace looked like she was on the verge of a nervous breakdown.

"Just don't tell Amy yet," Edward insisted. "Maybe Lance is planning some kind of surprise. You know he likes to make an entrance."

"Right," Grace said thinking back to when Lance proposed to Amy a few months earlier. "That proposal was quite a surprise indeed. You know, you might be right."

"Right," Edward said. "No need to worry yet."

Grace appeared to have been comforted by her thoughts.

"I'm going to see Amy in the holding room," Grace said. "Let the festivities commence as is. Do not tell anyone. I'm sure he will show. It would be unlike him to get cold feet."

Grace walked out of the room and up a hallway down to another room in the church.

"What's the matter?" Amy said automatically as soon as her mother walked in. "I know that face. Something is wrong."

"Dear, there is nothing wrong. Let's get your wedding party ready," Grace said while not meeting eyes with her daughter. "Jill—ladies—follow me to the entrance of the chapel."

One by one, the bridesmaids walked out of the room so Amy could be left alone in the holding room. She was beginning to feel nervous. She looked over at the clock and felt as if that particular clock was moving faster than normal. She reached for a glass of champagne that Jill had left for her and drank it all in one gulp to calm her nerves.

"There's still no sign of him," Edward whispered to Grace a minute before the pianist that was hired for the wedding was to begin playing the *Wedding March*.

"Mr. and Mrs. Avery!" Edward called to Lance's parents as they walked into the church.

They both looked flushed. Mrs. Avery's make-up was blotching because of sweat and Mr. Avery's white hair looked tousled from a run.

"I hope this is not one of his tricks," Mrs. Avery said. "And call me Marissa, Edward."

"He is nowhere on the church grounds," Mr. Avery said.

"George," Grace said to Mr. Avery, "do you have a spare key to his apartment? You could go in and look around."

"I don't," George replied. "Amy does however, but I did not want to ask her for it because it would worry her. I don't want her to worry unless there is a real reason to."

"But Lance is not here and—" Grace began but the *Wedding March* began to play on the piano. "There is every reason to worry. It's show time!"

"Shit," Marissa said. "Something must have happened to him."

"Cold feet?" George suggested.

"Amy knows her cue to come out of the holding room," Grace said. "When she comes out and sees that we are all still here, she's going to be heartbroken and upset."

"We need to cancel or at least hold off the wedding," Marissa said. "He's not here. I do not know what happened."

A door down the hall opened and Amy walked out holding up her wedding dress slightly so that it would not drag on the ground. She had a look of concern when she spotted her family and the wedding party's worried faces.

"What's happening?" Amy said. "Why isn't anyone in there?"

"It's Lance..." Edward began.

"What happened?" Amy cut in.

"He hasn't shown up," Edward said while not trying to meet her eyes.

"Is he calling off the wedding?" Amy asked with tears forming in her eyes.

"Dear," Grace said, "we haven't heard from him all day. He's missing."

"What?" Amy exclaimed. "Oh my God! What if something happened? Who was the last one to see him?"

"Me," Edward said. "We parted ways after the groomsmen met for a drink at a bar down the street from where we had the rehearsal dinner."

"Wait, he came over to the cabin last night," Amy said. "He surprised me, but I kicked him out and told him he was not allowed to see or be with me the night before our wedding."

"We need to find out if he made it home though," George said.

"Mr. Avery, I have a spare key," Amy said.

"I know," George replied. "That's what I was going to ask you next."

"Grace," Marissa said, "Come with me and we will address the guests and let them know that we are temporarily holding off the ceremony until we find Lance."

Marissa received a text message on her phone. Her eyes went blank and she began to shake with nerves as she walked out with Grace in the direction of the chapel.

"I hope he's ok," Amy said grabbing onto Edward's arm.

She reached for her cell and tried to call Lance. When there was no answer, she ended her call and began to cry.

"Let's get you out of that dress and we'll go to Lance's apartment," Jill said. "Edward, why don't you come with us?"

Amy changed out of her dress and walked out the back of the church so as not to see any of the wedding guests. Edward drove his sedan to the back alley of the church and picked up Jill and Amy who was now wearing a sundress and flip-flops. Her mascara had run from crying and subsequently made it look blotchy underneath her eyes.

"This isn't like him," Amy kept saying over and over on the car ride to Lance's apartment in Austin.

"I know," Edward said. "I haven't been able to reach him. Neither have his parents. Maybe something serious happened?"

"I hope he's ok," Jill said nervously with her hands holding Amy's tightly.

They arrived at Lance's apartment, which was near Lake Austin. Amy pulled out the spare keys from her purse and ran up the stairs to the second floor of the complex. She nearly ran into two movers who were carrying a couch down the stairs. They let her pass through. Once she arrived at Lance's apartment door, she hastily inserted the key and opened the door. The apartment looked clean and undisturbed. Jill and Edward followed her into Lance's room. Hanging on the doorknob of his closet was Lance's tuxedo still in the bag from the department store from where he purchased it.

"He never got dressed," Amy said, tears forming down her eyes.

"I don't think he ever came back home last night," Jill said.

"What do you mean?" Amy asked.

"His car is not in the carport. I can see where he parks from his window," Jill said. "And his alarm clock is blinking like it went off, but was never shut off. The sound has stopped on its own accord, but if you press this button—"

Jill pressed the button on top of the alarm clock, and the time stopped flashing on and off.

"There," Jill said. "He didn't sleep here. His bed isn't even undone."

"Maybe he made it in the morning?" Amy said hopefully.

"I don't know," Jill responded.

"Do you know the password to his laptop?" Edward called from Lance's bedroom.

"I think it's just my name," Amy said.

"You're right," Edward replied. "I'm in."

"What are you looking for?" Amy asked when she walked into Lance's bedroom.

"I want to see if—aha his emails have not been checked either," Edward said. "His bank account is logged on as well. There's been no activity with his debit card since the bar from last night. He didn't try to skip town then."

"Should we call the police?" Amy asked.

"We probably should," Jill said.

"I'll get them on the line," Amy said, and she ran out of the room and dialed for the police on her phone.

"Hey, he's also logged onto his iPhone finder app," Edward said. "We can track him!"

"We can?" Amy said with her phone in one hand, and then she ended the call with the police. "They did not answer yet."

"Ok, it's searching for his GPS," Edward said after clicking the "track my iPhone" button on Lance's laptop application.

"Anything?" Jill asked nervously.

"Holy shit!" Edward said, and he stood up from Lance's desk chair so quickly, he knocked over a desk lamp. "He's at the church!"

"What?" Amy and Jill said in unison.

"Did he not get the memo on what time the wedding began?" Edward said in disbelief.

Amy instantly dialed Lance on her cell, but after a minute of no answer, it went straight to voicemail.

"Why is he not answering?" Amy asked in frustration.

"The dot on the map showing his location is still," Edward said. "He's not moving. Let's haul ass back to the church."

The sun was beginning to set when they finally arrived back at the church. All the wedding guests had dispersed from the church leaving it eerily quiet and dark.

"It's closed," Jill said.

"The door is unlocked!" Amy said after reaching for the doorknob to the entrance of the church.

They walked into the church and entered the chapel. All the pews were empty and a soft orange glow from the setting sun was the only source of light illuminating the space.

"What the hell?" Edward said when he spotted an out of place object down the aisle at the alter.

"Is that a coffin?" Amy asked in shock.

"Are they planning a funeral tonight in lieu of the canceled wedding?" Jill added in disgust.

"This is some kind of joke, right?" Amy said while beginning to cry.

"I'm going to try Lance again," Edward said reaching for his phone.

There was a muffled ringtone coming from the direction of the coffin. Edward ended his call and the ringtone stopped. Amy, Jill, and Edward shared a look of concern, and without a word, they made their way down the aisle that Amy should have walked down earlier in her bride's dress.

"There's something on top of the coffin," Jill whispered. "A rose."

When they were ten feet away from the coffin, they saw the rose. It was on top of a music sheet. Amy recognized the music on the sheet as the *Wedding March*.

Amy began to cry. Her heart was racing with what she felt she was about to discover. Amy pushed the rose and music sheet off the coffin carefully. It fell to the ground. A muffled ringtone was coming from inside. Amy sniffled a sob and opened the coffin.

Chapter Two

Six Months Earlier...

Lance and Edward walked out of a jewelry store in downtown Austin with smiles on their faces.

"She's going to freak out at dinner tonight," Edward said. "She has no idea that you are going to propose to her tonight at her birthday dinner."

"I'm so excited," Lance said waving his shopping bag around that contained a rose gold engagement ring with three diamonds that he purchased for his girlfriend.

"You sure you are ready though?" Edward teased. "Marriage is till death do you part."

"Well, considering my last girlfriend—whose name I will not speak—she's the whole package. For one, she's normal."

"Agreed," Edward said. "Onward and forward with the future. And it has been almost three years that you have been living back here in Austin. I have to say you've adjusted well."

"Yeah," Lance said. "I don't miss Seattle at all."

"So, I'll see you at the restaurant. She thinks she is meeting you at seven-thirty, right?" Edward asked.

"Correct," Lance said. "We need to be there by seven. She has no idea all of our friends and family will be there."

"Amy's gonna flip out," Edward said. "I hope she says 'yes'. Ha!"

"I'll see you later," Lance said, and he walked over to his car that was parked at a meter.

Lance arrived at his apartment complex and parked in his carport. He stepped out of his car at the exact same time as one of his neighbors. The neighbor was holding two heavy-looking grocery bags with one in each arm. She used her foot to close the door to her car.

"Do you need some help with those?" Lance asked.

"Oh," the woman, who looked to be in her late twenties said. "That would be kind."

"Here, let me grab both of them," Lance said reaching for her grocery bags. "What floor are you on?"

"The second floor in this building," she said. "I'm Dana."

"My name is Lance. Lance Avery," he said. "Did you just move in here?"

"Actually, yeah," Dana said. "I moved in last week. This was my first trip to the grocery store."

"No way," Lance said. "I see you have Washington license plates."

"Oh yeah," Dana said. "But I moved here from California."

"I see. Are you originally from Washington?" Lance replied. "I used to live in Seattle about three years ago, then I moved back here to Austin."

"No," Dana replied. "The car belonged to an old friend. I bought it off her."

"Got it," Lance said. "Well, I'll follow your lead."

"Of course," Dana said, and she sounded flustered.

Lance followed Dana up to her apartment. Her apartment was three doors down from Lance's apartment. Lance followed her into her kitchen and set the bags down on her countertop.

"That was so nice of you, neighbor," Dana said with a big smile. "I'm new in town. Maybe we could grab coffee some time?"

"Sure. Yes. I mean why not?" Lance said awkwardly because he was getting the impression that Dana was flirting with him.

"You free tonight?" Dana asked. "I have nothing going on."

"Actually, I'm not," Lance replied. "I'm having a surprise dinner party for my girlfriend."

"Oh," Dana said suddenly. "That's very sweet. I just got out of a relationship myself. That was part of why I moved. Well, that and I got a wonderful job offer that I could not refuse."

"Where do you work?" Lance asked.

Dana was quiet for a few seconds before responding, "I work for a tech company that specializes in mobile apps."

"That's a booming business here in Austin," Lance said.

"Yeah, it really is," Dana added. "And for freelance I'm a make-up artist. I do weddings and what not."

Lance made a mental note to ask her about her wedding services for the future.

"Well, I need to unpack my stuff and whip up something for dinner. Let's do coffee soon," Dana said. "I really am going stir crazy not having many friends. I figured knowing a neighbor would be nice. My parents would be happy to know there's at least someone friendly where I'm living now."

"Of course," Lance said. "I'll stop by some time this week and we can grab some coffee down the street. There's a great place on the lake that I really love called Beethoven's."

"I looked at reviews on Yelp," Dana said. "Been dying to check it out. Sounds like a plan."

Lance bid farewell to Dana and went back to his apartment to shower and change for Amy's birthday dinner. He stood in front of the mirror debating on how he should style his hair.

"Combed back? To the side and parted?" he said to himself.

Lance decided to part his hair. He added a bit of hairspray once his hair was combed to his liking, and he put on his favorite button shirt and tie. His heart began to race with nerves. He would be asking the love of his life to marry him.

"The love of my life..." he muttered aloud and his mind went into an old memory.

The weather kept Lance indoors and on his computer in his one bedroom apartment in Seattle where he could stay dry. The grey skies and the downpour of rain outside made him miss his hometown of Austin, where it did not rain as much. He was instant messaging with his then girlfriend who was at work.

"I'm sorry about our fight yesterday," Lance typed into the chat box. "I love you Claire."

"You have been so selfish with our relationship," Claire typed back. "I'm so tired of you not meeting my expectations when clearly I've let you know what they are. I need you to be there for me. I know right now you don't have a job and that's tough, but you'll get a new job soon."

"I've been so depressed," Lance typed onto his keyboard and pressed enter. "It's not easy to sit here in my one bedroom apartment during the day with nothing to do. I'm going stir crazy. I feel so useless. It has been several months of unemployment. I keep dipping into the trust left behind for me by my dad. It will eventually run out. I keep spending money out of boredom. I'm not happy in Seattle. It rains too much, and I don't have anyone else here but you."

"You have my friends," Claire wrote back.

"YOUR friends. Not mine," Lance typed.

"Then you should meet people and get out," Claire wrote. "However, stay off dating sites and apps. That's not a good way to meet people. People on those sites only want to date or hook up."

"Sometimes people actually use it to make new friends," Lance wrote.

"Are you kidding me? How would you feel if I was still using the dating sites I had before we met?" Claire wrote in haste. "You would feel betrayed."

"That was months ago," Lance wrote. "Can you let it go? I'm done using those sites. You know that. I'm not cheating on you."

"I'm afraid you will leave me," Claire said. "I don't want you to have to move back to Austin."

"If I don't find a job here, I'll have no choice," Lance typed.

"I see long term with you," Claire wrote instantly.

Lance thought for a second before he punched the keys to type his next message.

"I do too," he said. "I see us getting a house together, a dog, and maybe having kids. I want to grow old together. Get married. I want all that, but right now it is not realistic. I'm having a hard time. I know I probably have to move back to Austin."

"I know of a job opening at a friend's company," Claire wrote back. "I'll e-mail you the job description. We'll get through this. We always do. You and I will stay in Seattle. We'll be happy."

"Ok," Lance wrote back trying to feel hopeful.

"You're the love of my life," Claire said.

"You are too," Lance wrote back. "It would hurt me so much to leave you."

Lance shook his head as if the memory he had just relived could be easily erased and forgotten. He looked at himself in the mirror with a feeling of disgust. He had not seen his ex-girlfriend Claire Carpenter in nearly three years since their break-up and his move from Seattle.

Lance's phone rang, and he answered it.

"Hey baby," he answered.

"Hey," Amy's voice answered from the other line. "I'm starving. Seven-thirty seems so far away."

"I know, but I need to finish up some documents for work," Lance replied.

"Are you still at the bank?" Amy asked.

"Yeah," Lance lied.

He had taken the day off from his job so that he could purchase Amy's engagement ring.

"You finance people tend to work late," she teased.

"Our work lives are so enthralling though," Lance said sarcastically. "I'm doing some amazing formulas with Excel."

"You can tell me about it at dinner," Amy said. "It's my big three-O. Thirty years old today."

"You're so old now," Lance teased.

"You'll be thirty in a few months, so shut up," Amy laughed.

"Don't remind me," Lance said. "Ok, so meet me at Mr. Lobster's Bar and Grill at seven-thirty. See you then!"

"Love you. Bye," Amy said, and she hung up.

The January winter Texas skies were grey that day. Thunder was clapping in the distance and the weather reports forecasted a high chance of rain, which Lance had learned over his car's radio. As Lance pulled off the freeway down the exit to the restaurant for Amy's birthday, it began to rain. The drops started to fall on the metal hood of his white BMW sedan softly. Within minutes, the drops were pounding hard, and the asphalt of the road went from dry to flooded in seconds.

"Oh great," Lance muttered as he turned on his lights and windshield wipers.

Lance locked his car and zipped up his jacket over his button shirt. He put on the hood of the jacket, as he had not thought to bring an umbrella. He walked into the restaurant and realized he was the first one to arrive from his party.

"Hello. I'm checking in for the reservation under Lance Avery," Lance told the restaurant's hostess.

"Mr. Avery, right this way. I'll lead you to the private room."

Lance followed the hostess into the back private room. There was one large table with about thirty seats. There was a giant cake in the middle and plates set and ready to be served on. The room had a rustic feel to it. There were even Christmas lights hanging from the ceiling that had not been taken down from the previous holiday month.

"It's perfect," Lance said to the hostess.

"Wonderful," she replied. "I'll make sure to send your party guests here. Enjoy."

As the hostess walked out, Amy's friend Jill Evans walked into the room.

"Lance!" she said. "I can't wait! Amy is going to be so excited."

"I'm nervous," Lance said.

He pulled out the ring and wrapped it in clear plastic wrap. He then proceeded to put it under the frosting on one corner of the birthday cake he had ordered for the event.

"I'll cut the cake and she will get the end with the ring hidden in it," Lance said.

"I hope she doesn't choke on it," Jill teased.

"Me too," Lance laughed nervously while fixing the frosting with a butter knife and covering the ring. He attempted to make it look like a hole had not been dug into it.

The guests began to arrive right around seven sharp. Amy's mother Grace arrived with Lance's parents, Marissa and George.

"Mom! George." Lance said. "I'm so glad you could make it."

"Can I have a private word with you?" George asked Lance.

"Um, sure," Lance said.

The two men stepped outside of the restaurant to a back smoking patio. George pulled out a cigarette and lit it. He took one puff and then spoke to Lance.

"I know I can never replace your father," he said, "but I'm trying really hard here. You did not sound so enthusiastic to see me walk in here."

"I apologize," Lance said awkwardly. "I'm still trying to get used to my mother being married to my uncle. It's plain weird, if I may be blunt."

"Well it has been almost a year now since we exchanged vows," George said. "She's very happy. You know that. She's been open with me since we started dating two years ago about the depression she went through when your father—my brother—Jeremy passed away. She was alone for so long raising you during your teens. How old were you again when he passed?"

"I was fourteen," Lance said. "Why are we talking about this now? I'm about to propose to my girlfriend at her surprise 30th birthday party. I don't think going down memory lane and talking about one of the hardest parts of my childhood is something I want to get into."

"I'm sorry," George said. "I don't want you to think it is weird."

"She probably only wanted to date you because you remind her of my dad," Lance said sternly. "It's disgusting to me. You were Uncle George growing up. Now you're stepfather George. I don't support it and my mother knows that. But we can all fake smiles. Everyone else in that room is. Our families are too, but don't think for a second that when we all turn our backs, they aren't talking shit about this situation."

"It's been sixteen years since your dad was killed," George said. "You can't expect your mother to be single forever. And I'm sure it was nice that she could keep her married last name."

"Cause you shared the Avery name with your brother—my dad," Lance said through gritted teeth. "Don't ruin this day for me. You are boiling my blood."

Lance's mother Marissa walked out onto the patio.

"What are you men talking about?" she asked suspiciously.

"How weird it is that you married Uncle George," Lance snapped. "Grandpa and Grandma Avery must be turning in their graves."

"Lance," Marissa said sternly, "don't you dare talk to me that way. Not after everything I did for you."

"Right, or everything dad's money did for us," Lance said, and he knocked an ashtray off one of the patio tables.

"I did not raise you to have this temper," Marissa said clenching at her shawl in shock while her diamond bracelets dangled against each other.

"No you didn't," Lance said on his way back towards the door to the restaurant. "The nannies took care of me while you were away on business. Now if you will excuse me, I have a life to make for myself and my future wife will be walking into this restaurant in about five minutes."

Lance opened the door into the restaurant and slammed it shut.

"I think it's best you try to warm up to him a different way," Marissa told George. "And perhaps on a night when he is not planning to propose to his girlfriend. He seems rather stressed."

"Shhh!" Jill told everyone in the room. "I saw her walk in. The hostess is about to bring her in."

"You ready?" Edward, who had arrived while Lance was having a heated conversation with his mother and George, said to him after clapping him on the back.

"Yeah," Lance said nervously.

The lights in the room were turned off. The door opened and framed in the doorway was Amy. The lights went on instantly and everyone yelled in unison.

"SURPRISE!"

There was applause and cheers and Amy's name being chanted by all the party guests.

"Oh my God!" Amy said putting her hands to her mouth. "Lance, you sneaky little monkey!"

Lance and Amy exchanged a passionate kiss to the sound of jeers and whistling in the crowd. Once they broke free of the kiss, they sat down in their seats and waiters brought dinner for all the guests.

When dinner was over, Lance stood up to address the party.

"Who is ready for cake?" Lance asked.

Everyone clapped and murmured in anticipation.

"It's your favorite," Lance said to Amy. "Red velvet."

"Yum!" Amy replied.

Lance reached for a knife and cut the corner of the cake that the wedding ring was hidden in. The room became quiet as they waited with bated breath. Amy looked around at the room as they were all staring at her. Lance began to sweat bullets around his forehead. His heart began to beat against his tie.

"Try it babe," Lance said.

Amy gave him a suspicious look and put her fork into the cake. She scooped up a piece of the moist red velvet cake, then pulled out the ring from the frosting and unwrapped the plastic off it. Chills shot up and down Lance's spine as tears began to pour out of the corners of her eyes.

"Oh my God!" she yelled with the ring in her palm high enough for the whole room to see.

Lance knelt down on one knee and took the ring off her palm and grabbed her other hand.

"Amy Aberdeen, will you marry me?"

Chapter Three

The room was quiet. The silence was broken by a small cough in the background and the awkward shuffling of dinnerware on someone's plate.

Lance stared intently into Amy's eyes. They began to glisten into what looked like tears. Her look of shock from when she first saw the ring disappeared as her lips formed into a wide smile.

"Yes!" Amy uttered into the silent room.

The entire party erupted into claps, cheers, and hollers. Lance took a sigh of relief and put the ring on Amy's finger.

"Thank goodness you said that," he lovingly whispered to her and ended his sentence with his lips pressed against hers.

"Mr. and Mrs. Future Avery!" Edward cheered.

Later in the evening, Lance's mother Marissa asked Lance for a private word in the patio where he had had a heated conversation with George earlier.

"Can you try to be peaceful with George?" Marissa told her son as they stepped out onto the cold patio.

Lance could feel his nose turn red from the chilled air. He rubbed his hands together for warmth and debated what he would tell his mother next. After a few tense minutes he spoke up.

"I grew up knowing him as my uncle," Lance said harshly. "That's all he will ever be. He's not my stepfather."

"I'm not telling you to consider him as one," Marissa snapped. "I'm only asking for respect. At least give *me* some. I've been through enough. Your father's death still haunts me to this day. I want to close that chapter of my life and start a new one."

"Dylan didn't even show up," Lance said through gritted teeth while clenching his cold hands.

"I'm sorry," Marissa said, and her expression of frustration disappeared into one of sorrow. "Your brother had to work late at the bank."

"He works for the same bank as I," Lance said. "There's no way he has to work later than I. He's at the same branch."

"Don't be so hard on him," Marissa said. "He's the one who helped you find a job. In this economic climate, you get what you can take. Business has been rough, even for me."

"You're still driving your nice Mercedes," Lance said sarcastically. "And your new penthouse probably doesn't have as great a view of downtown Austin as you would have liked, but I'm sure you are dealing and getting by."

"Lance!" Marissa snapped. "I've had enough of this. You are lucky to have what you have because of all the hard work your father and I put into giving you a good life. And George has done well for himself as well, picking up the slack after your father's death to help with our realty business."

"Father's slack?" Lance said. "That's cheap. Even for you to say."

"I'm sorry," Marissa began to cry. "I did not mean it that way. I want you to be happy. Amy and her family are lovely. We are lucky to have them in our lives."

"You're happy because she comes from money too," Lance snapped. "My last girlfriend—Claire—was not as privileged and you never really accepted her. You never made an effort to meet her because she wasn't established financially."

"I never said that," Marissa gasped.

"You did not have to," Lance spat, and he stormed through the door of the restaurant. "It was written all over your face."

Lance walked into the restaurant and closed the door shut. Marissa was left with her jaw open in shock at the final words that Lance said to her.

Jill, Amy, Edward, and Lance were the last ones to leave Mr. Lobster's Bar and Grill. It was almost midnight when the hostess bid them farewell and locked the restaurant's doors behind them as they walked onto the parking lot.

"It's starting to drizzle," Jill said. "I thought the rain was over."

"Maybe it'll turn to snow," Amy said hopefully. "Just for my engagement day."

"Wishful thinking in this unpredictable Texas weather," Lance responded. "Oh, by the way Edward, you'll be my best man."

"Without question!" Edward said and winked.

"Jill, you're my maid of honor," Amy said, and she gave Jill a tight hug.

Jill looked like she wanted to break out in tears, but she contained herself. The look of happiness on her face was more than words could express.

Lance and Amy took off in separate cars, but Amy followed Lance's BMW up the road in the direction of his apartment.

"I'm excited for them," Jill told Edward as he walked to her yellow Volkswagen Beetle. "Two years of dating. That's enough time."

"It is," Edward agreed. "So much better than his crazy ex."

"You met her, right?" Jill asked.

"Two or three times," Edward said. "When I went to visit Lance in Seattle during the time he was having difficulty adjusting to the city."

"Was she really crazy?" Jill asked. "That's what he tells Amy."

"Um, well," Edward said scratching his head. "I'm not at liberty to really talk much. There were parts of her that were acting out of hurt. I think maybe both were at fault in the breakup, but I can say—and don't you dare tell Amy or Lance—that Lance didn't handle the situation well. He could have done more for the poor girl."

"It *was* his fault, huh?" Jill added.

"The past is the past," Edward said. "She won't be a bother to him anymore nor has he heard from her since a few months after the breakup. I think everyone has moved on just fine."

"Since we are on the subject of secrecy," Jill continued, "can I tell you something. I received a weird email a few days ago with what appeared to be a fake email address created for anonymity. Can I show it to you?"

"Yes, of course," Edward said.

Jill scrolled through her iPhone until the email pulled up on the screen. She handed it to Edward. He took the phone and put it close to his face. The glow of the phone lit his face blue in the dark parking lot.

Dear Jill,

I can't tell you who I am, but I want you to know that your friend Amy is dating someone with deep, dark rooted issues and secrets. Be wary. A friend of a friend once dated Lance, and he betrayed her trust. I would not be surprised if he has other girlfriends on the side. Do whatever you can do make sure that Lance does not succeed in proposing.

"It's not signed by anyone," Edward said. "This is beyond creepy. You need to tell Lance. For all we know, it could actually be Claire—his ex. It wouldn't be the first time she sent fake emails to friends of his."

"Interesting," Jill said.

29

"The weird thing is," Edward said. "Even if it were her— and she has no way to keep up with Lance's life as he blocked her out of all his social media—how would she have known he was about to propose to Amy?"

Edward thought about his statement for a minute before continuing.

"Only people who were invited to the party tonight would have known it was a surprise engagement, and even they were all sworn to secrecy. Maybe it was someone in our circle? Who else dated Lance that would know someone that was at the party?"

"I know of two girls who are friends of Lance's that were in attendance," Jill said. "I know he dated these two girls briefly after his Seattle girl and before he started dating Amy again."

"Again," Edward said more to himself than to Jill. "It's so crazy that Lance actually dated Amy for five months way before he moved to Seattle or met Claire. I guess it's fate that years later the stars aligned for them."

"It's late," Jill said while stretching and yawning. "Time for bed.

"Get some rest. Wedding planning galore is ahead for you in the next six months," Edward teased.

"They haven't picked a date though, have they?" Jill asked.

"By tonight Lance will have proposed a six month engagement for them, and he'll let Amy know that he actually has a church picked out too. It's symbolic or something."

"Oh," Jill said. "Six months is not a lot of time. Damn."

Lance parked his BMW under his carport, and then got out of his car in haste so that he could beat Amy at opening her door. Lance then opened it for her.

"Aw, how sweet my handsome fiancé," Amy blushed.

Lance and Amy walked hand-in-hand up the steps to his apartment. He glanced over at his neighbor's apartment and saw that the lights were on. He pulled out his key and unlocked his door. A rush of warm air met their faces as they escaped the cool winter night into Lance's warm and cozy apartment.

Lance pulled Amy by her hips and brought her closer to him. He caressed her back and began to unzip her dress.

"Let's take this to your bedroom, shall we?" Amy said seductively.

Amy pulled Lance by his tie and led the way into his bedroom. She pushed him onto his bed and untied his black dress shoes and threw them to the ground. She pulled off his tie and began to unbutton his shirt from the top down until his chest was exposed.

Amy admired Lance's well-toned physique. She rubbed her hands over his abs and then reached down for the buttons on his slacks.

"You are going to be an amazing wife," Lance panted as his heart began to race.

"I will make you very happy," Amy smiled and then she pulled off his pants leaving Lance in his boxers.

Lance had a flashback in his mind for a few minutes to a memory of when he and Claire shared a passionate moment outdoors in a meadow just outside of Austin. He was reliving the first time he took off Claire's clothes and her red hair fell down to her shoulders. Her soft, silky porcelain skin glistened with sweat as they lay on the grass after an intense first night of passion. Lance enjoyed every second of it and believed it would only be a one-night stand as she was leaving home for Seattle the next evening.

Lance put his arm around Claire and began to spoon her. For only having just met, they shared an intense chemistry. They cuddled for a long while. The high he was on continued for the rest of the evening. His sweat that drenched his entire body from their sexual encounter began to dry and cool off as the outdoor breeze caressed his skin on that hot summer night. Claire spent the rest of the night at Lance's apartment that evening after he asked her to go home with him.

"Morning," Lance said when Claire stirred at sunrise.

31

"Hi," she said, and then began to kiss Lance feverishly as if they had not seen each other in days.

"Want to go at it again?" Lance teased.

"Oh, yes," Claire said and she wrapped her naked body over Lance.

"I thought I lost you for a moment," Amy said to Lance as she rolled off his sweaty body and got up to use the restroom.

"What do you mean?" Lance asked.

"You always look at me during sex with these intense eyes," Amy said. "It felt like you weren't there with me at that moment this time."

"I was," Lance lied. "So much was on my mind about our future. I was imagining how we would be doing this in a shared house one day."

"That would be nice," Amy said. "I guess we need to pick a date now, don't we?"

"June 17," Lance said.

"This June?" Amy asked while reaching for the bathroom door handle. "As in six months from now?"

"It's a special day to me," Lance said.

"Why?" Amy said.

"It changed my life and brought me closer to you," Lance said.

"We started dating in December, two years ago," Amy said.

"We ended things with each other the first time we dated a few springs ago during June," Lance said. "I thought I lost you then when we fought and ended our relationship, but it was only the beginning."

"How is that special?" Amy asked curiously.

"It just is…for me," Lance said. "I'm tired, let's go to sleep."

Amy walked into the restroom and shut the door. Lance turned over on his side and pulled up his covers. When Amy came back to bed she put her arms around Lance and squeezed him tight.

Lance tossed and turned throughout the rest of the night. Around four in the morning, he got up to go to the kitchen to get a glass of water. He looked out the window of his living room and thought he saw a silhouette move on the other side. He walked up to the curtains, which were drawn shut, and opened them. There was a woman walking down the steps with a dog on a leash. Lance recognized the woman as his neighbor Dana.

Lance put on a jacket that he found in his closet and quietly walked outside for fresh air. He walked downstairs and saw Dana sitting on a bench near the carport.

"Fancy seeing you out here this late," Dana said.

"Or early," Lance replied. "Depends on how you look at it. What are you doing up so early?"

"I could not sleep," Dana said. "So I decided to take my pup Marley out."

Lance knelt down to pet the Yorkshire Terrier, which was jumping around with excitement.

"Cute dog," he said.

"Thank you," Dana replied. "I'm trying to get her used to our apartment complex since we just moved here."

"I see," Lance said putting his hands in his pockets.

"How was the dinner?" Dana asked.

"It was good," Lance said with a big smile. "I proposed to my girlfriend. She said yes."

"Congratulations," Dana said while sending a text message on her phone.

"You are texting someone this early in the morning?" Lance asked.

"Nosy, aren't you?" Dana teased. "It's a good friend of mine. She was supposed to meet me for lunch at this new spot tomorrow, but I told her some things came up with work."

"Oh, which restaurant?" Lance asked.

"The Pork Belly," Dana said. "You should stop by sometime. It's delicious."

"I've heard of it," Lance said. "I have never tried that place."

"So, why are _you_ up early?" Dana asked.

"Couldn't sleep," Lance said. "I have sleep issues. And issues in general I guess."

"What kind?" Dana asked. "Sorry if that's asking too much. We only just met."

"I've just been dealing with things from my past," Lance said. "The issues always surface when I make commitments. I'm sorry I should be telling this to a therapist, not you."

"That's fine," Dana said. "I actually know someone in town who is a therapist. I could refer you to her. It's always nice to have someone to talk to."

"I don't know," Lance shrugged. "Maybe not right now. I'll let you know if I change my mind."

"I strongly recommend it," Dana said. "It does wonders. I'll give you her card. Here."

Dana pulled out a business card from her wallet. She handed it to Lance who accepted it and read the name on it.

"Rose Finley, MFT," Lance read aloud. "Thanks. If I decide I need a therapist, I'll call Rose."

A few days later, Lance walked into the bank where he worked. He went into his office and found his brother waiting for him.

"Dylan!" Lance said in surprise.

Dylan was wearing trendy black glasses and had a five o' clock shadow. He had the same features that Lance had, yet his eyes looked tired. There were shadows under them as if he had not slept in days.

"I'm sorry I've been MIA lately," Dylan said. "Some weird things have been happening to me. I keep getting these blocked calls in the middle of the night. I keep screening them, but it's driving me nuts. I'm having the phone company look into it, but they said they can't trace it."

"I'm sorry to hear that," Lance said. "Who did you piss off?"

"Maybe a client," Dylan said. "I have no damn idea. Anyways, I wanted to apologize for missing the engagement dinner. Mom said it went well."

"It did," Lance said. "Wish you could have made it."

"I'll make it up to you," Dylan replied. "Let's do dinner later this week. I've got to run upstairs. I have a meeting in ten minutes, but I wanted to catch you before."

"Ok," Lance said. "Talk soon."

Lance shuffled some documents on his desk and turned on his computer. When the screen came on, he smiled at the desktop wallpaper of himself and Amy hugging from a trip to California that they took the previous year.

Someone in the hall yelled, "Excuse me, can I help you? Excuse me!"

A frail-looking man walked into Lance's office. He was a balding Hispanic man. The man was holding a cup of what appeared to be hot coffee judging by the steam it was letting off from the top. He was wearing a torn up shirt and jeans. He had on sandals that looked a size too big. The man appeared homeless and his eyes were blinking fast.

"Are you him?" the man asked.

"Him, who?" Lance asked, pushing his chair back and reaching for his phone. "Who are you?"

"Are you him?" the man repeated.

"I'm sorry sir, but this is a place of business. You need to leave," Lance insisted.

One of the bank's security members walked into Lance's office and put his hands on the man's shoulder. The man shook a

35

bit out of fright and then threw his coffee at Lance. The coffee splashed all over his desk, computer, and Lance's white button shirt. It was scalding and once it made impact with Lance's skin, he jumped up and yelled.

"What the hell!" he roared.

The security yelled for help and handcuffed the homeless man. Lance reached for a water bottle from his drawer and poured it on his skin that was burned from the coffee. The homeless man was immediately apprehended by police officers and taken outside and into a police car.

"Are you ok Mr. Avery?" the security officer asked.

"I'll live," Lance said flustered. "I'm going to have to leave to change into clean clothing. Who let that vagrant in?"

"He just walked in sir," the officer replied. "We will make sure that does not happen again. He could have been a customer."

"With clothes like that," Lance said angrily, "I don't think he has two cents to deposit."

Lance pulled out his phone and texted Amy to meet him for lunch after he had finished changing.

"Let's eat at The Pork Belly," he texted. "I have a story to share with you about what happened to me at work this morning."

Amy responded almost instantly. "Yes, I'm starving. I'll see you there. I hope it's exciting news."

"No, not the promotion I want," Lance wrote back. "A crazy man walked into the bank. I'll explain over lunch. See you soon."

Amy got into her car and adjusted her rearview mirror. She noticed that her glove box was opened and had been ruffled through as if someone had been in there, yet there was no sign of a break in or anything missing.

"Weird," Amy said to herself. "Maybe I left it open?"

Amy pulled out of her workplace's garage and proceeded through a back road in a residential area to avoid the lunch rush traffic. The street was practically empty except for a black sedan behind her. When Amy turned a corner to get onto a different street that would take her to the restaurant she was meeting Lance at, the car behind her followed. She looked into the rearview mirror but could not see who was driving. The windows were deeply tinted. Amy picked up speed and so did the car behind her.

Amy reached for her phone and proceeded to dial Lance.

"I think I'm being followed," Amy blurted when Lance picked up.

"What do you mean?" Lance said through the car's speakerphone.

"I just turned a corner, and this black car did the exact same turn. It has been following me through this neighborhood," Amy said. "I'm scared."

"What neighborhood are you in?" Lance asked.

"Westlake," Amy replied. "Oh my God it's speeding up now and tailgating me."

"Call the police," Lance insisted.

"Lance, this car is getting closer and closer," Amy cried.

"You need to hang up with me and dial 911," Lance insisted.

The car was about five feet away from Amy's rear bumper. She hit the gas pedal to accelerate faster. The sedan then moved onto the opposite lane until it was parallel to Amy's car. Amy looked over at the car and could not see through the dark tint. She sped up again and was now going over seventy miles per hour in a thirty mile per hour residential street. The black car was keeping up seamlessly with her.

"What is this person trying to do?" Amy cried into her car's speakerphone.

"Try to lose it," Lance pleaded.

Suddenly, the sedan sideswiped into Amy's car. She screamed and lost her connection with Lance. Her car veered off the road and crashed into a streetlight, which broke and fell onto the roof of her car. The black sedan sped off and disappeared onto another street and out of sight.

Amy moaned and tried to yell for help. She searched for her seatbelt to unbuckle herself, but before she could, her airbags deployed and pushed her back against the seat.

In the distance, she could hear sirens blaring and people shouting. Her vision became blurred and all that was left was darkness and silence.

Chapter Four

Police tape, traffic cones, an ambulance, and several police cars blocked off the street in the neighborhood where Amy crashed. Lance arrived at the scene of the accident and rushed out of his car.

"That's my fiancé!" he shouted as the paramedics lifted Amy onto a stretcher.

An officer nodded his head and allowed Lance to cross the police tape to run to Amy's side.

"Is she going to be ok?" Lance asked worriedly.

"Yes sir," a female EMT replied. "The airbags saved her, but she has a small concussion. We need to take her in for some X-Rays in case she broke something."

"She was on the phone with me," Lance said. "She told me that someone was tailgating her. It was a black car. It ran her off the road. Were there any witnesses?"

"As a matter of fact there was," the officer that allowed Lance to come to Amy's side said.

"I'm officer Grant," he said. "Here is my card. This has my cell phone number. I'm going to have the witness come into the station for questioning later on in the day. We would like you and your fiancé to come when she is out of the hospital to talk to us. The witness said that a black car did in fact intentionally run her off the road at high speeds. May I quickly ask you if you know of anyone that would try to intentionally hurt your fiancé?"

"I don't," Lance said racking his mind. "I have no idea who would have done that. She has no enemies that I'm aware of."

"Ok," Grant said. "We will also check any nearby stop light surveillance video to get a license plate number."

"Grant!" a female officer yelled. "We found the car. It was left abandoned by the lake. It was a reported stolen yesterday."

"Does that mean you won't be able to get an ID of who it was?" Lance asked.

"Chances are slim since the car was stolen," Grant said sounding defeated.

"Well, we'll be speaking soon," Lance said. "I'm going to follow her to the hospital."

Amy came around a few hours later. She was lying in her hospital bed with Lance, Jill, Edward, and her mother Grace by her side. When she looked at them, she began to cry. She shifted up slightly on the bed so that she could sit up.

"Your X-Rays came out fine. Nothing is broken," Lance said. "How are you feeling?"

"Like I wrapped my car around a streetlight," Amy said as tears streamed onto her bed sheets. "Who would do that?"

"The cops are going to find out," Jill said with her arms crossed. "That maniac will pay."

"I'm so glad you are ok," Grace said with relief. "Your father and I spoke on the phone. He's concerned, but I'll call him back tomorrow. It's already night time in China where he's located right now on business."

"Ok mom. And thank you for coming to my aid, Lance," Amy said putting her hand on Lance's and squeezing it tightly.

"I'm so glad you are ok," Lance said kissing her forehead. "And alive."

Lance looked out of the hospital window and thought back to a car accident he had a few years back.

Lance was driving around Seattle and running errands for a film producer for which he had been hired to be a personal assistant. The producer was filming a documentary in Seattle about a local rock band that had made it to mainstream radio. Lance was still new to Seattle and could not find his way around with out the GPS in his car. He had been trying to enter the address on the GPS screen of his car, when he passed a stop sign by accident and hit a truck. The entire hood of his BMW was smashed in.

"Shit!" Lance cursed.

There were two men in the little pickup truck that he hit. They were speaking in Spanish and sounded angry.

"I'm so sorry," Lance said. "Don't worry I can help pay for the damage. No need to call the insurance."

Lance was pretty sure that the men did not have insurance, and he was not even positive if they were legal residents. He gave him his number and said that he would get a check out to them.

"No need to call police," Lance assured them.

"Policia?" one of the men said. "No policia. You pay for scratch. No policia. No."

"Yes I will pay," Lance said. "No policia."

The men took off in their truck, leaving Lance alone in a random neighborhood with a busted car. He called Claire on his cell phone.

"Babe, I just had a really bad car accident," he said. "I'm going to need to get towed to the nearest car shop."

"Where are you?" Claire asked.

"I'll send you my GPS in a screenshot text," Lance said.

"Ok I was just about to go into work, but I'll come get you baby," Claire said lovingly. "I'm glad you are ok. That's scary. I'll come get you and we can go to the BMW dealership to get a rental for you."

"Thanks Claire," Lance said.

Lance sat in his car and waited for Claire to arrive. He was fighting the urge to cry and call his mother. He knew she would be mad and would be the one who would help him pay for the repair.

The doctor walked into Amy's room and gave them the all clear for her to go home.

"She has bruising and a few scratches, but everything else seems fine," the doctor informed Lance. "Take it easy for the rest of the day Miss Aberdeen."

"I will," Amy said softly.

The following morning, Lance and Amy found themselves sitting in the waiting room of the Austin Police Department for about half an hour before Officer Grant was able to finally meet with them.

"Thank you so much for coming," Grant said while brushing his handlebar mustache. "Follow me."

Lance and Amy walked hand-in-hand as they followed Grant down a hallway to an office. His cowboy boots echoed with every step he took. When they arrived at the office, they found a sign outside of it that read "Detective Ross."

The man sitting in the office was wearing a navy blue tailored suit and had red hair and green eyes. He was clean-shaven and well maintained.

"Mr. Avery...Miss Aberdeen...this is Detective Ross," Grant announced his office guest.

"Hello," Detective Ross said. "Please take a seat."

Lance and Amy sat on a couch that was in front of the detective's desk. Officer Grant pulled up a wooden chair that was up against the wall.

"The witness said they could not get a description of the driver," Grant said. "The surveillance cameras we checked were not helpful either because the car's windows were really tinted."

"Dammit," Lance said under his breath.

"The next step is to really dig deep into who could have possibly wanted to run you off the road ma'am," Detective Ross said.

"I don't have any enemies," Amy said.

"This could have been a completely random incident," Detective Ross said, "however, the car was abandoned and whoever was driving it left on foot. The car was stolen and the windows were tinted. Someone went through the trouble of not getting caught. My gut is telling me that this was strategically planned and not random."

"Your name came up in a police report of an incident that happened yesterday morning, Mr. Avery," Grant said.

"What?" Amy said curiously.

"Oh, right," Lance said. "My bank had to file a police report because I was attacked by a homeless man who came into the bank and threw coffee at me."

"The security said that the homeless man was asking you something along the lines of 'are you him.' Is that correct?" Grant asked.

"Yes," Lance said. "He seemed delusional."

"The homeless man said he was paid to put a coffee hit on you," Grant said. "He was found with a twenty dollar bill in his pocket."

"Really?" Lance said sounding nervous. "Who put him up to it?"

"He said he was sworn to secrecy or this person would find him and kill him," Grant said. "He sounded really scared. I think he'll crack and we can get an ID on this person. It's very strange that two isolated incidents happened to both of you only a few hours apart on the same day."

"Do you both share a common enemy?" Detective Ross asked.

"What about Claire?" Amy said slowly turning to Lance who returned a shocked look.

"What about her?" Lance asked back.

"Who is Claire?" Detective Ross asked with peaked interest.

"Claire Carpenter," Amy said. "I've never met her, but she was Lance's ex girlfriend. She cyber stalked Lance after they broke up and he moved to Austin from Seattle where they had dated for over a year. Somehow through a photo on Instagram on one of Lance's friend's pictures, she figured out he had started dating me and she even found my email address. She wrote me an email posing as someone other than herself telling me that Lance had given her a sexually transmitted disease and that my life was in danger. It was all crazy talk obviously. And it was scary."

"My mother and I put a restraining order on her," Lance said. "She was harassing me for four months after we broke up and I moved here. I cut off all communication. She was even emailing my mother even though my mother had never met her."

"Well, this is a possible lead," Grant said. "When does the restraining order end?"

"Beginning of June of this year," Lance said.

"Is it possible she's doing it again?" Amy asked. "Could she have been the one who nearly ran me off the road?"

"I haven't heard from her since the restraining order was put in place," Lance said. "It would be illegal for her to break it."

"Is it possible to get some kind of protective watch on us?" Amy asked. "Just in case this happens again?"

"Until we have proof that yesterday's incident was actually personal, I can't get approval to do that," Grant said. "Mr. Avery, may I ask why your relationship with Claire Carpenter ended?"

"Um," Lance shifted uncomfortably. "She was very jealous and did not allow me to make my own friends in Seattle. I essentially lived there to please her and be her full time boyfriend. I was depressed and wanted out. She became upset with me and got drunk one night and said horrible things to me that made me nervous. I moved out of Seattle while she was away one weekend for work and vowed to cut off communication."

"I see," Detective Ross said staring intently into Lance's eyes. "Well, I can do some checks on this Claire woman and see if I find out anything. I assume she still lives in Seattle?"

"I would imagine so," Lance said, "but it has been nearly three years since I've last seen her."

"We will look into this, and keep you both posted," Detective Ross said. "Here's my card should you notice anything suspicious."

Amy and Lance walked out of the station and into the parking lot where Lance's car was.

"I think Claire has moved on," Lance said. "There's no way she even knows where I live or work. That's crazy to think she could still be stalking me."

"You never know," Amy said. "It's crazy to think she actually knows who I am and we've never met."

"Let's just drop it," Lance said. "I'll take you to the car rental place and then I've got to go see my mom. She wants me over to have dinner with her and George. This should be really awkward."

"Ok," Amy said and she was about to get into Lance's car when she backed away suddenly and ran in the direction of the station.

"What is it?" Lance asked in shock.

"Sorry," Amy said hurriedly. "I saw a bee. I'm deathly afraid of them."

"Oh," Lance tried to hold back laughter. "I think it's gone now."

Lance arrived at his mother's downtown condo. He left his car at the valet and took the elevator to the penthouse level. When he arrived at the door, he saw a package sitting on top of the doormat. He picked up the box and knocked on his mother's door. Marissa answered and smiled at the sight of Lance.

"Good to see you son," Marissa said. "How's Amy holding up?"

"She's still shaken up, but she's a strong girl," Lance said. "Here...there was a package for you."

"Oh I wasn't expecting anything," Marissa said. "It might be from your aunt. Leave it on the kitchen counter."

Lance walked into his mother's magnificent penthouse condo. The walls were all glass and it overlooked downtown and the lake. The sun was setting in the distance and the sky was turning pink and burnt orange.

"Ah, hello there engaged man," George said to Lance.

Lance returned a forced smile and nod, then placed the package on his mother's counter.

"What's for dinner?" Lance asked.

"My meatloaf special," Marissa said. "It's going to be quite the treat."

"I do love your meatloaf," Lance said honestly.

"George dear, could you run to the room and bring the candles I left on my vanity. I want to light them up for the dinner table," Marissa said.

"Sure thing," George replied, and he left the kitchen to enter their bedroom.

"What's that foul smell?" Lance asked.

"I'm getting a whiff of that too," Marissa said, and she began to sniff the kitchen air in order to find the source of the pungent smell that began to permeate the condo.

"I smell that too," George said when he walked back into the kitchen with a handful of candles. "Even over the scent of these."

"It might be that package," Lance said. "Maybe there was food in it and it perished?"

"There's no return address either," Marissa said. "But your aunt always forgets to leave one."

Marissa pulled out a pair of scissors and sliced open the taped edges of the small brown box. She reached for the flaps and opened the box. As soon as the lids were open, the foul smell grew stronger. Marissa let out a scream and recoiled from the box as if it were about to attack her.

"What the hell?" George had a look of disgust. "That's a cow's heart!"

Inside the box was a raw and bloody heart from a cow. There was no note and only a bit of rolled up parchment paper that was used to pad the inside of the box.

"Who would do such a thing?" Marissa asked with anxiety.

Lance shifted uncomfortably. There were several abnormal occurrences in the last forty-eight hours. His only thought was that these events were some how related.

"I'll throw it down the garbage chute outside," Lance said.

Lance walked out of the condo and into the hallway. He found the garbage chute and tossed the entire box with the raw cow's heart.

"Disgusting," he said. "But Claire can't be doing this. She may have stalked me, but she never mailed me anything."

When Lance returned to his mother's condo, he found her drinking straight whiskey from a glass while sitting on her couch.

"I've lost my appetite," she said. "I'm going to call my lawyer tomorrow. I think this might have been sent from a client that we did not close a deal for because they could not get financing. The person was angry with me even though it was not my fault."

"Oh," Lance said hoping that his mother's guess on who the culprit behind the delivery of the cow's heart was not who he originally believed it to be. "Well, I'll just take some of the meatloaf to go. I'm hungry, but I'm also very tired."

"Yes, help yourself," Marissa said.

Lance arrived at his apartment. He was about to unlock his apartment door when he saw Dana walking up the steps with her dog.

"Hey neighbor," she said cheerfully.

"Hi," Lance said in a monotone voice.

"Everything alright?" Dana asked.

"It's been a weird couple of days," Lance said. "I'm not really having a good day."

"Did you call Rose?" Dana asked. "I'm sure she could help. You should call her. I insist."

"Now?" Lance asked.

"Yeah," Dana said. "She'll take your call. She works all the time. She takes her last client at 10:00 pm. It's only eight now."

"I guess I will," Lance finally decided that the crazy last two days of his life required some kind of mental health release.

"I'll shoot her a text to let her know to expect your call," Dana said. "Oh, and can we do coffee soon?"

"Oh, right," Lance said. "How about next week? I've got my plate slightly full right now."

"Yes, no problem," Dana said.

Lance walked into his apartment and sat down on his couch. He pulled out the therapist's business card from his wallet and dialed her number on his phone.

"Hello?" Rose answered her phone after one ring.

"Hello Rose, my name is Lance Avery," he said. "My neighbor Dana said she's a good friend of yours."

"Oh yes!" Rose said. "As a matter of fact she texted me a second ago saying you were going to call. How can I help you Lance?"

Lance felt comforted by Rose's voice. It was very friendly and warm. He had a good feeling in his gut that going to therapy was a step in the right direction after procrastinating from going to it after his break up with Claire.

"I would like to schedule an appointment to come in," Lance asked. "When is the earliest I can see you?"

"Let me look over my schedule. I'm going to put you on hold for a second," Rose said.

"Ok," Lance replied.

"Ok, I'm back," Rose jumped back on the line after a few seconds. "How about tomorrow morning?"

"I get into work at nine," Lance replied. "Are you available at seven?"

"I am," Rose said cheerfully. "I'll put you down. Make sure to bring your insurance card if you have one. I look forward to meeting you."

"Thank you," Lance said.

Lance spent the rest of his evening cleaning his apartment and watching TV. The show he decided to watch was a series about a substance-abusing nurse, which he started watching a few years ago because Claire had introduced it to him. Lance's thoughts fell on a memory of his high school days during a time he began to frequently use cocaine months after his father was killed. He had been clean for several years, but those days in high school still haunted him. He made a mental note for himself to talk about it in his therapy sessions.

Chapter Five

Lance arrived at an area of downtown where there were several older houses that were turned into businesses, shopping boutiques, and law offices. He walked up the steps of a wooden green house that had "Rose Finley Counseling" written on the awning of it. He had arrived for his first therapy session, and his heart was beating against his rib cage more out of fear than nerves. He had always avoided going to therapy even after his break up with Claire because he did not have his own medical insurance at the time, and he did not want to ask his mother for money. When he was in high school he went to two sessions of therapy, but decided to stop going.

"Here goes," Lance said to himself before taking a deep breath.

He walked into the building and sat on a sofa in the waiting room. He picked up one of the tabloid magazines on the coffee table to keep him occupied as he waited for Rose to finish with her current client. He could hear muffled voices coming through the door that led to the office.

An old woman with shopping bags walked into the building a few minutes later. She had a confused look on her face.

"Excuse me sir," she said to Lance. "I seem to have walked into the wrong building. I'm looking for Sally's Salon. Do you know which way it is? I could have sworn this was it."

"I'm sorry, I don't," Lance said. "I can look it up on my phone using the maps application."

The woman looked at Lance as if he were speaking in another language. Lance assumed she was not technology savvy. He typed in the name of the business that the woman was looking for and a pin dropped in the exact location they were in.

"Hmm," Lance said. "That's odd. You are at the right place—oh there's a note on the information section of Sally's Salon's Google information. It appears as though the shop closed and has moved to 4th street. That's two blocks south. We're on 6th."

"Oh," the old woman said. "I haven't had my hair done in a while, so they must have moved since I last made a visit. Thank you sir. May I have the Salon's new address number?"

"446," Lance said.

"Thank you," the woman said, and she walked out of the building.

Ten minutes later, the door to the office opened. A man walked out and shook the hand of Rose Finley. The man nodded at Lance on his way out. Lance locked eyes with Rose. She was a very beautiful woman with strawberry blonde hair that reached to her shoulders, but she currently had her hair in a simple ponytail. She had green eyes and very tan skin. She was wearing a business skirt and a matching blazer jacket. She wore red high heels that made her look taller than she was.

"Hi," Lance said nervously as he tried to avoid gazing below her chin as she was very toned and fit.

"Ah, you must be Lance Avery," she said with a warm smile. "Thank you so much for coming by. That was so nice of Dana to offer my services to you. I just moved into town like her and I'm trying to get a good pool of clients."

"Where did you move from?" Lance asked.

"Los Angeles," she replied. "Everyone says that Californians are making an exodus to Austin. This city is amazing, and I really love it. I found this adorable place for lease. It used to belong to a hair salon, but they wanted more space so they moved down the street."

"Well, I like what you've done with the place," Lance said. "The style is very modern contemporary. That's very much my style."

"Thank you," Rose said. "Won't you come in and have a seat?"

Lance followed Rose into her office. Her walls were aligned with bookshelves and they were stacked high up to the ceiling.

"I read a lot," Rose said following Lance's gaze. "The human mind is both my profession and a hobby. I love studying it. And studying how people work."

"Well, I have a lot of characteristics that need studying," Lance said jokingly.

"Please, take a seat. Make yourself comfortable," Rose said.

Lance sat on a couch that was directly across from Rose's leather armchair. She crossed her legs and pulled out a pen and a pad of paper.

"So what brings you here," Rose said with her soft and warm voice.

Her beauty took Lance by surprise because he envisioned a therapist who would be old and average looking. Rose was about Lance's age and it made him feel nervous.

"So many things," Lance mumbled. "Lately, there have been some strange events in my life that have brought me to remember a past relationship with an ex girlfriend that I never had closure with. I recently became engaged, and I also have a strained relationship with my mother and her new husband."

"Well," Rose said, "we have a whole hour. I would like to start with your family background. We can move on from there."

"Ok," Lance said and he crossed his arms.

"You mentioned you don't get along with your mother's husband," Rose said. "I imagine your parents are divorced then?"

"My father was killed when I was fourteen," Lance said. "I believe there was foul play in his death. He was found in a full suit in a pool at a house he was trying to sell. He was a real estate agent. The autopsy revealed that there was a high alcohol blood content in his system, and it was first thought he might have slipped into the pool while drunk, leaving him to drown. My mother and him were not divorced officially, just separated. They owned the business together, so it made things difficult with work. His assistant Victoria, who was half his age, was beginning an affair with him. She was also the last person to have seen him alive. My family thinks that she got him drunk and drowned him. She was arrested at first, but then let go because there was not enough evidence."

"Does this woman still live in Austin? Assuming this happened here?" Rose asked.

"She does, but she's in hiding and doesn't leave her house," Lance said. "She's keeping a low profile."

Rose was silent for a few minutes as if she were contemplating what to say next. Lance continued.

"My brother Dylan and I found out over breakfast. We got a call from one of my dad's business managers. He called our house and my mother answered it. She was running late that morning, which I'm thankful for because she would have been the one to find his body as she was supposed to head to that house he was found in. It was really hard for us to deal with. My mom had to carry on caring for us and raising us alone. She had the help of hired nannies to watch over us even though my brother and I were in high school. The glorified housekeepers were there to make us dinner, wash our clothes, and clean the house because my mother had to travel around Texas as she began to expand the business to keep up with the wealthy lifestyle she wanted to maintain. Even though we were all given a huge trust from my father's death, she was a smart woman and knew that to stay rich she would have to keep working and making more money. I do credit her on that and not becoming a house mom living off my dad's money."

"Do you feel that if your dad was still around, your home life would have felt more normal?" Rose asked.

"God yes," Lance said. "My dad was very traditional. We always ate meals together. When my parents were happily married she carried on with traditional motherly tasks even if we did have maids from time to time. I know she was depressed from his passing because they were trying to work things out even though they were separated. Then again, there was that woman who was allegedly having an affair with him. She was torn between not having closure with the affair, and anger about the uncertainty of how to deal with her feelings."

"How did you go about continuing with your everyday life?" Rose asked.

"Not well," Lance said. "It was shitty. There were articles all over the newspaper and stories splashed on the local news stations. Everyone at school looked at me with pity. Then to top it off, I was sexually abused at a mall a few months later by an older man."

Lance stopped immediately. He had never told anyone about the incident at the shopping mall he had in a fitting room with one of the sales associates who coerced him into doing a sexual act with him.

"Sexually abused?" Rose asked looking very intrigued by Lance's statement.

"It was by this man named Marvin," Lance said. "He worked at a department store in a mall here in town. I was shopping with my mother for back to school clothes, and I ventured off on my own. Marvin was very nice to me. He helped me find some trendy clothes so that I would look cool in school. He followed me into my dressing room and said that if I let him give me oral sex, he would give me is employee discount. I was scared and he was playing mind games with me. I felt so ashamed."

"Why didn't you tell your mother or someone at the store?" Rose asked. "He could have gone to jail. In the state of Texas, because you were fourteen, it would have been considered statutory rape."

"Rape?" Lance said. "I never thought about this incident as rape."

"Sexual abuse. Child molestation. Rape," Rose said. "Call it whatever you want, but the effects on someone at that age are very detrimental."

"I was too embarrassed," Lance said. "I was afraid of the whole world finding out. This incident didn't happen once though."

"He made more advances in the future?" Rose asked.

"I went back two more times," Lance said. "We used the family bathroom in the department store as it was a single private stall. He locked me in. I was beginning to think I was homosexual. At least the guy wanted me to think that. He really messed with my head, but I knew that I was attracted to girls at my school."

"What did he make you do in the bathroom?" Rose asked.

"Oral sex...and he touched me," Lance said, and then he began to cry. "I'm sorry, this is the first time I'm saying this out loud. The hurt is coming back to me at full force."

"There, there," Rose said, and she passed Lance a box of tissues.

Tears rolled down Lance's face. He felt disgusted with his terrible memories. He could imagine himself in that stall at that moment. He could see it in his head as if it had only happened yesterday.

"I never saw him again after the third time," Lance said. "It was the only time I was ever with another man...sexually. I did kiss another boy in high school one time. It was a friend, and he ended up coming out later in life, but I think a part of me wanted to experiment to figure out if that was the lifestyle that was normal for me. I realized it was not, and I ended up dating this girl for two years."

"The effects of child sexual abuse never really go away," Rose said with a serious tone. "Victims are haunted by it into adulthood. That man had a power over you. Some people experience the inability to trust, depression, lack of sexual desire, and some people have suicidal thoughts."

"I experienced all of those," Lance said. "Sometimes even now. I tried to kill myself when I was seventeen."

"Because of what happened to you?" Rose asked.

"I was experimenting with drugs. Mainly pot and cocaine," Lance replied. "I tried so hard to fit in with the cool crowd at school. Drugs were recreational at all the parties I would go to. One night I stole Vicodin from a friend who had broken his leg. I enjoyed the high from it, but I become addicted. One night I had taken too many pills and hits of cocaine. I was so depressed. My girlfriend found me sick on my bathroom floor. My mother was away and the nanny had stepped out to buy me alcohol since I was under twenty-one. I was taken to the hospital. I could have died that night, and I really wanted to. I hated how my mother was never around. My brother Dylan was the favorite and excelling at everything in college. I wasn't happy. I was that poor little rich kid who had everything, but lacked affection and love."

Lance was silent for a few seconds. He held back more tears, but he looked like he was at the point of breaking down. Rose eyed him intently with concern.

"You're very brave to talk about this," Rose said. "I want you to know that. We can work through all the hurt together. We can do one session a week. It will take time, but therapy is the best method to coping and healing from these major incidents of your childhood trauma."

"Yeah," Lance agreed. "I feel like a weight is slowly lifting off my shoulders."

"Exactly," Rose said. "And everything is in complete confidence. You mentioned earlier that there were recent events that happened to you that you said triggered you to remember an ex girlfriend?"

"My fiancé was run off the road by a car," Lance said. "Intentionally. On the same day a homeless man threw hot coffee on me at work. Apparently someone paid him to do it, the police learned. But the homeless man didn't give them any specifics on who could have put him up to it. Someone is intentionally trying to hurt my girlfriend and me. And my mother received a raw cow's heart in a package that was left at her door. I think it is my ex girlfriend Claire. She's the only person from my past that would have a vendetta against me. There's currently a restraining order on her, but it ends in a few months. I had to put one on her a few months after we broke up because she kept texting, emailing my friends, my family, and me mean and threatening words. She was very angry and I felt unsafe. When we were together, I never saw the crazy side of her. We broke up because I was sexting an old fling on Facebook, and she logged onto my account through my phone one night when I was asleep. The break up was my fault, and I genuinely felt horrible because I was actually in love with her. Even though I did not have my life together, I could see myself marrying her. I moved to Seattle for her. I met her in Austin through a mutual friend. We had a few drinks at a party and I ended up having a passionate night with her. We clicked. Her name was Claire Carpenter."

Lance closed his eyes and remembered the day he met Claire for the first time.

"Hey Josh, it's Lance, I'm a few minutes away from your ranch. I brought chicken for the grill," Lance said over his cell phone.

Lance turned off the highway and onto a dirt road that led to his friend Josh's ranch in the hill country. He was meeting up several friends for a summer barbecue for the Fourth of July. He pulled up to the ranch house and found several cars and trucks parked outside.

"Lance!" Josh called.

Josh had a cowboy hat on along with an American flag button down shirt.

"You look like the Fourth of July threw up on you," Lance joked.

"Shut the hell up and get yourself some beer. There's a keg on the back porch," Josh said while shaking Lance's hand and then giving him a half hug.

"Sounds great," Lance said.

"Oh, this is my old college dorm neighbor Claire. Claire is visiting from Seattle," Josh said.

"Nice to meet you," Claire said with a smile.

She was a very attractive woman. She had bright green eyes and beautiful reddish auburn hair. Her physique was slim. She was wearing a cotton dress with cowboy boots. She had a white flower in her hair held up by her right ear.

"Hi there, welcome to Texas," Lance said while shaking her hand.

Later into the evening, Lance was walking to a meadow a mile away from the ranch house. Claire and Lance had escaped the party to find somewhere quiet. They had also had a few beers and were slightly intoxicated. They kept laughing at each other's words and their flirting became more and more prominent. Lance put his hands in Claire's as they approached the meadow. A white wooden fence bordered the meadow. There were a few white sheep grazing on the well-irrigated green grass.

"They look so peaceful," Claire said. "I love sheep."

"They are bahhhhhh-utiful," Lance said and he broke out in laughter at his own joke.

"You're stupid," Claire laughed back.

"You're baaahhh-utiful too," Lance said.

"You're not so bahhhh-d yourself," Claire joked back.

They looked into each other's eyes and began to kiss feverishly and passionately. Lance reached for the bottom of Claire's dress and pulled it off her. He began to unbutton his shirt. He had just met Claire for the first time and shared a first kiss with her on that meadow. The evening proceeded with the first time they would be intimate.

When they finished, Lance zipped up his pants and began to dress. Claire did the same.

"It's a shame you fly back to Seattle tomorrow," Lance said. "That was really amazing."

"You're very talented," Claire said, and she began to blush.

Lance reached for her hands and held them tightly. They sat down on the grass and looked out onto the meadow as the sun began to set.

"The Texas hill country is gorgeous," Claire said.

"Why don't you move here?" Lance joked.

"I can't," Claire replied. "Work has me bound to Seattle. I do marketing for a coffee company, and I just got an amazing promotion. I need to get a few more years under my belt."

"I finished school a few months ago," Lance said. "Also with a marketing degree and a minor in finance. I'm trying to find a good gig here in Austin, but the job market has been difficult."

"This economy is rough," Claire said. "Our parents' generation had it much easier. I thank my lucky stars just to survive layoffs every year."

"I hear you on that," Lance said. "We graduated from college at a really difficult time."

Claire gave Lance a side hug and kissed his cheek.

"The alcohol is wearing off and I still think you look attractive," Claire teased.

"Ha," Lance laughed. "You're still as hot as when Josh introduced us."

"Is that a black sheep?" Claire asked pointing at the herd of sheep grazing in the meadow.

Every single sheep in the fenced meadow was white, except for a black one that stood out above the rest.

"How funny," Lance said. "I wonder if they intentionally bought one black sheep. I've always felt I was the black sheep of my family."

"What do you mean?" Claire asked with peaked interest.

"Oh nothing much," Lance said trying to think of a way to change the subject. "My family can be a tough one to survive through. I've always been the different one. My older brother gets all the attention and has a swanky job at a bank in town."

"I'm the oldest of four girls," Claire said. "I feel the pressure is always on oldest to do everything first and be the guinea pig at adulthood."

"I suppose," Lance said. "Anyways, when are you coming back to Austin?"

"Better yet," Claire added, "when are you coming to see me in Seattle?"

"There's a concert happening there in two weeks that I was thinking I could check out," Lance said. "Maybe I can look up tickets for flights and the show so that I can come see you?"

"That would be amazing," Claire said. "That's also the weekend of my birthday and I'm having table service at one of my favorite brunch restaurants. You could stay at my apartment."

"This sounds like a really good plan," Lance said excitedly, and then he extended an invitation to her to stay over at his apartment for the rest of the night before her flight.

Lance took a break from telling the story of his first encounter with Claire. Rose appeared to be in deep thought as she wrote down a few notes in her notebook.

"Do you still talk to this friend Josh?" she asked.

"No," Lance said. "After my breakup with Claire, there was a rift in our friendship, and I had to abandon that circle of friends because I did not want to see or know anything going on with Claire's life. I haven't seen Josh around town in a long time."

"Is Josh still friends with Claire?" Rose asked.

"I'm not sure," Lance said. "I want to say I heard through the grapevine that their friendship kind of faded."

"I see," Rose replied. "So you were drawn to Claire immediately after your first meeting?"

"Yes," Lance admitted. "I would say it was love at first sight. We were instantly taken with each other. It's so weird to think about that first night we had together. After our time at the meadow, I invited her to my apartment in town. The next morning, we ended up having brunch before she took off on her flight to

Seattle. It feels like yesterday. Things were so different. We talked and texted everyday until I went up to visit her for her birthday. However, because I was iffy about a long distance relationship, I was still talking to other girls and went on a few dates in that two-week span before meeting up with her again. I had sex with one of the dates as well. She never knew about this until close to our breakup when she went through my texts and Facebook messages and put a timeline of those days together. Was I wrong to have hooked up with someone else, even though I knew there was something special about Claire?"

"Well, you all were not in an official relationship," Rose said. "It would only be considered cheating if you were boyfriend and girlfriend."

"I had sex with someone days after I got back from my Seattle trip," Lance said. "It was with a girl I had met through an online dating site, and we never had a chance to connect before I went up to Seattle to see Claire. We went to a movie, and I figured it would be harmless, but she ended up coming back to my apartment. I was official with Claire then. I felt very guilty, but I kept it to myself."

"Well," Rose said softly, "that would be dishonest and considered cheating. It appears you have a need for sexual encounters. Do you have any idea why?"

"Flattery," Lance said. "I needed confidence. I liked when girls went after me because when I was younger, I had these awkward teenage phases and was never able to get a girlfriend. At least, not until I was almost done with high school."

"That is what my thoughts were," Rose said. "Much of that comes from the effects of child sexual abuse. People who are victims cheat and find ways to justify it as innocence in their minds. Have you ever cheated on your current fiancé?"

Lance was quiet for a few seconds before he could muster up the courage to tell the truth.

"Almost," Lance said. "I did kiss another woman and we almost hooked up, but I stopped myself. I had only been dating Amy for a few months. She doesn't know I kissed another girl during a vacation I went on with my best friend Edward."

"I see a pattern," Rose said. "We will work on all this moving forward so that you stay honest with your future wife. If you want longevity and happiness, then we have to overcome the tragedies of your past. You will become stronger. I have faith in you because you are doing something to help yourself. Do you know what that is?"

"Coming to therapy?" Lance asked.

"Yes," Rose said. "You're finally admitting to yourself that you wronged people in your past because of the dark skeletons in your closet. You know that you are at fault for destroying your relationship with Claire, and you don't want to make the same mistakes with Amy."

"That's right," Lance admitted. "I want to be a better person. I have so many issues to be worked out."

"What has been your method for closure on that relationship?" Rose asked.

"Silence," Lance said. "Cutting off communication was the only thing I could think of doing. And now she can't legally contact my mother or me in any way shape or form."

"Do you think you will ever reach out to her in the future?" Rose asked.

"No," Lance said. "The ending of that relationship was too sour. I don't want to stir the pot with her again. I think it is best the way things are and that we've gone our separate ways in our lives. Besides, we also live in different parts of the country."

"I see. Well, the hour is up," Rose said, "but let's get you in the books for next week. How does next Wednesday sound at six o' clock?"

Lance pulled out his iPhone to look at his calendar.

"That would work," Lance said. "Could we make that a standing meeting?"

"We can," Rose said. "I only work Mondays through Thursdays in Austin in case you need to shift around days in the future."

"Where are you the other days? Off?" Lance asked.

"I travel up north to see clients in Dallas," Rose said. "I have family that lives there so I can be close to them too. So Friday, Saturday, and Sundays I'm working from my office in Dallas."

"That must put a lot of mileage on your car," Lance said.

"Well, I've really only started," Rose said. "I'm sure it will grow tiring. But business is great."

"Well, good," Lance said. "It was a pleasure talking with you today."

"You too Lance," Rose smiled. "I want you to type up a document with bullet points of things you want to talk about for our next session. Print it or email it to me. That way we can make the most of our weekly sessions."

"Will do," Lance said, and he bid Rose goodbye and exited her office.

Chapter Six

As the weeks passed, Lance was becoming more and more confident in his therapy sessions. He was breaking new grounds and felt comfortable talking to Rose. He was also feeling safer as there had not been any strange occurrences in his life since Amy's accident. The police had closed the investigation, as there were no evidence or leads on the person who ran Amy off the road. Lance's mother still insisted the cow's heart came from a former client out of spite, and he was not sure who would have paid the homeless man to throw coffee at him. The man was questioned in jail, but it was ruled that he was bipolar due to his behavior. Therefore, the police believed that he was not actually paid by anyone to throw coffee at him.

"I guess it was all just a strange coincidence," Lance told Edward over beers at their favorite sports bar by Lake Austin.

"I mean if nothing weird has happened in the last month since the incidents, then I guess it's safe to say that crazy bitch was not behind them," Edward said referring to Claire.

"Yeah," Lance said. "And I feel so calm right now with the therapy sessions I'm doing weekly. The wedding planning isn't even stressing me out."

"That's because Amy is taking that load off you," Edward laughed. "You know she's a control freak and wants it to be perfect."

"Well, yeah," Lance admitted.

Lance's phone vibrated on top of their table. It was a text message from his brother Dylan. The text read "Sorry. Late meeting. I'm coming to the bar to meet you. 5 minutes away."

"My brother is almost here," Lance said.

"Good ole Dylan," Edward said. "Are you two doing fine working for the same company?"

"Well it is because of him I have the job," Lance pointed out. "But yeah, the sibling rivalry has waned in our adulthood. Although, I must admit I think he is jealous I'm getting married first since I'm the younger kid."

"Same Dylan," Edward said. "You guys would fight so much when we were kids."

"I know," Lance said. "We've become closer now that we both are not in favor of my mother's marriage to our Uncle George."

"That's really weird," Edward said.

"It was the talk of the country club," Lance laughed. "Momma Marissa stopped going there every weekend because the other women were gossiping about her. She's since found a new social circle. The other housewives were such bitches."

A few minutes later, Dylan walked into the bar. He was wearing his suit, but he had taken off his tie. He was holding a briefcase with him. He had shadows under his eyes and looked as if he had not slept in days.

"Rough day?" Lance asked. "I just ordered you a beer."

"May need more than just one beer," Dylan said. "Thanks kid."

"No problem," Lance said. "Why did you bring your briefcase in?"

"I have some valuables in here that I don't want to leave in my car," Dylan said without meeting Lance's gaze.

"Have you talked to mom?" Lance asked.

"Not in a few days. Why?" Dylan asked.

"She's thinking of selling some of dad's farmland. She wanted our opinion," Lance said.

"Oh," Dylan said. "She should sell it. We can split the profit. Speaking of which, can I borrow a hundred and forty dollars?"

"Why?" Lance asked.

"So nosy," Dylan snapped. "I mean, I'm short on cash and I need to pay my maid. She's not a legal resident so I pay her in cash under the table."

"Didn't we just get paid?" Lance asked.

"I have had a lot of bills lately," Dylan said. "Mortgage stuff. Etcetera."

"Ok, can I write you a check and then you can cash it?" Lance asked.

"Yes," Dylan said. "I'll be right back. I need to go pee."

"Your brother seems kind of distracted by something," Edward blurted out when Dylan was out of earshot.

"He looks like he's very jumpy too," Lance added.

"Open his briefcase," Edward said while grabbing it from under the table.

"No," Lance said. "It's not my business."

Edward ignored Lance and opened the briefcase. His eyes widened in shock before he closed it back up quickly.

"What?" Lance asked curiously.

"Dude," Edward whispered. "There's a bag of coke inside. And not the soda either. Cocaine…"

"Are you serious?" Lance said, and he reached for the briefcase and opened it. "Holy shit."

Lance closed the briefcase and quickly put it back the same way it had been placed under the table.

"Your brother is on crack, man," Dylan said. "That's probably why he needs the cash, so he can buy more drugs."

Dylan came back from the bathroom looking as if he had washed is face. He fidgeted with his phone and looked at his watch. He grabbed his beer and drank it really fast.

"Easy there," Lance said.

"I'm going to order another round of beers for the table," Dylan said. "We can put it on mom's tab."

"Are you using one of her credit cards again?" Lance asked.

"She let me borrow it," Dylan said.

"Of course," Lance groaned.

As the night progressed, Dylan became inebriated and was no longer able to drive. Edward had to leave because he was tired and had an early meeting. Lance was left with his drunk brother and had no other choice but to drive him to his condo.

"I can drive bro," Dylan slurred his words.

"I'm going to take you home," Lance said. "You can get a taxi to bring you here in the morning to pick up your car at the bar's parking lot."

"Ok, fine," Dylan said.

Lance arrived at Dylan's downtown condominium. He parked his car in a meter outside the entrance of the building and helped Dylan walk up into the lobby of his complex.

"Where's my briefcase?" Dylan said worriedly as they walked into the lobby.

"I have it here," Lance showed Dylan.

"I'll hold it," Dylan said, and he forcefully pulled it out of Lance's hands.

"Good day Mr. Avery," the doorman said to Dylan. "Long night?"

"Very," Dylan murmured.

"I'm going to walk him up to his room. He's had a bit to drink," Lance whispered to the doorman who nodded back.

As soon as they were inside Dylan's condo, Lance pulled the briefcase out of his hands and opened it in front of him. Dylan's face turned red and his eyes narrowed in anger.

"What the hell?" he snapped.

"You want to explain what you are doing with these drugs?" Lance asked.

"I have needs," Dylan said angrily. "Don't you dare tell mom. When you did this stuff in high school, I kept it quiet."

"I thought you gave this stuff up," Lance asked.

"I had withdrawals," Dylan said. "I found some chick to deal it to me, and it has been keeping me awake during my long nights in the office."

"People at work are going to notice you're on something. You look like shit right now," Lance said. "You need to get off crack."

"Why don't you chill out and do a line with me?" Dylan teased, but he opened the bag of his drugs and poured a portion of its contents on his coffee table. He pulled out a small blade and shaped the white dust into two individual lines.

"No," Lance said.

"Just one time," Dylan pleaded. "Consider it my apologies for missing your engagement since I was pretty messed up."

"You were high, weren't you?" Lance said angrily. "That's why you missed my engagement."

"Well...yes," Dylan admitted. "My bad."

Lance looked at the lines of coke on the table. He had not done it since he was in high school, but he remembered the excitement it brought to his senses.

Lance was sixteen years old when he had first done a hit of cocaine. His mother was out of town on business as usual, so he had the housekeeper buy his friends bottles of vodka. He decided to throw a party at his mother's condo, where he was living at the time.

"You want to get lucky tonight?" his then girlfriend Chelsea asked him as they were making out in his bedroom to the loud blasting music coming from the living room that was filled with most of his close high school friends.

"Yes," Lance said drunkenly.

"You need to try this stuff," Chelsea said, and she pulled out a small sandwich bag with white powder.

She used her credit card to make two individual white lines on Lance's nightstand.

"Ok, just snort it now through your nose," Chelsea said. "I'll demonstrate."

Lance copied what Chelsea did and breathed in the white powder through his nose into an instant euphoric feeling. That night Lance was on a whole new kind of level and the beginning of his teenage drug addiction had begun.

"Are you going to try it?" Dylan teased. "Don't be a party pooper."

Lance jabbed Dylan playfully on the shoulder and proceeded to get on his knees in front of the table. He thought about what he was about to do for a minute before he finally decided to partake in the euphoria of using cocaine for the first time in over thirteen years.

Dylan had fallen asleep on his couch still wearing his suit. Lance was wide-awake and alert. The extra adrenaline gave him the push to drive home. He had not consumed much alcohol so he knew it would be safe for him to drive to his apartment. He had a few text messages from his neighbor Dana, but he had ignored them so that he could focus on the road.

At last, he arrived at his apartment complex and saw Dana waiting by his carport with her dog.

"Did you get my texts?" she asked as soon as Lance had come out of his car.

"I haven't read them," Lance admitted.

"Are you ok?" Dana asked. "You look a little jumpy."

"No—yes I'm fine," Lance said and he pulled out his phone.

"I came by your apartment a few minutes ago to see if I could borrow some milk," Dana said. "I heard shuffling in your living room, but you never came out. I checked to see if your car was parked and it wasn't. I think someone was in your apartment. They might still be in there."

"What?" Lance said.

He ran up the stairs and straight to his front door. He turned his doorknob.

"It's unlocked!" he shouted.

"I'll call the police!" Dana said while reaching for her phone. "Don't go in there!"

Lance ignored her and walked into his living room. It did not appear as if anything was taken, but several items looked as if they had been shifted. A few drawers were open and items had been taken out and not put back in their place. Lance's heart began to race as he walked into his bedroom. His sheets had been undone on his bed. There were creases in his pillows as if someone had laid in it. His underwear drawer was left open and several pairs of his boxer briefs were scattered on the floor.

Lance investigated his bathroom, which was inside his room, and saw that several of his cologne bottles had been left open with the tops left on his kitchen counter as if someone had decided to smell or sample each one. His medicine cabinet was also left ajar. The only items that appeared to have been touched were his prescription anti-depressant medications, which he was trying to wean off. He had another prescription medication next to it, but the label on it was not his name. It read "Patient: Amy Aberdeen."

"Is there anyone in there?" Dana called from his front door.

Lance opened the door to his walk-in closet and saw that most of his clothes had been taken off their hangers and left in a pile on the ground. It was the last place in his apartment that could have been used for someone to hide.

"I don't think so," Lance called back. "Are the cops on their way?"

"They are," Dana said by his bedroom door as she had walked into the apartment with her dog before he answered.

"The window is open," Lance pointed at his bedside window, which was left open.

"It's a one story drop," Dana said. "If someone jumped out, they could have hurt themself."

"Not if they used a ladder," Lance said after looking out of his window and realizing that a ladder was left thrown on the ground."

"Oh my," Dana said. "I never heard or saw anyone suspicious."

"I feel so violated," Lance said feeling the euphoria of the cocaine wearing off. "Someone went through my stuff. I don't think anything was stolen. All my valuables are still here."

The police knocked at the front door and announced themselves.

"Austin PD," a male officer called.

"In here," Dana said.

"Hi, do you both live here?" the officer asked when he entered Lance's room accompanied by another male officer.

"Just me," Lance said. "I'm Lance Avery. This is my neighbor Dana."

"I'm Officer Mendez," the man said. "This is my partner Officer Ruiz."

"Hello," the other male officer said.

"Is anything missing?" Mendez asked.

"No, I don't think so," Lance replied. "It does appear as if someone was looking for something specific, but I don't know what."

"Well you may eventually find out something went missing," Ruiz said. "Should we dust for fingerprints, Mendez?"

"That would be a good idea," Mendez responded. "Could I ask you a few questions while Ruiz checks for prints?"

"Sure," Lance replied.

Mendez walked to the living room and sat on Lance's armchair. He pulled out a pen and pad and proceeded to ask Lance and Dana a few questions.

"You were here at the time of the break-in?" Mendez asked Dana.

"I was," Dana said. "I did not hear or see anything out of the ordinary. I came to knock on Lance's door, and then I heard shuffling inside. Nobody ever answered so I figured he did not want to come out. I proceeded to take my dog downstairs for a walk and noticed Lance's car was not parked in his assigned spot. I sent him a few texts, but he pulled into the complex a few minutes later. Whoever was in his apartment escaped out of his room window within ten minutes of Lance arriving. I did not hear anyone leaving through the window, but there was a ladder left abandoned out back by where his window is."

"Ruiz," Mendez called. "Can you do a perimeter search of the complex? It was probably twenty minutes ago that the perpetrator was inside this unit. He or she might still be on the grounds."

"Yes sir," Ruiz said, and he ran out of Lance's apartment with his flashlight raised in front of him.

"Has there been any other break-ins in this apartment community recently?" Dana asked the officer.

"I looked at a few reports before arriving," Mendez said, "but nothing recent came up. This could be a random incident."

"Or targeted," Lance said mysteriously. "I mean it appeared as if they were looking for something of mine."

"That's what I was going to say in conjunction with my previous statement," Mendez replied.

Lance folded his arms and then wiped some sweat off his face. He was hoping that nobody would notice that he was slightly off due to his recent drug use. The last thing he wanted was for the cop to discover he had been high a few minutes ago.

"I honestly don't know who could have done this," Lance said. "A few weird things happened to my girlfriend and me a month ago, but nothing out of the ordinary has happened since."

"What happened?" Mendez asked.

"Someone tried to run my fiancé off the road, and a homeless man threw coffee at me," Lance said. "As nothing had happened since, I just figured it was all a strange coincidence."

"Do you think someone would try to hurt you or your fiancé?" Mendez asked.

"I don't know," Lance said even though his mind raced to thoughts of Claire.

The officer followed up with a few questions before he decided he had enough information to take with him to the station to fill out a report. His partner, Ruiz, came back with nothing to report. They both left, leaving Lance and Dana alone in the ransacked apartment.

"Do you need anything Lance?" Dana asked. "Coffee or tea? I feel terrible that this happened. I can even help you put things away."

"No, it's ok," Lance said. "I need sleep right now. I can clean up this mess in the morning. It's really late and I'm thinking of calling in sick tomorrow."

"Are you going to tell your fiancé about this?" Dana asked.

"I'm not sure," Lance replied. "I don't want to worry her right now. I want her to go to work and continue as normal. The accident she had when she was run off the road really made her anxious. She's already stressing what with all the wedding planning we are doing. I might keep this quiet. I know you haven't met her yet, but you will eventually. Can we keep this between us?"

"Of course neighbor," Dana replied. "You have my word."

"Thank you," Lance said.

The next morning, Lance called into work and asked for a personal day. His boss said if he and his brother had planned the day off because Dylan had called in sick as well. Lance explained that his house was broken into and wanted to clean up the place. It took him until the afternoon to finally put all his things in order the way they were before he had left his house the previous day. Nothing appeared to be missing. All of his watches and rings were still in their cases and drawers. The only weird thing he discovered was a white marker on the floor that he found by the desk in his room. He opened the top of it to reveal the tip was white. He pulled out a red index card from his desk and scribbled on it with the marker. No ink came out.

Lance shrugged and absentmindedly threw the marker into one of his drawers even though it did not work. He looked at his watch and realized he had three hours before one of his therapy sessions with Rose. He decided he needed some kind of spiritual guidance after the episode from the night before.

Lance arrived at the Austin cemetery an hour later to seek that guidance. He parked his car near his father's gravesite. He walked over to his father's grave and sat on the freshly lawn grass.

"Hey dad, it's Lance," he said to the grave as if he could talk to his father's spirit. "I hope you are watching over me. I'm sorry that Dylan and I are a mess right now. Last night was just a one-time thing. It won't happen again. Mom would be so pissed. She'd probably take us out of her will. Anyways, I wanted to ask you to watch over me. I've been under so much stress lately. I don't feel as healthy as I should be. I'm still on my anti-depressant medications. I can't seem to get off them, and if I stop cold-turkey, it would be bad for me. I have to admit the high I got last night really made me feel so much better. I haven't felt so alive and happy in a long time. My meds don't even do that for me. Not even the Vicodin I took from Amy that she was prescribed after her car accident. She doesn't know, but after she stopped using them when her pain subsided, I took them from her and said they are addictive and should be thrown out. I kept them for myself. They are in my medicine cabinet. I miss you dad. I need help. Therapy might not be enough. I feel a nervous breakdown coming, and it scares me."

Lance looked away from his father's tombstone abruptly at the sound of a strange clicking noise in the distance. A few yards away was a woman dressed in all black. She was wearing a slim dress with black high heels, which were the source of the clicking sound. She also had a long black veil over her head that extended a few inches above her shoulders and covered her face. It was attached to a pillbox hat. She was wearing long satin gloves that extended to the halfway point of her arm above her elbow. In one hand, she was holding a single red rose. She stopped dead in her tracks at the sight of Lance. For a minute she did not move. Lance shifted uncomfortably and stood up. The woman turned on her heels and walked away without a backwards glance. By the time Lance arrived at his car, the woman was nowhere in sight.

Chapter Seven

Sweat was pouring down Lance's forehead as he ran two blocks to the location of Rose's office. There was unexpected traffic on the highway that caused him to be a few minutes late. Once Lance had arrived at the front door, he saw Rose waiting for him clad in a bright green dress that brought out her eyes. She was stunning and simply beautiful.

"I was about to give you a ring," Rose said with a warm smile.

"Traffic," Lance huffed and tried to catch his breath.

"No worries," she replied. "Come on in and take a seat."

Lance took his place on the couch and Rose took her usual seat directly in front of the couch on her black leather chair.

"My house was broken into last night," Lance said. "I've been off all day."

"Oh my goodness," Rose said in surprise. "Was anything taken? Are you alright?"

"Nothing was stolen, which is fortunate," Lance told her. "But I can't shake the feeling that something—someone is out to get me."

"Do you still think the incident with Amy and that car as well as that man attacking you at work has something to do with an enemy?" Rose questioned.

"I don't even know," Lance said pushing back his hair. "I did something bad last night. I found out my brother has been using drugs for some time, and I did some cocaine with him. The feeling made me the happiest I've been in months, but only for a short amount of time."

"Ah," Rose said while scribbling notes in her notebook. "If you feel you have self control right now, it would be best to not try it again or you might fall into another addiction."

"I know," Lance said with feelings of shame. "Being under the influence was what led me to suicidal thoughts as a teen."

Lance had briefly explained his brush with death at age seventeen, but at that moment he began to relive it in his mind.

Lance's mother was gone again on business, and the housekeeper had cooked him a meal. His brother Dylan, who was in college at the time, stopped by the house to have dinner with him. After they finished eating, Dylan went upstairs to Lance's room and pulled out a bag of marijuana.

"Let's get toasted little brother," Dylan said.

"I've been waiting to get high," Lance said excitedly as his brother clicked his lighter and the tip of his joint began to burn.

Dylan inhaled deeply and then coughed out smoke. Lance grabbed the joint from Dylan after he was done and took two large puffs from it. He breathed out the smoke and it began to cloud his room.

"You should open one of your windows," Dylan said.

"What if Maggie smells the smoke?" Lance asked.

"She's busy doing housemaid chores downstairs," Dylan said. "She used a ton of pots and pans to make dinner, so she'll be a while. You know she prefers to clean by hand instead of the dishwasher."

"Right," Lance agreed and he took another puff from the joint.

Lance's mind began to rest. His body felt heavy as if it were sinking through his bed sheets. He looked up at the ceiling and imagined the stars and outer space above him. He turned his head to the right to see his brother sitting at his desk staring out the window and not moving. He was zoned out. Lance turned his head back towards the ceiling and felt as if it took all his energy to make such a minimal move.

"I'm baked," Dylan said. "I'm going to head to my dorm. See you later bro."

Dylan walked out of Lance's room and closed the door. Lance's arms were too heavy for him to lift up or say "goodbye." He felt too lazy to even open his mouth to say anything.

Finally, he decided to move. He opened his nightstand drawer and pulled out anti-anxiety medications that he had stolen from his mother's medicine cabinet a week before. He opened a water bottle and took ten pills. After he swallowed them all, he reached for a handle of vodka that was hidden under his bed. He twisted off the top and threw it across his room. He began to chug the vodka as if it were water. The vodka that did not make it into his mouth began to drip down his chin and onto his shirt. Lance began to cry into his pillow. He held his breath. He could feel his intestines squirming and pleading in agony as the vodka coursed through his body. His throat felt as if hot coals were stuck in it and it was on fire. Before his mind became clouded, his last thoughts were that he made this choice to end his life because he could not deal with the lifestyle of a mother he felt did not love him, and the stress of not living up to the prestige of his older brother.

Lance tried to stand on his two feet to run to his restroom, but his legs felt like jelly. He collapsed onto the ground and hit his head on the corner of his nightstand. He was instantly knocked unconscious.

It was by luck that at the same time he collapsed, his then girlfriend Chelsea rang the doorbell to the condo. The housekeeper Maggie answered.

"Hello Miss Chelsea," Maggie greeted politely. "Mr. Lance is up in his room. Should I call him down?"

"No, I'll go up and see him," Chelsea said.

Chelsea was not the thinnest girl, but she was not that large either. She was curvy and looked as if she was in between stages of losing or gaining weight. She had short curly brown hair.

"I'm here Lance," Chelsea knocked on his door.

There was no answer, so she reached for the doorknob and opened it.

"Lance?" she called.

Chelsea noticed that the bed sheets looked ruffled. She walked to the other side of the bed and saw Lance unconscious on the floor. She screamed, and minutes later Maggie arrived at the room. They called 911 and in the interim of waiting for the ambulance to arrive, Chelsea kept slapping Lance's face while crying heavily onto his chest.

"I woke up in the hospital the next morning feeling as if I had a massive hangover," Lance told Rose. "My entire body ached and I reeked of liquor. They pumped my stomach. The doctors told me I was this close to dying. My mother had to fly back down from her business meeting to see me in the hospital. She was furious about having to lose time with a client, but when she learned that the doctors suspected I tried to commit suicide, she broke down and cried. It was the first time I saw my mother cry since my father passed away. She hugged me and said I needed therapy. She also said she was going to fire Miss Maggie because she neglected to care for me. I felt bad that Maggie lost her job because of my lapse in judgment. It was not her fault nor could she have prevented it. I still would have tried to do the same thing to my body had my mother actually been home."

"Why did you feel like death was the only escape?" Rose asked seriously.

"I felt like damaged goods," Lance said. "I was addicted to pain killers, anti-anxiety medications, pot, crack, and I had experimented with ecstasy the week prior. I also knew I was not in love with my girlfriend, and I could not get the courage to break up with her. She wasn't really my type and she had gained so much weight since we started dating. I know it sounds shallow of me, but I didn't want to end up marrying her. I wanted to date someone I was actually attracted to. I was battling my spoiled vain needs, and my good-natured human heart. I could not find a happy medium."

"Are you happy that Chelsea found you?" Rose asked.

"Yes," Lance said. "In retrospect, she was my guardian angel. That night strained our relationship and eventually we broke up. I wasn't in love with her, like I said. I felt that this incident was the beginning of a new chapter of my life. It was a wake up call to focus on my grades, so that I could get into a decent college and find a career of my own."

"If you feel that your addiction could be coming back, I can recommend you to a wonderful rehabilitation center in town," Rose said.

"I just got high once last night," Lance said. "I don't plan to do it again. However, maybe I can recommend rehab to my brother."

"It's called the Austenite Support Center," Rose said. "I do not want Dylan to become your enabler."

"I won't let him," Lance said. "I'm thinking he will need an intervention. I've worked so hard to build myself up after college and my break up with Claire to find some semblance and norm in my life. I will not lose it."

"That's good," Rose said. "You mentioned your mother wanted you to go to therapy, and I believe you mentioned before that you did go for a few sessions in your youth. Why did you stop?"

"I went for two visits," Lance explained. "On my second visit, I went deep into talking about my father's death and a few anecdotes of the difficulties I had with my mother after his passing. He went berserk all of a sudden and said that I was damaged goods and that I would never change. He said there were long-lasting consequences in my life, which stemmed from the tragedies I experienced. It would be difficult for me to truly love someone, because I did not love myself. At least that's what he told me."

"That's not professional," Rose said with curiosity. "He should never have said that."

"He was having a breakdown," Lance added. "Later that night he was arrested for domestic violence with his wife. He had confessed that he had been disloyal in their marriage—apparently he had some dark issues in his past—and their altercation became physical. He lost his license and I took that as a sign to stop therapy and not search for a new therapist. I was also freaked out that he called me 'damaged goods.' The therapist was damaged goods himself, and I felt as if I would be constantly comparing myself to him."

"Well everyone is different," Rose said in a comforting tone.

"I know," Lance shrugged.

"How are things with Amy?" Rose changed to the topic.

"Things are great," Lance said. "She's been pretty stressed with the wedding plans. She's still frantically searching for a wedding dress. The planning is causing a bit of tension so we've been spending less time together. I'm letting her do most of the planning."

"Weddings can be stressful," Rose said, "but you must remember that this is also a good time to make your relationship stronger. These next few months could define how the rest of your relationship will grow."

"My apartment lease is up in a few weeks," Lance said. "That's a good thing too since I feel so violated from last night's break in. I'm thinking of asking Amy over dinner if she would like to start finding a house or apartment to move in together. We've never really lived together. I don't count our countless sleepovers as cohabitating."

"That would be a good idea," Rose said. "Find a place together because people really learn about each other once they share a home. May I also suggest taking a weekend trip together alone soon to take your minds off the wedding planning?"

"That's not a bad idea either," Lance said. "Amy's family has a cabin in the hill country we can easily escape to for a weekend getaway on Friday afternoon after work."

Lance arrived home that evening to a feeling of unease in his apartment. He sat on his couch after warming up a frozen mac and cheese dinner, and turned on his TV. His phone began to vibrate in his pocket. It was Amy.

"Hey babe," Lance answered.

"How was therapy today?" Amy asked.

"Not too bad," Lance said. "How was dress shopping?"

"Hell," Amy said sounding irritated. "Jill keeps suggesting I should get a more well known designer. I want something that fits and feels right. I rather save the money and put it towards other expenses."

"Like a house…" Lance said slyly.

"Huh?" Amy was caught by surprise.

"I wanted to wait to talk about this in person," Lance began, "but with my lease ending soon, I've been thinking all day that we should find a place together."

Amy was silent for a few minutes before she replied.

"Yes!" she said excitedly. "I was wondering if you were going to suggest that. Oh baby you made my day! I would much rather be apartment hunting or house shopping in the next few weeks to take my mind off this wedding."

"How about we also take a weekend trip to your parent's cabin?" Lance suggested. "Let's go this Friday?"

"Yes, yes, yes!" Amy cheered over the phone. "Oh, we can have all sorts of fun in that cabin."

"We sure can," Lance said with a large grin on his face.

Lance's phone began to beep. Dylan was on the other line.

"Hey Amy," Lance cut in, "I'm going to have to let you go. Dylan is calling me."

"Ok, love you," Amy hung up.

"Hey," Lance answered Dylan's call.

"What the hell happened," he said, and he sounded high.

"You should probably stop with the drugs," Lance urged him.

"Yeah," Dylan said, and he sounded sad. "I just used some of the stuff before bed. I need to get back to work tomorrow. Did you call in sick?"

"Yes," Lance said. "However, I only called in sick because my apartment was broken into."

"What?" Dylan exclaimed. "Was anything stolen?"

"That's the weird part. Nothing was taken, but someone was definitely looking for something," Lance said.

"I keep getting calls from a blocked number," Dylan said. "I'm thinking it's my drug dealer calling from a private line. I'm hoping he did not go over to your house to try and steal back the coke he sold me."

"How would he know where I live?" Lance said in outrage.

"He's a drug dealer," Dylan said. "They know everything."

"Well get rid of your stash and don't let me find out you are still getting high," Lance said. "I'll kill you if you miss my wedding."

"I won't miss it," Dylan said in an irritated tone. "Let's just keep this between us. I'm going to dump the stash down the toilet. I don't want this to affect my work life."

"Thank you brother," Lance said with relief. "Love you. I'm gonna let you go. I have some TV to catch up on."

"Night," Dylan hung up.

Lance put his phone in his pocket and looked over at the living room window that overlooked the entrance of his apartment. His heart dropped and the hair on the back of his spine rose. There was a silhouette of a person bent over and looking into his apartment through a crack in the blinds.

Lance got up immediately and ran to the door. Whoever was watching him saw him move suddenly and disappeared. Lance swung his door open and saw that the person was gone. He ran back into his apartment and opened his utility closet. He found a flashlight and checked to make sure it worked. Once it lit up, he ran out of his apartment door and locked it behind him. He proceeded to run down the stairs and listened for any noises. There was nothing but the sound of crickets and cars driving down the nearest highway in the distance. It was a clear night and he could see the stars and a full moon.

He walked over to the leasing office of the complex. The lights were off. He noticed there was a security camera above the entrance.

"I never thought to ask the office if they could check the cameras from last night," Lance said thinking about how the footage from the previous night could show the possible intruder of his unit.

Lance walked to the community gym. There were a few people on the elliptical machines working out and watching the TVs that were mounted on the walls. One woman that had been working out walked out of the door and stared at Lance curiously. Lance gestured for the woman to take off her earphones.

"Yes?" she asked.

"Did you see anyone running by the windows a few minutes ago?" Lance asked.

"Yeah," she said. "Why?"

"There was some creep looking through my blinds," Lance said. "And last night someone broke into my apartment."

"Is that why there were cops last night?" she asked sounding interested. "I was wondering about that. Did you tell the community manager?"

"Not yet, but I plan to go first thing in the morning," Lance added. "Was the person who walked by male or female?"

"It was hard to tell," she replied. "The glare from the gym lights make it hard to see who is walking outside. It could have been anyone though."

"Right," Lance said with a defeated tone. "Well, just keep an eye out for anything suspicious. I'm not going to be able to sleep now."

"Yeah, that really creeps me out," the woman replied. "Have a good night and make sure you lock up."

"Thanks," Lance said, and he pushed back his hair in frustration."

He walked down a path that led along the gated community pool. He heard a few dogs bark in the distance and the continued sounds of crickets. Lance rubbed his arms to keep warm as he walked along a path, because the temperature kept dropping. He reached a dead end. He arrived at the fence that encompassed the entire apartment complex. There was no sign of any movement in the vicinity. Whoever had been looking through his window had vanished.

Lance was about to turn and head back to his apartment when the shine of his flashlight hit a section of the fence that looked as if it had been cut with bolt cutters. He examined the opening on it. It was about four feet high, which was enough for an adult to fit through. Lance tested it and went through the gate. On the other side were a bunch of trees that led into the woods and to Lake Austin. Lance's heart was racing and despite his fear and feeling of cold numbness, he decided to continue into the woods. He walked slowly so as to remain as quiet as possible so that he could listen for the slightest of sounds. There was no other source of light, so if there were anyone in the woods they would need a lamp or a flashlight to navigate.

"Ah!" Lance said suddenly.

Some kind of flying insect had flown into Lance's face, making him jump. He dropped his flashlight and it rolled into a bush. Lance got on his knees to reach for it and found a crumpled piece of paper. He grabbed his flashlight and reached for the paper on the ground. It was a print out of a map that showed a satellite view of his apartment complex. The building that Lance lived in was circled in red ink with the label, "Lance's Apt."

"Holy shit," Lance said realizing that this was evidence that someone had in fact intentionally broken into his apartment and had been watching him. "Claire?"

Lance felt a foreboding feeling and put the paper in his jacket pocket. He ran back up towards the gate and desperately looked for the part of it that was cut open. Finally, he found it and to his surprise it had been closed up with zip ties.

"Shit…" Lance whispered into the night.

Someone was near him. He moved his flashing light three hundred and sixty degrees around him, but he did not see anyone. Whoever had gone through the trouble of sealing back the gate, had done so ever so stealthily because he had not heard anything.

"Is there anyone here?" Lance called into the darkness. "I know you were looking through my window. What do you want? What are you looking for?"

There was nothing but the sound of crickets and a couple of birds chirping in the distance.

Lance flashed his light through the fence towards his apartment complex. He could have sworn he saw someone running in the distance, but it was too dark to tell if it was male or female. The light hit someone's back and for a second, and the person hid behind a tree. Lance realized that whoever had sealed the gate, had gone back into his apartment complex and was probably going back to his unit.

Lance reached for his phone and was about to call the police, when he noticed that his phone's screen read "Not in service."

"What the hell?" Lance swore.

He took off at a run following the fence to the nearest street. Once he was on the street and out of the woods, he ran up the sidewalk all the way around until he reached the entrance of his apartment complex. His phone still had the "Not in service" message. He attempted to dial 911, but an operator on the phone said, "This line has been disconnected or no longer in service."

"I paid my bill!" Lance said into the night.

He walked back up the stairs to his apartment. He reached for his doorknob. It was still locked. He opened his apartment door and everything looked the same as he had left it. He felt uneasy and nervous. He debated calling Amy and asking if he could stay at her apartment, but then decided he was making himself feel anxious. He decided that since he could not sleep, he would see if his neighbor Dana was awake.

Dana answered the door after a few knocks. She was wearing a robe and her glasses.

"I'm sorry to bother you," Lance said. "Someone was peering through my blinds while I was home."

"Oh my God!" Dana said.

"I ran out to try to find this person, but I came up empty handed," Lance said.

He decided to keep the printed out copy of his apartment complex with his name on it a secret as he did not want to tell the story of what he had just experienced.

"You need to go to the leasing office tomorrow and—" Dana was saying.

"I'm going to," Lance cut her off. "There are cameras around the complex. They are bound to have recorded this intruder."

"Do you think someone is targeting you?" Dana asked.

"Yes," and then he decided he would show her the printed out map and explain to her what had happened to him when he went into the woods.

"Oh my…" Dana said, and she looked alarmed and scared.

"You're fine," Lance assured her. "It's someone looking for me. No need to worry."

"But who?" Dana said.

"I have my suspicions," Lance replied. "But I'm keeping them to myself. And to Rose of course. I met with her today and we talked about the break-in."

"How are your sessions going?" Dana tried to ask calmly.

"Very well," Lance said. "Look, keep your doors locked. I'm going to wake up first thing and talk to the manager on the premises. I want them to look through the footage. I'll even call the police after. I want to see if someone was taped that should not have been here."

"Ok then, good night," Dana said.

Lance took one of his strong anti-anxiety pills after he brushed his teeth. He swallowed it with a glass of water and then jumped into his bed. Within minutes, he began to feel drowsy and his mind was put to ease. He slipped into a dreamless and restful sleep.

His alarm went off at seven in the morning. Lance woke up and felt comforted that the sun was out as he looked out of his window. He quickly got up and brushed his teeth, and then put on his slacks, shirt, and tie for work. He ate a banana and ran outside of his apartment. When he opened the door he saw that a newspaper had been left at his doorstep. Lance was caught off guard by it because he did not have a subscription to the Austin Chronicle.

He picked up the newspaper and nearly dropped his banana in shock. The headline read "Real Estate Agent Found Dead in Open House's Pool."

"What the..." he mumbled.

The newspaper was dated fifteen years ago and had the yellowing effect on the pages that happens to old newspapers. Lance's heart dropped and tears began to pour out of the corners of his eyes.

"Someone is screwing with me," Lance said. "It has to be that bitch, Claire."

Lance opened his apartment door and flung the paper onto his armchair. He double locked his door and marched to the leasing office.

"Good morning Mr. Avery," the community manger Terrance replied.

Terrance was wearing a white button down shirt with suspenders. He had short black hair and dark brown skin. His wide smile revealed very white teeth. He was flamboyant in nature and looked alert and awake for it being seven in the morning.

"Terrance," Lance said. "I did not report this yesterday, but I had a break in two nights ago in my unit. I filed a police report. Last night someone was peering through my window. Is there any way you can check the camera footage?"

"Oh my goodness. Why, yes, of course," Terrance said looking worried and less cheerful. "Why don't you follow me to the back office."

Lance followed Terrance to his office. There were several small circuit televisions that showed different angles of the entire apartment complex community. Terrance pulled out a few tapes from the closet and began to rewind them. A large flat screen TV that was divided by six different screens, showed the various areas of the complex where the cameras were stationed.

"You can help me by being another set of eyes," Terrance said. "Around what time did this happen two nights ago?"

"Close to 10:00 PM," Lance answered.

The tapes took about twenty minutes to rewind to the exact time frame that Lance had said. When they got to the nine o' clock hour of that night, they began to play the tape in real time. Terrance pushed a button that made the video fast-forward slowly, but not fast enough to where small details could be missed.

"Do you see anything weird?" Terrance asked.

"Not yet," Lance said.

"Wait, did you see that?" Terrance asked suddenly.

He rewound one of the screens that showed the gated entrance to the complex. A person walked in and pushed the pedestrian gate open. The person was dressed in black but was wearing a dress and heels; it was apparent that the person was female.

As the woman walked into a clearer view of the camera, her whole body was captured in the light. She was wearing a veil that covered her face with a small pillbox hat on her head. She glanced at the camera, but the veil and the shadows of the night kept her face hidden. Even though the video was recorded two days previously, Lance had the uneasy feeling that the woman was looking at him straight in the eyes in a shroud of mystery.

Chapter Eight

Terrance picked up his phone and called someone. He had a look of worry on his face.

"Gustavo," Terrance said into the phone, "can you please come to my office? I need to show you something."

Terrance hung up the phone and turned to Lance who had a look of anxiety on his own face.

"That woman," Lance said. "I saw her at the cemetery yesterday afternoon. I think she was following me. She must be the one who broke into my apartment. I might even know her identity. We should show this to the police."

"I don't think this is who broke into your apartment," Terrance said. "We've seen images of this woman on our footage for the past few months. She always walks into the complex and then disappears into the darkness. My coworker Gustavo will explain her appearance. I'm not sure if you are a believer of the supernatural or paranormal, but after hearing Gustavo's story, you might become a believer."

"Excuse me?" Lance questioned with a raised eyebrow. "Paranormal?"

"That woman is a ghost," Terrance said in a serious tone.

Lance wanted to let out a sarcastic laugh, but the look on Terrance's face was intense and worrisome.

Gustavo walked into the office carrying a rake. He was sweating with dirt and grass stains on his white shirt. Gustavo was a portly man with salt and pepper hair and a small mustache.

"Que pasa Terrance?" Gustavo asked.

"It's her again," Terrance said while rewinding the footage of the woman in the veil walking through the front entrance of the apartment complex.

"La Viuda!" Gustavo exclaimed.

"La what?" Lance retorted.

"The widow," Gustavo said. "Viuda in English is widow…The Widow."

"This is not a ghost," Lance insisted. "This is the intruder who broke into my apartment two nights ago."

"Amigo," Gustavo continued. "She is the ghost of a Hispanic woman who murdered her husband in their home at a house down the street. She then took her two twin sons to the lake by the woods and drowned them before killing herself. Her ghost walks through our complex grounds and the lake behind us. She mourns her children and husband that she murdered. Her spirit has not been able to rest."

"I'll admit this woman did go to the lake," Lance said, "but a ghost does not print out Google maps!"

Lance pulled out the crumpled page he found out in the woods near the lake.

"What do you mean?" Terrance asked while taking the paper from him.

"I found this last night," Lance said. "Someone was looking through my window and I chased them out to the back of the complex. The fence was cut open easily enough for someone to slip through. I walked through the opening and found this by a bush. Then, when I tried to get back onto the apartment grounds, the fence's opening was closed shut with zip ties. Someone locked me out long enough to keep me away from my apartment. They may have attempted to break in again, but they didn't in the end."

"Are you serious?" Terrance said. "Gustavo we should go check the fence."

Lance led the way out to the back of the apartment complex to the section of the gate that had been cut and then zip tied. Once they arrived, Lance put on an I-told-you-so look.

"See!" he said and pointed at the part of the fence that was zip tied together.

"Dammit," Gustavo cursed. "This is going to cost us to fix."

"It's not a ghost," Lance said. "Ghosts don't cut through fences."

"I always thought maybe he was too superstitious," Terrance whispered into Lance's ear so that Gustavo could not hear."

"What happened then?" Gustavo asked. "This might have been someone else. La Viuda is real. I'm telling the truth. Es la verdad."

"I'll call in a police report and maybe we can have some extra eyes at night," Terrance said. "This woman is a suspect. We will find out who she is."

Gustavo looked offended by Terrance's change of heart of his belief in Gustavo's alleged folklore. He swung his rake over and took off to continue his yard work without another word.

"Thanks for helping," Lance said. "Keep me posted on anything you learn. I also wanted to mention that I'll be moving out in a few weeks too. I'm going to find a place with my fiancé. After these crazy experiences here, I think I need a change of scenery."

"I'll get that paperwork started," Terrance said. "I'm sorry to see you go. Can I ask you a favor?"

"Um, sure," Lance replied.

"Can you keep this mysterious woman a secret?" Terrance said. "I don't want to start a panic across the community here."

"Ok," Lance agreed.

Lance woke up on Friday morning feeling refreshed and less on the edge. He did not have any strange visitors peeking through his window, and when he stopped by Terrance's office before he went to work, Terrance had confirmed that the veiled woman had not showed up overnight. With that satisfying news, Lance went to work feeling much more relaxed than he had all week. He did take his anti-anxiety medication the night before to allow him to sleep, so he assumed the medication was working well to calm him.

The workday went by in the blink of an eye. One second he was walking in and having his morning coffee, and the next he was bidding his tired-looking brother Dylan farewell on his way out the door. Lance picked up Amy from her apartment and then they were on their way to her parent's vacant cabin for a much needed weekend getaway. Lance had chosen not to tell Amy about the woman from the cemetery and his apartment complex so as not to worry her. The irksome feeling resonated in his mind, but the prospect of Amy and him moving in together in a completely different zip code, was enough to make him get through the one-hour drive into the hill country. When Amy and him were not talking and there was silence, Lance's mind would wander off into the memory of road trip he had with Claire a few years back.

"I can't believe we are driving all the way to San Diego from Seattle," Claire said over the loud music blasting from her car stereo.

"Driving through California is beautiful...like you," Lance replied.

They had been driving through the Pacific Coast Highway all day, and the sun was beginning to set below the horizon of the ocean. The sky was bright pink and orange. The windows of Claire's Jeep were down and her beautiful red hair was blowing into the wind. Her hands were interlocked with Lance's on the center console. Lance had never felt so happy and lucky. He kept looking at Claire and knew she was the one for him. They were celebrating their one-year anniversary of being a couple. They had taken a few short trips around Washington in the past, but this was their first major trip together, he thought as they drove down the west coast of the United States.

"I love you," Claire said to Lance, and she reached over and kissed his cheek.

"I love you more," Lance replied.

They exchanged a happy laugh and began to sing the lyrics to the song that was blaring on the radio, while not caring about the other cars behind them that were giving them judging looks for how silly they may have appeared.

"Can you lower the volume of the radio," Amy shouted when Lance had turned it up when his favorite song was playing.

"Oh come on," Lance said playfully. "Let's sing-along to this."

"I want you to focus on driving safely," Amy said. "It's getting dark."

"Live on the wild side," Lance said in a defeated manner.

"It's hurting my ears," Amy said pointing to both her ears. "And I can't talk to you over it."

"Fine," Lance said bitterly.

"I'm sorry," Amy said after a few minutes of silence. "The wedding stuff is still going through my head. I feel so bad not working on planning during this weekend."

"That's the point," Lance said, "We want to get away from it all and have Lance and Amy time."

"Yeah, I know," Amy said. "I'll text Jill to go dress shopping and send me photos."

"No," Lance said. "You can do that when we get back."

"It'll help me narrow down options," Amy pleaded.

"Lance and Amy time only," he said. "The rest can wait. Please baby?"

"Ugh," Amy groaned. "Fine."

They arrived at Amy's parent's cabin that evening. It had already been fully stocked with groceries by Amy's parents a few days ago when they stopped by to upkeep the house. Lance carried their travel bags and put them in the master bedroom of the cabin. Amy rummaged through the cabinets looking for food options. She decided she wanted to cook for their first dinner of their weekend stay.

"I'm thinking we should make a pasta," Amy suggested when Lance came back into the kitchen.

"Yum," Lance said while rubbing his stomach. "That sounds like a plan to me."

"Do you remember when we dated the first time?" Amy said. "You wanted to cook me a dinner for the first meal. I was hesitant at first because I thought that meant you wanted me at your apartment so that I would be easy access for a hook up."

"And it turns out you were," Lance teased.

"Shut up," Amy said.

Lance thought back to the three months he dated Amy nearly five years from that day and a year before he met Claire. They broke up because Lance and Amy had a fight that was taken out of context. He believed Amy was saying negative things about him to one of her friends behind his back. Later, he found out that he misunderstood a conversation he overheard, and even though they had stopped seeing each other romantically, they remained friends. Lance had eventually met Claire and then moved to Seattle, but they had kept in touch every once in a while.

When Lance moved back to Austin after his heart-breaking and stressful break up with Claire, he felt alone and scared. He was so used to having someone to love and the feeling of being loved, that he was desperate to seek out someone. He reached back out to Amy and let her know he was back in Austin. They went out for a drink at a bar on Sixth Street, and ended up spending the entire night at her apartment. For those few weeks he was able to hide the pain of his recent break up. He never considered Amy a rebound, but as Rose, Lance's therapist, had told him in a recent session, he should have given himself more time to enjoy a single life as he had always rushed to be in some kind of relationship whether it was emotional or just sexual. Lance knew that Rose may have had a point, but he also knew that reaching back out to Amy rekindled his old feelings and the stars aligned for them once again.

Lance and Amy recounted the tail of the night they rekindled their romance over the pasta and salad they cooked together. Lance had never felt more in love and more comfortable than at that moment knowing that he was with someone whom he could trust and would not be fueled by crazy jealous intentions like his former lover Claire. They toasted each other and their glasses of red wine clinked. The blaze in the fireplace was lazily licking the logs and giving off a warm glow to the cabin.

After they finished their meal, they retired to the living room couch where they began to kiss feverishly and slowly they went from fully clothed to naked on the couch with only a fleece sheet over them to add to the warmth of the friction already caused by their bodies as they made love into the quiet night in the hill country.

The alarm clock on Lance's phone began to ring. It scared both Amy and Lance who had fallen asleep on the couch.

"Turn it off," Amy groaned.

Lance stretched and reached for his cell on the coffee table. He turned off the alarm and got up to get dressed.

"I'll make you breakfast baby," Lance said.

Amy smiled and stretched, then closed her eyes.

"I'm going to sleep some more," she said. "I never get to sleep in."

Lance proceeded to cook a delicious breakfast that consisted of scrambled eggs, bacon, French toast, and fresh squeezed orange juice. He presented it on a platter and made it look as though it was being served at a restaurant. He brought it into the living room and set it on the coffee table in front of Amy. She woke up once the smell of the food reached her nose.

"Wow," Amy said with delight. "I could get used to this in marriage."

"You'll have to cook for me too, you know," Lance teased.

"This is the twenty-first century," Amy retorted. "None of this macho stuff. I want us to be equal. That's what marriage is about. There should always be equality in the relationship. You meet me halfway…always."

Lance closed his eyes to those words. He recalled a scenario where he was in a heated argument with Claire during the time they were together.

"It's always about you and when you want to have sex and when you want to go out. All you want to do is stay in," Claire said angrily in Lance's one bedroom Seattle apartment.

"Claire …" Lance began, but he was cut off.

"Don't," she replied angrily. "I always do what you want to do. You never meet me halfway. It's not fair!"

"I moved across the country for you!" Lance snapped. "You know I'm having trouble adjusting and I feel as though some of your friends don't even like me."

"That's because they don't know you!" Claire replied. "They want to get to know you, but you don't give them the opportunity to get to hang with you when all you want to do is stay in. I want our relationship to be equal. I want to be on equal footing, but if you don't make an effort to hang with my friends and become a homebody, then we will never be able to have a life outside the walls of your fancy luxury apartment that your mom helps you pay for."

"Ok, you crossed the line there," Lance snapped. "Just leave."

"I'm sorry," Claire pleaded. "I did not mean it that way."

Lance pushed Claire out the front door of his apartment. She began to cry and plead for him to let her back in. He put his back to the door as she knocked on it and remained silent until she stopped and her cries became fainter and fainter as she walked out of his complex and back to her apartment, which was a block away.

"Yeah," Lance said to Amy. "Being equal is good. We are a team after all."

"Glad you agree," Amy smiled and she kissed Lance on the lips.

"What would you like to do with our Saturday afternoon?" Lance asked.

"Want to take the boat out on the lake?" Amy suggested.

"That sounds like a plan to me!" Lance agreed.

Lance and Amy spent the afternoon leisurely paddling the boat, owned by Amy's family, on the lake that was located a mile away from the cabin.

"It's nice to see that spring is finally around the corner," Amy said as she ran her fingers lazily through her hair.

"Yeah, the weather is getting warmer and the day light is sticking around longer in the evening," Lance said. "I can get used to this."

"You know what I just realized?" Amy said suddenly. "I still have a few more months on my lease. Dammit. There's no way we can move in until after the wedding or I'll be penalized."

"Well…that blows," Lance replied. "I guess I can do month to month at my place until your lease ends."

"Yeah," Amy said. "Anyways, I'd probably drive you crazy with the wedding planning if we lived together."

"That's so true," Lance agreed. "It'll be nice to live together once we tie the knot. It'll make it more official."

"And for the honeymoon…" Amy said while taking one of Lance's hands off the steering wheel of the boat to hold it, "I want to go somewhere exotic and warm."

"I've always wanted to visit Australia," Lance said. "Maybe we can go down there?"

"Well, our wedding is in summer, which is their winter down under," Amy said.

"Oh right," Lance replied. "Maybe something in the Caribbean?"

"Perhaps," Amy said. "Oh look at us talking about wedding stuff when we agreed we were going to take our minds off the planning."

"Guilty," Lance smiled.

They docked the boat around dinnertime and walked back up to the cabin. When they arrived, Lance began to pull out pots and pans from the cabinets.

"How about we make pasta...again?" Lance suggested.

"We have ingredients for spaghetti," Amy said.

"Let's do that," Lance said. "I'm starving."

Lance and Amy spent the evening making their dinner and sharing a bottle of wine. They fell asleep on the couch to a TV marathon of one of their favorite shows. Lance was awoken when he heard his cell phone vibrate on the coffee table. He reached for it and saw that it was his brother calling. Lance got up from the couch stealthily so as not to wake up Amy.

He walked outside onto the porch and dialed Dylan back.

"You called?" Lance yawned.

"Sorry to call you so late, Lance," Dylan replied and he sounded out of breath. "I'm in a bit of dilemma."

"What's going on?" Lance said with a feeling that he was not about to hear good news.

"I got really drunk earlier and ended up going over to Victoria Price's house," Dylan said.

"You what?" Lance sounded agitated.

"I know it's crazy," Dylan said. "I wanted to get closure because I'm so angry she got out of jail and wasn't found guilty for dad's death. It was murder after all."

"Dylan," Lance said. "You can't just go to her house unannounced...or at all. Our lawyers advised us to have zero communication. Mom will be pissed. What did you say?"

"She threatened to press charges because I was allegedly harassing her," Dylan said. "That's what I'm worried about. I didn't mean to open Pandora's box. Mom will in fact be pissed."

"Ok, calm down for a sec," Lance said. "You need to stop with the substance abuse first of all. Secondly, let me do damage control."

"Are you going to meet up with her and talk to her?" Dylan asked.

"I'm more level headed than you right now," Lance said. "I'll go Monday after work. I'm staying at Amy's parents' cabin just outside of the city limits. We are heading back into town tomorrow."

"Ok, you're better with words than I," Dylan admitted. "Thanks little brother."

Lance ended his call and jumped at the sight of Amy.

"How long were you standing there?" Lance said.

"For a bit," Amy said sleepily. "I heard your voice and it sounded like you were having a heated argument."

"It was Dylan," Lance said. "He went over to the house of the woman who allegedly killed my father."

"Is he insane?" Amy said in shock.

"He's been using again," Lance confessed. "He needs rehab or an intervention. His addiction is getting pretty bad."

"Oh God. Do you think the woman will do anything to retaliate?" Amy asked.

"Personally, I think she wants to remain low key," Lance said. "There was so much negative press on her, and I know my mom would hate having the spotlight on us again."

"Well, maybe this woman won't try to press charges," Amy said. "After all, she has been cleared of murder charges."

"That's my hope," Lance said. "However, I feel like I can relate to what Dylan was going through. My mom shielded us from much of the press and kept us out of the courtrooms. George was very helpful and by her side a lot of the time during that really difficult point in our lives. That's probably why they became so close and eventually married almost a decade later. Anyways, maybe I need to see this woman. Maybe I can get answers."

"I honestly think you should let the dust settle," Amy advised. "It's not worth it to open old wounds. Maybe she won't really do anything. Don't go."

"Maybe. You're probably right," Lance said, yet he had already made the decision to pay Victoria Price a visit.

Lance avoided Amy's gaze because he could not look at her with honesty knowing that he would be going to visit Victoria against her wishes.

Chapter Nine

Monday evening had arrived at last. It felt like the longest day of Lance's life. He packed up his briefcase when the clock struck 6:00 pm and darted out the door.

"Lance!" Dylan called out to him when he was almost at the elevator to the parking garage.

"Are you going to talk to her?" Dylan asked.

"Yes," Lance said. "But this stays between us. Amy doesn't even know."

"Ok good, because I got a call from her lawyer saying he wants to speak with me," Dylan said. "He left me a voicemail, but I have yet to return it. I'm nervous about it."

Dylan genuinely looked nervous. He was fidgeting with his watch, and he still looked like he had not had any sleep. There were dark circles under his eyes, and his hair looked as if it had not been washed in days.

"Are you sober?" Lance asked.

"What?" Dylan whispered. "Yes...yes of course I am."

"Stay that way," Lance said. "I'm going to drive to her house. She lives up north right?"

"Yeah," Dylan said. "I wrote down the address. Here."

Dylan handed Lance a Post It note with Victoria's home address.

"Thanks," Lance said. "I'll talk to you later tonight."

The drive down to Victoria's house was very nerve wrecking for Lance. He had not seen Victoria since he was a teenager. He was not sure if she would look the same or if time had aged her. Lance's mind rested on a particular memory of Victoria.

Lance was thirteen when Victoria was hired as his father's assistant. His mother was not keen on her hire because she felt threatened and insecure next to her. Victoria was in her early twenties and was a former beauty pageant model. Lance had arrived home from school and saw Victoria sitting on the living room couch.

"Hi," Lance said awkwardly because he had developed a small crush on her.

"Hey there Lancey," Victoria said playfully. "Your parents are upstairs."

"Ok," Lance replied without making eye contact with her.

Lance walked upstairs and could hear muffled voices coming from his parents' bedroom. The door was closed. Lance walked closer to the door then pressed his ear against it to hear the fight his parents were having.

"She dresses like a slut," Marissa spat. "Why did you hire her, Jeremy?"

"She's very talented," Jeremy said. "You have nothing to worry about. I can tell by your tone that you're threatened."

"Do I have anything to worry about?" Marissa snapped.

"Of course not honey," Jeremy replied and he sounded offended.

"Why did you bring her to the house?" Marissa asked. "It's a little unprofessional and any work that needs to be done can be done in the office, right?"

"I was going to do a driving tour of a neighborhood I want to get some of our properties on," Jeremy replied. "We stopped by the house since we were in the neighborhood. I just needed to grab some paperwork from the home office."

Lance heard footsteps approaching the door, so he quickly ran to his room. Just as he was opening his door, he turned around as his father addressed him.

"Didn't hear you come in," Jeremy told Lance.

"Hey dad," Lance said. "Are you going to be home for dinner tonight?"

"Need to work late," Jeremy said.

Lance brought his attention back to the road. He was in an unfamiliar neighborhood. The memory he relived in his head was the day he began to suspect his father was having an affair. Lance felt that had his mother not shown up at the house almost at the exact same time as his father and Victoria, his father would have been caught in the act with Victoria. Lance knew his parents' relationship was strained. They lived and worked together. They rarely had time off. These factors were getting to them. Lance had feared divorce was inevitable and eventually they had a separation. Lance never knew for certain if his father had started the affair prior to the separation. Even though his parents were apart, they were still legally married, and Jeremy was definitely seeing Victoria romantically by then.

The neighborhood where Victoria lived in was very quiet and peaceful. It was in the north part of Austin in a very suburban area where every house looked the same. He arrived at her address and parked his car directly in front of the house. There was an old silver Toyota Corolla parked outside.

Lance mustered the nerve to open his door and walk up the front step. He pressed the doorbell and it rang. He heard shuffling inside and then saw a pair of eyes peeking through the curtains of the side window of the house. The door opened slowly to reveal someone that did not look like the former beauty pageant winner he had met over a decade ago. The woman had unkempt blonde hair and looked like she was over weight. The Victoria Lance once knew was really slim and was always dressed to the nines. The woman before him was wearing an oversized shirt and sweat pants. She was at least a hundred pounds heavier than when he had last seen her. While she looked dramatically different, there was no mistaking it was her. She had wrinkles and looked older than her real age, which would be her late thirties or early forties.

"Can I help you?" the woman asked.

"Victoria Price?" Lance asked.

"That's me," Victoria replied.

"It's Lance. Lance Avery," Lance replied expecting the door to be shut in his face.

Tears began to pour down her face.

"Why do you boys feel the need to bother me?" Victoria cried. "I am not really going to press charges. I had my lawyer call just to scare your brother. I don't want trouble. I want to be left alone. I have been living off welfare for years. I'm ugly. I'm fat. My life has been ruined. Is this not torture enough? Have you come to gloat at my pathetic sloppy mess?"

"I wanted to clear the air," Lance said, but he could feel anger surging within him.

While it did appear that Victoria's life had taken a dark turn for the worst, he knew that no matter what had happened to her, she was still alive and his father was not.

"I did not do it," Victoria sobbed. "I know you want to ask me. I know you want to hear it. Look at me. I have nothing to live for. At least in jail I would have interaction with people. I'm alone. But I did not kill your father. I loved Jeremy."

"Don't say that," Lance snapped. "You are the reason my parents divorced."

"They fell out of love," Victoria said.

Every word she uttered was making Lance angrier.

"You are a home wrecker," Lance said. "You were the last one to see him alive. He did not fall into the pool drunk and drown himself. My father was a swimmer in high school."

"I went home early that day," Victoria said. "Your father said I could do so."

"Weren't you two living together?" Lance asked.

"I still had my own place," Victoria replied. "Yes, we spent many evenings together, but I was still living on my own. He was not my sugar daddy like the press made him out to be."

Victoria opened a drawer near the door and pulled out an old newspaper clipping and showed it to Lance. The headline read "A Price To Pay."

"Victoria Price, paid the price," Victoria sobbed. "Of an accidental death I did not commit. I was in jail for three years before I was let out because there was no sufficient evidence."

"Be honest with me," Lance said sternly with tears forming at the corners of his eyes.

"Why don't you come inside and we can talk," Victoria said. "I'll tell you everything you want."

Lance accepted the invitation, yet he felt uncomfortable the minute he walked into the house of his father's alleged killer. Two cats hid under a couch at the sight of Lance. He sat on a rocking chair in her living room. The house looked worn down. The walls were lacking pictures or artwork and the furniture did not match. It looked as if she was given hand-me-down furniture. Her home also appeared as if it had not been cleaned in months. There were plates on the coffee table full of scraps of food.

"I fell in love with your father," Victoria began. "I would never have wanted to hurt him. Your mother harassed me when they separated. She kept insisting I resign, and of course Jeremy would never have fired me. She was angry because she had no control over my hire as I only assisted Jeremy. I promise to God I was not the one who killed your father. Only God, your father, and I know the truth. I was not his killer."

Lance was feeling frustrated. He was sure that he could get closure. He wanted to hear the truth. He knew that at this point, jail was not really and option for Victoria. He knew she was being punished in a way for her crime, but he also knew that nothing could bring his father back.

"Tell me the God damn truth!" Lance snapped again.

"I have," Victoria said. "What do you want me to do? Lie to you? I have nothing to lose. I'm being honest."

Victoria broke down into hysterics. She was crying loudly. Lance looked at her with pity. This was a woman who had lost everything: looks, money, youth, a social life, friends, and much more. The tears that were pouring onto her food-stained shirt were not an act. There was something about the look of genuine sadness in her eyes that spoke the truth. This was a woman who had been broken and perhaps her act of adultery was the only sin she was guilty of. Lance's heart dropped. He felt that he was in fact getting closure and that perhaps the courts were right to let her go. There was no proof. She was really in love with his father. She gave up everything to be with him and at the price of being scorned by the Austin upper class community that knew his father.

"Victoria…" Lance began awkwardly. "I'm sorry for your loss."

Victoria stopped crying and gave him a look of confusion.

"Excuse me?" she asked.

"I think we were so caught up in the heat of the tragedy and from anger at my father's infidelity, that we were blind," Lance admitted. "You really did love him. You never intended to drown him in that pool."

"I did not Lance," Victoria said. "My word is honest and pure. I have nothing to lose."

"I don't know what to say," Lance said feeling awkward. "Your life was ruined. Our lives were turned upside down. We all lost so much."

"That house never sold," Victoria said. "Nobody wanted to buy the house where an alleged murder had occurred. Eventually it was torn down so they could rebuild a new house because the neighbors complained it was an eyesore. Before it was torn down, I went back there to find my own closure. I was never able to attend your father's funeral, naturally. I've even visited his grave. I am sorry for splitting up your parents. I was young and naïve. I was drawn by your father's good looks and power. It was terrible of me to do that. For that I will always pay. It ruined me."

"I don't want any more trouble Victoria," Lance said in a comforting voice. "We will leave you alone. Thank you for your time. I hope this has been closure for you as it has been for me."

"Thank you," Victoria sniffled. "It has been. I only wish I could get closure with your brother and mother, but that might be pushing it."

"Yes," Lance said while making a mental note never to speak of the details of his meeting with Victoria because his mother and brother were dead set on their thoughts on her guilt.

Lance walked to the door. He turned around and looked at Victoria. She gave a forced smile for about a second before returning to a frown.

"Have a good life Lance," Victoria said.

Lance nodded and left her house. The walk to his car felt like several miles. So many emotions came rushing back once he stepped outside into the crisp evening. Lance never would have thought he would come to terms with believing that Victoria was not behind his father's death, but the conversation he had with her felt like the truth. He left the home of a very broken woman who had nothing left to live for.

Lance's attention was drawn to a white Mercedes that pulled up next to a neighboring house. It felt very out of place in the very quaint lower income housing community. The car was familiar and Lance's heart dropped when he saw the woman who came out of it.

"Mom?" Lance said in shock.

"I was phoned by Victoria's lawyer earlier that your brother had harassed her," Marissa said, and she had an angry look on her face. "What the hell are you doing here?"

"Damage control," Lance said. "I fixed it. I assume that is what you are doing here?"

"This bitch is the last person I want to see," Marissa said. "But if Dylan was stirring up trouble, I need to make sure she keeps quiet. She's done enough to embarrass our family. I don't need her to attempt to make herself look like the victim. You didn't see her in court. She played that character really well."

Lance was not sure how to respond. He began to think that perhaps Victoria was acting during his conversation with him. Had she hoodwinked him?

"No need to talk to her mom," Lance said. "It will be too difficult for you and you might lose your temper. Let's get out of here before someone sees you."

"What did you tell that whore?" Marissa demanded.

"We don't want trouble and that Dylan was intoxicated when he came to see her. I told her we will never make contact again," Lance lied.

"Very well," Marissa said curtly. "Then I guess thanks for clearing that up. However, next time come to me."

Marissa glared at the front door of Victoria's house with disdain. She turned on her heel and stepped into her Mercedes.

"Talk to you later Lance," she said, and without another word, she sped off.

Lance talked to Dylan on his drive home and left out most of the details. He did not want to cause him stress so he left out the part where he ran into their mother. Lance arrived at his apartment and found a package that was left at his door. There was no name or any kind of labels on it. It was a blank rectangular box. Lance stepped into his apartment and took out a pair of scissors to cut open the tape binding the box. Once the package was open, he pulled out its contents. It was a flashlight with a blue bulb. He had never seen anything like it. The flashlight's body was thin and silver and felt heavy. He clicked it on and it glowed blue.

"A black light?" he said peculiarly. "Who would have left this at my door?"

Lance had an uneasy feeling about this item. His night had already been really emotional, and he was hoping that the strange things that had been happening to him would cease.

He turned off his living room light and turned on the black light. The entire living room glowed blue. Anything that was white became brighter and pronounced by the light. Then Lance discovered the most bizarre thing. There was text written on his wall that was only visible via the black light.

"What the hell?" he gasped.

Written on his wall was the sentence:

"To the untrue man, the whole universe is false- it is impalpable- it shrinks to nothing within his grasp. And he himself is in so far as he shows himself in a false light, becomes a shadow, or, indeed, ceases to exist."

And there was another quote below that one:

"...if truth were everywhere to be shown, a scarlet letter would blaze forth on many a bosom..."

"*The Scarlet Letter...*" Lance realized that the quotes were from Nathaniel Hawthorne's well-known novel.

Lance flashed the light around the room to look for other messages and at last he found one final message:

"Like father, like son."

Lance turned his living room light back on and sank onto his couch. He felt scared, unhinged, and anxious. Whoever had broken into his apartment had written these messages on the wall. It was not to steal anything. It was to leave a deliberate message. Lance remembered the white pen he found near his desk that night. He walked over to his desk and pulled the pen from it. He drew a circle on the back of his hand. His hand remained blank as if no ink came out of the pen. He flashed the black light over his hand and saw the circle he drew. The intruder had left it behind, whether intentional or by mistake.

"Oh my God," Lance said with worry.

The only person in the world who he felt could do something like that was Claire. He had cheated on her. She knew that his father had had an affair before his untimely death. He was being mocked in his own apartment.

"She knows where I live," Lance said in fear. "She's in town. She's been watching me."

111

"What do I do?" Lance said later that evening to Edward who had come over to see the scribe on his wall.

"This is messed up," Edward said. "She's crazy. She's back. You have a restraining order. Do we call the cops?"

"I think I'm going to pay a visit to my lawyer tomorrow during my lunch break," Lance said. "He can give me advice on how to proceed. We'll need proof it's her. I want to be sure."

"Who else would it be?" Edward asked matter-of-factly.

"I know, but I can't jump to conclusions or even contact her out of the blue," Lance said.

"This is really insane," Edward sighed. "You saw Victoria tonight and then this happened. There's some bad energy in your life and you need to cleanse it."

"Keep this between us," Lance insisted. "I don't want to worry my family or Amy for that matter. I'll handle this. My lawyer will be able to help me. If she's stalking me again, it's time to put the law into my hands."

Chapter Ten

Lance's lawyer's office was located a few blocks away from the branch he worked at. Once it was time for his lunch break, he took a short walk to where the office was located.

"Avery!" a man in line for a food truck outside of the office building called.

"Roger," Lance said. "I'm a few minutes early for our meeting."

The man was Lance's lawyer. He was dressed in a well-fitted navy blue suit with a black skinny silk tie. He had dirty blonde hair and bright blue eyes. He was clean-shaven and his hair was perfectly parted.

"Do you want anything from this truck?" Roger asked. "They have the best tacos in town."

"I'm fine," Lance said. "Thanks. I actually brought my own lunch and ate it at my office before coming here."

"Ok," Roger said while shaking Lance's hand. "Let me get my lunch and we'll head on up."

Fifteen minutes later, they arrived at Roger's office. A name plaque at the entrance read "Roger Cohen Law Firm." There was a young female receptionist at the front desk who greeted them with a "hello" and a friendly smile.

"Right this way Mr. Avery," Roger said.

Roger's office was much like the way he dressed. The entire room was clean, neat, and well organized. Lance took at seat in front of Roger's large oak desk. Roger took a bite of his taco and wiped his mouth before speaking.

"So your message said you might have been harassed by Claire Carpenter again?" Roger asked.

"I think so," Lance said.

"She would be in breach of her restraining order," Roger said matter-of-factly while taking another bite of his taco.

Lance explained to Roger what had happened to him within the last couple of weeks from Amy's car accident to the break-in of his apartment and the black light ink invisible writing on his wall.

"...and the only person whom I know would have written such a message, is Claire," Lance finished.

"Did you file a police report updating them on the writing?" Roger asked.

"Not yet," Lance said. "It was late last night and I had to be up early. I did not have time."

"I see," Roger said, and he got up from his desk and paced back and forth in thought. "We'll need proof. Obviously I do not want you to contact Claire directly. We need to see if we can find out what she is up to. I'm going to have a private investigator friend of mine do some digging into if she's been flying or driving into Austin. Perhaps that will be a good start. If we see something suspicious, then we'll notify the authorities because she could be mentally unstable if she has gone through the lengths you are alleging."

"How long will it take your private investigator?" Lance asked. "Or at least what do you think the estimated amount of time would be?"

"Could be days or weeks," Roger said. "It is the best we can do until we have actual proof."

"I guess so," Lance said.

Lance walked out of the office and made his way back to his bank. Before arriving at his office, he decided to call his old friend Josh who had introduced him to Claire over four years ago.

Lance found Josh's contact information in his phone's contact list and pressed his name. It rang five times before Josh picked up.

"Lance?" Josh's voice answered.

"Josh. Hi, I know this is random but..." Lance replied.

"I haven't heard from you in a long, long time," Josh said and his voice sounded cold.

"You know I had to cut off communication with you after my break up with Claire," Lance said.

"I heard bits and pieces of it," Josh said. "Claire was vague on details but she took it pretty hard. It was pretty shitty of you to cheat on her."

"I know," Lance said. "I was not in a good place. I need you to keep this between us, but what is Claire up to these days? Is she still in Seattle?"

"I don't talk to her much either," Josh replied. "We're Facebook friends, so I see her posts from time to time and she looks happy. She posts a lot of pictures of her traveling the country. She mainly travels to the east coast for work."

"Has she been to Austin recently?" Lance asked.

"No, not at all," Josh replied. "If she did she would have called me up for sure. I know she would."

"I see," Lance said while not feeling assured.

"Is there a problem?" Josh questioned.

"No, no," Lance lied. "I was curious. I thought I saw a woman who could be her doppelgänger, so I wanted to ask."

"Ok," Josh said. "Well, maybe you and I can get drinks soon?"

"We should," Lance admitted. "I'm sorry you were a bit in the middle of things during our break up. I know you did not want to take sides as you were both our friend separately."

"Well, we are all adults and we can move on," Josh said. "And yes, drinks soon."

A few weeks had passed and Lance still had not heard any news from his lawyer. He was told that they were still doing some digging and would have a full report soon. Lance had not experienced anything strange since the night he discovered the writing on his wall and the package containing the black light that was left at his door.

Lance was also getting through many sessions with Rose. He had finally explained to her in his latest visit what had happened with Victoria Price, the writing on his wall, and how he reached out to his lawyer and Josh for help to see if he could get clues on if it was in fact Claire returning for revenge.

"You have to be careful," Rose said. "I'm glad you have not personally reached out. That would not be smart. Especially because you have a restraining order."

"I realize that," Lance said. "I'm just waiting on pins and needles until my lawyer, Roger Cohen, gets back to me."

"Very well," Rose said and she gave Lance a warm and comforting smile. "How are wedding plans coming along? You are about three months away from the big day, right?"

"Yes," Lance replied. "June 17th. Planning is coming along well, mainly because my fiancé is doing most of the hard planning. I finally picked out my suit and Amy has her dress selected. Our rehearsal dinner will be at a restaurant downtown. That should be nice. I'm ready for this to be done. We are going to the Virgin Islands for our honeymoon. It's not too far and we can still get our domestic cell phone reception."

"Sounds like things are coming along great," Rose smiled. "And if we may go back to Victoria Price for a moment...do you really believe she was innocent after all?"

"I do," Lance said. "The way she broke down in front of me was so honest and raw. I guess I may never know the real truth, but it could have very well been an accident."

"Well," Rose said, "if you had come to me first and told me you were going to pay her a visit, I would have told you it wasn't a great idea. However, if you feel it gave you closure and she's not taking any kind of legal action against your brother, then you should just move along and put that past behind you."

"I am going to," Lance agreed.

"Do tell me..." Rose continued, "You mentioned your mother showed up at Victoria's house as well, correct?"

"Yes," Lance said.

"Why?" Rose asked.

"To clear the air on behalf of my brother," Lance replied. "However, I'm glad it was me, because my mother hates her more than anything else on this world. It would have been a cat fight."

"Well, luckily you were there," Rose said.

"She likes to take matters into her own hands all the time," Lance said. "She has always done damage control for her sons every time we got into some kind of trouble. I had two DUIs when I was in college, and thanks to her connections, they don't exist on my record. I'm thankful for that, but I also know that I need to be more responsible for my actions. Dylan needs to as well."

"Ok, ok." Rose said. "Is there anything else you want to cover before we end our session?"

"Nothing else," Lance said.

"Oh, did you and Amy find a place to move into?" Rose asked.

"Oh," Lance said. "We are going to wait because her lease isn't up until right after our wedding."

"Spend as much time together practicing cohabiting," Rose said. "You'll learn more about her and see how living together is very different from dating. It'll be helpful for your marriage. It's just a thought."

"Thanks for the advice," Lance replied.

"Doing anything fun this weekend?" Rose asked casually.

"I'm going out with my friend Edward for drinks Friday night, and I invited my friend Josh—the one who I met Claire through. I have not seen him in a long time," Lance replied.

"That should be fun," Rose asked. "Drinks downtown?"

"Yes. Somewhere on Sixth Street," Lance replied.

"Well, enjoy," Rose said. "We'll do the same time next week."

Later that evening, Lance arrived at Amy's apartment. She and Jill were spread out on the floor with wedding invitations scattered around them.

"Addressing tonight?" Lance asked.

"Yes, you could help," Amy said curtly.

"Sorry, no need to be so moody," Lance said defensively.

"I'm sorry, I'm just stressed," Amy admitted.

"You can help though," Jill teased sarcastically. "It's so much fun."

Lance spent the evening helping Amy and Jill address the wedding invitations. Around 11:00 pm, Jill got up and stretched.

"I'm tired," she yawned. "I'll come back tomorrow to help you finish, Amy. I need my rest before work tomorrow."

"Ok, night!" Amy said. "Thanks for helping tonight."

"Mind if I stay over?" Lance asked Amy after Jill had left her apartment.

"Of course future hubby," Amy smiled and she gave Lance a kiss on the lips.

Lance had trouble falling asleep that night. He started to feel uncomfortably warm with Amy's comforter. She was fast asleep and breathing peacefully on her side of the bed. Lance stared up at the ceiling trying to count sheep in his imagination. His mind began to wander to that day he and Claire first kissed at the sheep's meadow at Josh's family's ranch. Then he was brought back to reality when his phone lit up. He reached for it. It was a text from Edward that read, "Plans have been finalized for Vegas. Next month we'll have the best bachelor trip ever."

Lance replied, "You're up late. Ok thx. Talk to you about it in person on Fri."

Lance placed his phone on the bedside nightstand and focused on the night Claire and he had their final fight...

It was three o' clock in the morning in summer. Lance had fallen straight to sleep in his bed next to Claire. They attended a concert and had VIP tickets that enabled them to attend an open bar prior to the show in downtown Los Angeles. Lance had become inebriated, and as soon as they arrived back at his apartment, he undressed and fell onto his bed.

"Good night," he mumbled sleepily to Claire who looked annoyed.

"Really?" Claire said with her hands at her hips. "Not even a good night kiss?"

Claire rolled her eyes and noticed his phone was on the floor. He had dropped it when he pulled off his pants to change into his sleepwear. Claire bent over and picked it up. Lance had recently put a passcode on his phone because of previous issues he had with Claire going through it. Claire had not gone through it in many months and had a suspicion that she should search it. The phone did not have a passcode that time, so she swiped it open.

The past few weeks were a little rough between Claire and Lance. Both of them had traveled to see their families and they had a few fights about trust. They were constantly bickering and Claire was starting to feel like she was at her wits end. She had marriage on her mind, and she was beginning to think that Lance was nowhere near even thinking about the next step. It left her frustrated and confused.

Her heart began to race against her rib cage as she scrolled through his text messages and Facebook app messages. She felt as though her heart was beating loud enough for Lance to wake up, but when she looked over at him and saw that he was in a deep sleep, she sighed a breath of comfort.

Claire came across a series of Facebook sexual message exchanges between him and a girl he had hooked up with prior to meeting Claire.

"Wait a minute…" Claire whispered to herself.

She looked at the date of the beginning of their message exchanges on his text history and realized that he had in fact met this girl a few days after she and Lance had become officially boyfriend and girlfriend.

"He had sex with her!" Claire gasped. "And only days after June 17th…the day we became a couple!"

Tears began to stream down Claire's face. She had gone through his messages before and knew about this one girl. He had contact with her a few times since they had been dating, but this only confirmed that Lance had in fact physically cheated on her while they were in a relationship. And his last message exchange with her was very sexual and had only happened two weeks prior. Claire began to cry silently into a pillow. She felt betrayed. The man she had opened her life and heart to, was sleeping next to her in a pile of his own lies. He had insisted he was always honest, but in black and white, before her eyes on his iPhone, was the truth she had always suspected.

"I've never been wrong about the guys who have cheated on me in my past," Claire said to herself. "Why? Why would you do this to me…"

She considered waking him up to yell at him. She had done it in the past when she had gone through his phone and discovered something out of the ordinary and suspicious. She decided that silence was going to be key. She dressed out of her sleepwear that Lance lent her and packed up her belongings. She gave Lance one last glance and then turned her head and walked out of his room and out of his apartment. She closed the door behind her and made her way back to her apartment, which was only a block away.

Lance woke up that morning to an empty bed. He shuffled around confusedly and rubbed his head, which felt like he had hit it against a rock.

"Holy hangover," Lance mumbled. "Claire? Babe where are you?"

Lance got up and looked into his living room. There was no sign of Claire. He walked back to his room and saw his phone on his nightstand. He opened it and saw that there were no messages.

He sent a text to Claire, "Thank you for last night. I didn't hear you leave this morning. I had an amazing time at the show."

Lance then sent her videos of the band that they saw perform. Minutes and hours passed and he had not heard back from her. Lance began to feel like something was wrong because she was so attached to her phone that she would text back almost instantly some times.

Lance opened up his Facebook application and his heart fell. It was left open to the message conversation he had had with this girl he had a fling with named Julia. He realized that Claire had gone through his phone. He instantly became angry and wrote to Claire.

"That's the last straw. You went through my phone again!"

Twenty minutes had passed and there was no answer. Lance knew he had really screwed up this time. He knew she was so fragile with trust and he had once again broken it.

Lance wrote another text to apologize and like fire, a few several heated texts from Claire came blazing through.

"You lied to me. You said you never hooked up with that Julia chick while we were together, but the dates of your message exchanges prove you did. You are a cheater, a loser, and you're pathetic. You need therapy. You need help. I've done so much for you. I can't do this anymore. We are DONE."

Lance began to cry. Claire was the only person he had in Seattle. He never made his own friends in the year that he lived there. He felt scared and alone. His birthday was two days away, and he was planning to fly back home to Austin to spend it with his family.

Another text from Claire came through: "Meet me at my apartment at 1pm during my lunch break. We need to talk."

Lance showed up at Claire's apartment at the time she asked him to appear. He was buzzed in and walked down the hallway to her unit. The hallway felt like the longest walk he had ever had to take as his guilt began to eat away at his heart. He stood at her doorway for a few seconds and took a deep breath. He knocked and she opened it with an angry glare.

Lance took a seat on her desk chair, while Claire sat in the middle of her bed with her arms and legs crossed. There was a book with several red letter A's on the cover that she pushed off her bed in anger.

"I'm pissed," she finally said.

Lance tried to get up to hug her, but she gestured for him to back off.

"I'm sorry Claire. I love you," Lance began to cry.

"Why did you do it?" Claire demanded.

"I screwed up," Lance said honestly. "I have a problem. I know that. I need to change, and I'm going to get help. I love you more than anything in the world. You're the most gorgeous girl in the world. You're the only one I want."

"I asked you a few weeks ago to be straight up honest with me," Claire said. "Remember? I noticed you had been to those dating sites again, and I asked you why. You said it was because you wanted to see if one of your exes was single and back on there. I even asked you if in the time between last June 17th and the present day if you had slept with anyone else other than me. Your answer was 'no,' but it turns out you lied. You always lie. Why can't you be honest God dammit? Be a man!"

"Claire, I'm s-s-sorry," Lance sobbed. "I know I have a problem. I want to fix this. I want to fix us."

"I don't need fixing, Lance," Claire shouted. "You do! We're done. There is no fixing this. You don't even want to talk about a long-term future. Is marriage even on your mind?"

"I need to get my life together," Lance said. "I need a job. I need friends here. I've had a rough time getting any of those here."

"You had chances," Claire said. "But you mess every opportunity up, and you always ask mommy for money. You're not independent. You need someone to take you by the hand and help you. I'm not going to be dragged into a depression because you are unstable and depressed. Your instability is rubbing off on me and making me feel horrible. You've degraded and embarrassed me. This is the last straw. We are done. There is no more Lance and Claire. Just...just leave."

Lance pleaded, but Claire gestured for him to leave. Lance shrugged his shoulders and wiped his eyes. He walked out of her apartment and did not turn back. He felt too ashamed to look her in the eyes.

Chapter Eleven

Friday arrived, and Lance could not have felt more excited for his night out with Edward and his reunion with Josh. They met at this bar in the warehouse district of downtown, called Dragon Fire. Its décor was oriental. There were Chinese lanterns and large dragons on every corner of the bar. It had purple velvet chairs and was very posh.

Lance and Edward arrived together. They saw Josh sitting on a chair in one corner of the bar alone. He was typing into his cell phone.

"Hey Josh," Lance said. "Good to see you."

They shook hands and exchanged smiles.

"This is my friend Edward," Lance said.

"Hey," Edward said while shaking Josh's hand.

"Glad we could meet up tonight," Josh said. "I'll get the first round. What will you guys have?"

"Vodka soda for me," Lance said.

"I'll do a scotch," Edward added.

The three chatted and laughed as they caught up and got up to speed on each other's lives. After a few rounds of drinks, Lance felt the courage to ask Josh a few questions about Claire.

"When was the last time you saw Claire?" Lance asked suddenly.

"I haven't seen her since you both broke up," Josh said. "I actually gave her a call after you and I spoke. Don't worry, I did not tell her we spoke, but I may have mentioned we were meeting up at a bar tonight for drinks. She sounded well and didn't really ask about you. I think she pretended like I didn't say anything about you. She's still living in Seattle and has been traveling out of the country for work twice a month. She has some clients in South America. She's working on something regarding a new coffee bean they are harvesting for her coffee company that she does marketing for."

"So she hasn't been to Austin then?" Lance asked.

"Not at all," Josh replied. "I told you, if she visited, she would have reached out to me. She did sound suspicious about our call though. I guess mainly because I called out of the blue."

"This place is getting packed," Edward said. "Josh, are you single? I am. If so, let's go meet some ladies. This one here is getting married and we need to catch up to him."

"Yep, I'm single," Josh laughed. "Let's do a loop around."

"I'm going to run to the restroom," Lance said, and he walked to the opposite end of the bar to where the restrooms were located.

When he finished and exited the restroom, he was surprised to see a familiar face walking out of the woman's restroom.

"Rose?" Lance said in surprise.

"Lance!" Rose said. Lance noticed she had a drink in one hand. "Oh my goodness, I was not expecting to run into patients."

"I thought you worked in Dallas from Friday to Sunday?" Lance asked.

"I took today off to hang with some girlfriends," Rose said. "I'm driving up in the morning. I probably should not drink too much. Oh! I'm with Dana. Come!"

Rose grabbed Lance's hand and ushered him to the part of the bar where Dana and another woman were having a conversation.

"Lance!" Dana said in surprise. "What are you doing here?"

"Having a guy's night out with my friends," Lance replied.

"And we are doing a girl's night out!" Dana said sounding like the alcohol was already affecting her.

"Can we get you a drink?" Rose asked. "Oh, and this is our friend Stephanie."

"Hi," Stephanie said.

She was slim and about a foot shorter than Lance. She had dark brown hair and eyes.

"Nice to meet you," Lance reached for her hand to shake it.

"I see you made some friends," Edward called to Lance and then patted him on the back when he arrived at the bar.

"Oh hey," Lance said. "This is my neighbor Dana, her friend Stephanie, and this is Rose…my therapist. Ha!"

They all let out a laugh.

"Should we not be hanging with you then?" Edward joked. "Can you tell us his embarrassing secrets?"

Rose looked annoyed at first, but then smiled and laughed, "Of course I can't."

"I'll get us all a round," Josh suggested and he gave the bartender his credit card and told him, "Keep it open."

One round became two rounds and two rounds became three. Lance had hit the point of drunkenness where he did not care about embarrassing himself. He was dancing to the songs playing and Rose kept staring at him intently. He felt uncomfortable with how she looked at him. Her smile was like a trap. He had always found her to be attractive, but to see her in a

126

slim black dress and not in work attire, made him realize how beautiful she really was.

"Can't keep up?" Rose whispered into Lance's ear.

"Watch me," Lance said and he took a shot of vodka from the bartender that Edward had passed to him.

It was 1:45 am when the bartenders called out, "Last call for alcohol."

"We're about to be cut off!" Josh exclaimed in a depressed voice. "Let's have an after party at my loft. It's not far from here."

"Looks like your friend Edward is getting cozy with our friend Stephanie," Dana teased.

Lance looked over at the other side of the bar and saw Edward and Stephanie locking lips in a very heated make out session.

"Oh gosh," Lance said rolling his eyes. "I think those two are going to—yep there they go."

Edward signaled to them that he and Stephanie were going to take off. They waved goodbye and headed out of the bar to catch a cab.

"I guess it'll be us four then," Josh said. "I'll go flag a cab for us."

A few minutes later, Lance, Josh, Rose, and Dana were headed a few blocks north of the bar to Josh's extravagant high-rise condominium. Lance was drunk and part of his mind was telling him how ridiculous it was that he had been out drinking with his therapist who was friends with his neighbor. Lance laughed to himself as they went up an elevator to Josh's floor.

"Wow, very nice place Josh," Dana said when they arrived at his unit.

Josh's apartment was very well maintained. It was very minimalist with the furniture set up making the living room look larger than it was. The walls were all glass and revealed the stunning skyline of Austin.

"I'll make us some more cocktails," Josh said, and he gave Dana a wink.

"I'll help you," Dana said in a flirtatious manner.

Rose and Lance sat on the couch and did not say anything for a few minutes. It felt awkward. Then Rose spoke up.

"Have fun tonight?" she asked.

"Yes. You?" Lance replied and he made eye contact with her.

"It was nice to let my hair down," Rose replied and she stroked her blonde hair.

Lance was trying hard not to look at her chest because she was wearing a low cut dress. He mustered a lot of energy to distract himself with a magazine that was on Josh's coffee table.

"Guys!" Josh called out from the kitchen. "Your drinks are here on the counter. We will, um, be right back."

Josh grabbed Dana's hand and they disappeared into his bedroom with the door shut.

"Well, that's my ride," Rose said. "Not that she can drink right now anyway. I should get going though. I have along drive to Dallas tomorrow."

"Right," Lance yawned. "I'm also kind of tired."

Lance's head felt so heavy. His vision was slightly blurred and his eyes were dry from wearing his contacts on so long. He kept squinting.

"Finding it hard to believe I'm sitting before you?" Rose teased as she made commentary on Lance's constant eye blinking.

"My eyes are tired," Lance said.

Rose placed her hand on Lance's lap and began to stroke his thigh. He felt a sensation of ecstasy and blood rushing through his veins. His heart began to race. Her beauty mesmerized him. Rose began to lean closer to him and then she pressed her lips against his and they began to kiss passionately.

Lance's mind was wiped blank. All he could think of in his head was that this was one of the most attractive women he had ever kissed in his life. Then his mind raced to Amy and his heart sank. He pulled away.

"What's the matter sexy?" Rose said seductively.

"You know I'm engaged," Lance said sadly. "And I'm your patient."

"Shut up," Rose said, and she pulled Lance by the collar of his shirt and kissed him again. Lance was very tense and tried to break free, but after a few seconds of feeling her rosy lips, he let go of the control of his body and put his hands through her hair. She shifted her head slightly and then grabbed his hands and pushed them over his head so that he was lying down. She climbed on top of him and continued to kiss him.

Lance moved one of his hands and placed it on one of her breasts. She pushed them aside quickly and got up off him. She ran her hand through her hair and began to breathe hard.

"I'm so very sorry," Rose said. "I should not have done that. You're so cute. I mean...never mind."

Lance could not pull two words together to reply. Rose shifted uncomfortably and then went to reach for her jacket.

"We were drinking," she said apologetically. "It was an accident. We're both adults. Let's, um, yeah let's just not bring this up. I'll...I'll see you soon. Tell Dana I took a cab."

Without a glance back, Rose left Josh's apartment leaving Lance looking like a deer in headlights. He ran his hands through his hair and wiped sweat off his forehead.

"What was I thinking," he muttered to himself.

His head was beginning to tinge with pain from the heavy night of consuming alcohol. He put his head against a pillow on the couch and relived the past few moments of his lapse in judgment in his head. He could not help but feel excited and alive when he kissed Rose. He only wished that they could have done more.

But what about Amy? He thought. *You can't cheat on her. I have a problem. I'm seeing a therapist to fix my problem, and now I just made out with that very therapist.*

Lance woke up the next morning to Josh shaking him.

"What happened?" Lance groaned.

"It's almost noon," Josh said. "You've been knocked out all night. Dana left this morning. She and I hooked up."

Josh sounded like he was in a good mood. He had a big grin on his face.

"Want me to make you breakfast?" Josh asked. "I was thinking of frying up some eggs."

"I should get home," Lance said while reaching for his phone. "Ah, I have a few missed calls from Amy. Yeah I'll catch a cab and head home."

"Thanks again for hanging out," Josh said. "It was more fun than I bargained for. I'm glad we can put the weirdness of our friendship behind what with your past with Claire and all."

"Right," Lance said. "Yeah, that's all water under the bridge. We'll hang again soon."

Lance spent the rest of the weekend keeping to himself. He ended his Sunday night by having dinner at his mother's house. When he arrived at her penthouse condo, George answered.

"Just in time," George greeted Lance.

"It smells good," Lance said.

"I made pot roast," George said. "And there won't be a serving of cow hearts tonight."

Lance tried to make his laugh to George's attempt at a joke seem genuine, but it ended up coming out forced. Lance walked in and saw his mother run into her room. Lance followed her into her bedroom. She appeared flustered and was looking through her dresser drawers as if she was searching for something.

"What's up?" Lance asked.

"What? Oh!" Marissa replied. She was surprised by Lance's arrival. "I was in the restroom and did not hear you knock. Sorry, my head's not here right now. I lost a book of mine that was a dear gift from your grandmother. I've been looking everywhere for it."

"What book?" Lance asked.

"Just some book," Marissa replied, and she seemed too distracted with finding it than to make small talk with Lance.

"I'll go help set the table," Lance said awkwardly.

"Ok," Marissa mumbled as she began to search under her bed.

Lance set the table, and George served the food on the plates. George and Lance sat at the table awkwardly while they waited for Marissa. Lance was on his phone to avoid having a conversation with George, and George was fidgeting with his utensils.

"Honey!" George called out to Marissa. "The roast is getting cold."

"Coming," she called out.

Marissa came out of her bedroom with her hair slightly disheveled. She brushed it with her hands to attempt to make it look neat after running around frantically looking for her lost item.

The entire meal was an awkward affair. George kept trying to make small talk with Lance. Lance kept trying to talk to his mother, and Marissa kept looking over at the clock on the wall and sipping on wine more than she was actually chewing her food.

"Close on any homes this week?" Lance asked.

"What? Yes, we are closed right now," Marissa replied absentmindedly.

"I didn't ask if you were closed," Lance said, "I asked if you closed any homes. Did anyone put in an offer that you accepted?"

"Oh, no," Marissa said, finally looking at Lance. "It was a slow week. Tomorrow I have several clients coming to look at a house on Lake Travis. It should be a good day."

"Is everything ok?" Lance asked. "You seem bothered."

"I'm fine," Marissa said while not looking like she meant it.

"She's been working a lot," George chimed in. "Care for dessert? I made cheesecake."

After they finished dessert, George grabbed all the dinner wear and started to clean the table and place the dishes in the dishwasher.

"I'm going to the balcony for a smoke," Marissa said. "Care to join?"

"I don't smoke, but I'll come outside," Lance replied.

They stepped out onto the cool spring air. There was the sound of cars honking in the distance as they were in the middle of downtown.

"Nice night," Lance said.

"It is," Marissa replied and she lit up her cigarette.

"What's really bothering you?" Lance asked.

"I'm annoyed I cannot find my book," Marissa responded.

"That can't be the only thing that is bothering you," Lance added.

"Dylan told me about his addiction," Marissa said. "He was supposed to join us for dinner, but we got into a fight. I told him I would pay for the best rehab center in Austin."

"He needs to fix this on his own," Lance said. "He's an adult. He needs to be responsible and mature and check himself in. I've tried."

"He told me you knew," Marissa said. "I understand why you did not tell me. You know how easily I get stressed out."

"Will he be going to rehab?" Lance asked. "I mean what did he say in response to your suggestion?"

"He wants to wait until after your bachelor party in Las Vegas," Marissa replied. "If he did a program before, he would not be able to attend your celebration. Since he's in the wedding party, he wanted to partake in the celebrations."

"Well, his health is more important," Lance said. "He and Edward have been working on planning it with my other groomsmen. I guess we can keep a close on eye on him so he doesn't fall into a dark hole."

"Everything alright?" George asked through the balcony door.

"Yes," Marissa said. "Thank you for an amazing dinner, honey."

Marissa smiled and gave George a quick kiss on the lips. Lance shifted uncomfortably.

"I should get going mom," Lance said. "It's getting late."

"Thank you for coming, honey," Marissa said.

The afternoon of his next session with Rose had arrived faster than Lance would have cared for. He had been dreading seeing her since he kissed her the previous weekend during a lapse of judgment. He decided he did not want to come in, but he felt that taking a session off would make things look awkward. Lance decided to call in with an excuse to cancel his weekly session in the end.

"Hello?" Rose answered her phone.

"Hey...it's Lance," he said.

"Oh hello Lance," Rose answered cordially. "How can I help you?"

"I won't be able to come in for our six o' clock today," Lance said. "Something with work came up."

"I see," Rose said. "Same time next week then?"

"Yes," Lance replied. "Thanks for being flexible."

"No problem," Rose said. "You were my last patient for today, so that means I have an early night off. Have a good rest of your week."

"Thanks...you too," Lance replied.

Lance decided to go for a run near a creek not too far from his apartment complex. He put on his running shorts and tennis shoes and strapped his iPod to his arm. He sprinted out the gates of his apartment community and down the road to a creek where there were small gravel trails. The trails led to the edge of the lake and into a wooded area nearby where many outdoor enthusiasts would take their dogs and children for physical activity. Edward was waiting for him at the entrance to the trail.

The spring evening was perfect for a run because the sun was now setting later and offered more sunlight to visitors on the trail. Lance and Edward sprinted down the trail until they reached the edge of the lake. They took a swig from their water bottles, and then proceeded up the trail into the wooded area, which became more of a hike because of a few steep hills along the path.

"Man, I'm tired," Edward huffed. "Let's take a break."

"It will get dark on us before we finish the trail," Lance pleaded. "Come on!"

Lance kept on running while Edward jogged behind. Eventually, they ended up at a part of the park that once had a zoo.

"The abandoned zoo!" Edward exclaimed. "I've heard of this place. There used to be a zoo here in the nineties, but it closed down after the it lost funding from the city."

"I've never heard of this place," Lance said scratching his head.

They walked a few yards off the hiking trail to find what appeared to be a giant rocky wall. When Lance put his hands on it, he realized it was not rock, but a hard type of plastic material.

"All for show," Edward said patting the wall. "This was probably the lion's cave. I see an opening over there."

There was an entrance into a cave a few feet away that Edward had pointed to. Lance looked around and saw that there were no other hikers or wilderness enthusiasts running about the trails. The sun was already beginning to set and could not be seen because of the trees surrounding them.

"We should probably go," Lance said. "The daylight is waning on us."

"C'mon," Edward insisted. "I'm going to go in."

Lance thought he heard the rustling of leaves and the click of someone's feet walking over rocks. He looked in all directions and could not see anyone. The sound eventually faded away.

"Did you hear something?" Lance asked.

"No," Edward said.

"Oh," Lance added. "I thought I heard someone walking up. Do you really want to explore this thing? It could be unstable and dangerous."

"Yeah," Edward said, and without another word, he ran into the cave's opening.

Lance followed behind, gingerly stepping over loose rocks on the ground. As soon as he was inside, he saw Edward walking up a staircase in a narrow hallway. The ceiling was so low to the ground that Lance had to hunch to walk up.

"These stairs were designed for animals," Lance said with a tone of frustration, and he dusted dirt off his shirt that fell on him from the ceiling.

Edward ignored Lance and kept on walking up the steps and he turned a corner once he had reached the top.

"Wait up!" Lance called for Edward.

Lance arrived at the top of the stairs and looked back down at the entrance. His heart dropped. Framed in the square opening of the cave was the woman he had seen at the cemetery and the same woman that his apartment managers insisted was "The Widow." She had her hands against the wall and her head tilted with her eyes shut.

As soon as Lance saw the veiled woman, he fell over backward onto the landing on top of the staircase and let out small yelp of surprise that echoed eerily in the lion's den. Lance got back on his feet and looked down. The woman had disappeared.

"Are you ok?" Edward had asked when he returned back to where Lance was attempting to stand.

"I saw something—*someone!*" Lance exclaimed. "We need to get out of here."

At that moment, a young boy had walked into the cave and looked at Edward and Lance in shock. The little boy gasped and began to walk back slowly.

Lance walked back down to the bottom of the stairs to meet the boy. He was taken by surprise and began to run out of the cave.

"Wait!" Lance called. "Don't be afraid. I have a question."

The boy stopped running and turned back to look at Lance who was standing at the cave entranceway.

"Did you see a lady wearing a black dress a few seconds before you walked into the cave?" Lance asked.

"No," the boy replied. "There's nobody here."

The boy walked away and ran down the path in the direction of the exit.

"Why do parents let their kids run around at dusk alone?" Edward said when he met Lance at the entrance to the cave.

"Beats me," Lance said, although he was pretty sure he saw a woman at the entrance.

Lance took a second to collect his thoughts before he followed Edward back up stairs. Lance had an unsettling feeling about being at the den.

That could not have been a ghost, he thought to himself. *I'm losing my mind. I'm tired. I'm seeing things. That's it.*

"Are you coming?" Edward called.

"I am!" Lance yelled.

They continued to explore the cave. There were random pieces of trash that littered areas of the floor. They found a few dead mice skeletons, and the walls were covered in graffiti. Metal cage doors blocked several of the rooms off. It was becoming increasingly difficult to see as the daylight began to fade. Edward turned on the flashlight feature on his phone so that he could see ahead of him. A sudden noise echoed in the distance and startled Edward. He dropped his phone on the ground. The room fell to black.

"Did you hear that?" he whispered.

"Yeah," Lance said. "I don't think we are alone."

"Maybe that kid came back?" Edward asked while picking up his phone to shine light at the hallway before them.

Edward picked up his pace and continued down the hallway. He looked back a few times to make sure Lance was behind him. Lance was following him closely with his own phone's flashlight feature lit up.

"It's practically pitch black," Lance said. "We need to get out of here. They close the gates to the trail at sunset."

"Shit," Edward cursed. "I was pretty sure there would be a way out of the caves from here. Maybe we should double back?"

"Yeah, that's probably a good idea," Lance said, and as he turned around he heard a crash in the distance coming from the direction that they came from.

Lance jumped and backed into Edward.

"Ouch," Edward whimpered as Lance had stepped on his toe.

"What the hell was that?" Lance said as his heart began to race.

Both Lance and Edward pointed their light at the path that they had come from that lay before them. One of the cage doors had fallen.

"Did someone do that?" Lance panted.

Lance took a deep breath and walked to the door. He put his hands around the bars and tried to lift it up.

"It's heavy," Lance cried. "We're locked in here!"

"Shit!" Edward cursed again. "Let's dial for help!"

"I have no reception," Lance complained.

"Dammit!" Edward blurted. "Me either. These damn thick walls aren't allowing us to get signal."

"Do you think someone closed the door on us?" Lance asked.

"It could have fallen on its own," Edward said. "This place is old, and maybe we shook the walls too hard or something."

"Hello!" Lance called out. "Is there anyone there?"

His voice carried down the hall and bounced off the walls. There was no response to his question.

"Shh," Edward said suddenly. "I hear something."

In the opposite direction of the hallway, they heard the shuffling of leaves against the floor. There were even what appeared to be faint footsteps in the distance.

"We're not alone," Edward whispered, and his voice sounded hoarse.

Lance gulped, "There's only one way to go."

"After you then," Edward said quietly.

Lance nodded his head and took the lead down the path that they originally intended to avoid. This time they had no choice. They walked slowly down the narrow hall. Edward was grasping Lance's shoulder so as not to lose him in the dark. Lance pointed his phone's flashlight on the ground and had to squint his eyes at what he saw before him.

"Is that a trail of rose petals?" Edward asked.

Chapter Twelve

On the ground were strategically placed petals in a trail that led down the narrow hallway to parts of the lion's den that they had not yet explored. Lance and Edward looked at each other with unease.

"This isn't right," Edward whispered.

"I think somebody followed us here," Lance admitted. "Remember the weird things that happened to me? This could be related. I mean there weren't rose petals on the ground earlier. I could have sworn I saw this woman at the bottom of the stairs earlier. She was wearing all black and a pillbox hat. She was dressed as if she was attending a funeral. I saw the same woman at the cemetery near my father's grave. She had a red rose. Now there are petals on the ground."

"Let's make our way forward," Edward insisted. "We have no other choice."

Edward bent over and picked up a loose rock from the ground.

"What?" Edward said when Lance gave him an inquisitive look. "I have no other way to protect myself in case there is some creep trying to kill us or something."

They began a brisk walk down the hall stepping over the petals as they loomed upon the ground with every step they took.

Lance shined his light on the brick wall. There was red writing on the wall: "He loves me."

"What the hell?" Lance muttered.

He put his finger on the writing and it smudged upon contact. It had a greasy feel to it. He smelled the red substance that stuck to his finger with his nose right over it.

"I think this is lipstick," Lance said.

Edward touched the writing as well and nodded in agreement.

"Was it freshly written?" Edward asked.

Lance shrugged, but he felt as though the answer was 'yes,' but he decided to keep quiet and continue their walk down the dark hallway.

A few yards away from the first writing on the wall, they found another written message in red lipstick. This message read, "He loves me not."

"Is this some kind of game?" Lance said aloud. "He loves me, he loves me not...and rose petals on the ground."

"Maybe it's some teenage girl who was playing here earlier today," Edward said matter-of-factly. "Yeah that's probably it."

As they continued down the path, they kept finding more messages on the wall. It would vary from "He loves me" to "He loves me not." The rose petals became scarcer and scarcer the further down they went until they arrived at the end of the hall. There was a narrow set of steps that led down to what appeared to be an exit.

"Yes," Lance punched the air in excitement. "Let's get out of here."

Lance and Edward ran down the stairs. With every step closer to the exit they took, they could feel the cool spring air of the outdoors hit their faces. When they exited the cave, they found themselves in an outdoor enclosed pit. They looked up and saw a railing. They were in another part of the old zoo's lion exhibit and the railing above them was where spectators would view the lions.

"Look!" Edward pointed at a large boulder in front of them.

The boulder had one petal on the ground in front of it and red writing on its side that read: "He loves me NOT."

The word 'not' was in all capital letters for emphasis.

"This is really messed up," Edward said. "Is this message supposed to be for you? Can it be Claire again?"

"I think it is," Lance admitted. "Who else?"

Somewhere in the dark corners of the pit, they heard a loud breathing noise that was followed up with a growl and the sound of earth being scratched by claws.

"What the hell?" Lance yelped in surprise.

A large male lion had apparently been woken up by their conversation and was now glaring at them from the corner of the pit. The light of the moon revealed the body of the magnificent animal.

"Oh my God!" Edward whispered loudly. "Why is there a live animal here? This zoo has been closed for almost two decades."

The lion snarled and positioned itself for an attack.

"It's going to pounce and maul us," Edward panicked.

The lion stretched and began its run and decent upon Lance and Edward. They both turned at their heel and ran back in the direction of the cave's entrance. As they entered and were about to ascend up the stairs, there was a yelp and cry from the lion behind them. They turned around and saw the large animal keel over and fall onto its side. The animal's large eyes gave them a look of horror right before its eyelids fell heavy and shut over its pupils. The animal's chest kept moving up and down and it began to let out grunts that could have easily been snores.

"It's not dead," Lance said while tiptoeing back out into the enclosure.

He got a closer look at the lion and saw that there was a dart sticking out of its side. Lance walked closer to the lion and realized that it was tranquilized. Someone had sedated it and saved them. Lance looked up at the railing above them and saw the silhouette of someone looking at them. By the time Edward had looked at the direction that Lance's eyes were fixed on, the person staring at them had disappeared into the shadows.

"There was someone up there," Lance said. "Someone who saved us."

"Nobody comes to this trail with a tranquilizer in their hands randomly," Edward said through heavy breaths. "What the hell is a live lion doing here?"

"I still don't have cell reception, but as soon as we get off this trail and I get a signal, I'm calling the cops," Lance said.

"We're still trapped here," Edward said. "We can't climb out of this pit, and that gate in the hallway is blocking our way back to the entrance we came in through."

"Well, we need to figure out something," Lance said. "This lion won't be sedated for long."

"I guess we can't yell for help either," Edward replied. "Might wake up this creature."

"Hey, why don't we go back into the cave?" Lance suggested. "This entrance has a gate too. We can close it and the lion won't be able to touch us. We might be stuck here until the morning it looks like."

"I hope someone sends a search party," Edward said hopefully. "It's kind of chilly and gross in this cave."

Lance and Edward had fallen asleep at the top of the stairs. Night had come and gone, and the sun was now peering into the cave from the entrance at the stairs. Lance immediately shot upright when he realized that the cave's gate was open.

"Holy shit!" Lance exclaimed, and he ran down the stairs to reach for the lever that would pull the gate down and protect them from the sleeping lion.

When he reached the foot of the staircase, he looked into the pit. There was no lion to be found and the boulder in the distance was wiped clean of the "He loves me NOT" message. Lance looked on the ground and could not find any flower petals either.

"What's the matter?" Edward called down to Lance who was scratching his head in confusion.

"The lion is gone. And so is the lipstick writing," Lance called up.

"Hey!" Edward said suddenly. "The door in the distance is open again…and it looks like the messages on the walls here are wiped clean too as well as the *Hansel and Gretel* trail of petals."

Lance walked back up the stairs to meet Edward. They walked back down the hallway in the direction that was blocked previously. There were no signs of rose petals or the messages that were written on the left and right walls of the hallway.

"Nobody will believe us," Edward said as if reading Lance's mind.

"I was just thinking that," Lance replied. "Somebody trapped us in here and nearly killed us with a lion."

"But if that same somebody was the one that tranquilized it," Edward added, "then why would they go through all this trouble only to keep us alive."

"I don't know what the mind of a crazy person entails," Lance stated. "We're lucky to be alive. This is beyond messed up."

They were able to exit the old abandoned lion's den easily without any obstacles on their path. They finally arrived through the opening they had originally entered and could see the hiking path in the distance already busy with early morning hikers.

Lance and Edward walked back to the main road at the entrance of the park. As soon as they arrived near the entrance, both their phones picked up signals and exploded with beeps from voicemails, texts, and missed calls.

"Amy has been calling me like crazy," Lance said. "My mother and George have as well."

Lance and Edward sat at a park bench and listened and replied to all of their messages to explain what had happened to them.

"…I know I should not have gone into that cave," Lance pleaded to a distraught Amy over the phone. "Don't worry we are ok."

Lance and Edward decided to keep the part about the lion and being trapped a secret as they had no proof and knew it would cause more worry and harm.

"It's beyond weird," Edward said. "You really think someone is out to get you?"

"All these strange coincidences," Lance said numbering each event he experienced on his fingers, "happened to me over the last few months. It's crazy."

Lance noticed he had missed one of his voicemails. It was from his lawyer, Roger Cohen. He clicked on his voicemail and listened to it.

"Hey Lance, it's Roger Cohen. I just got information back from my private investigator. He's been on the tail of your former girlfriend, Claire Carpenter. Apparently, she travels a lot for work around the country and keeps a normal routine. My P.I. said you have nothing to worry about. She's still living in Seattle and is apparently active in yoga and spin classes based on where she likes to frequent on her spare time. I guess you have nothing to worry about. Call me later. Bye."

Lance explained to Edward that he had his lawyer do some digging for proof that Claire could possibly be visiting Austin. He felt so defeated with the voicemail he had received. He was almost one hundred percent sure Claire was behind this, but how could someone be at two places at once?

"But last night was beyond crazy," Lance said. "That was done intentionally and unless you have an enemy I don't know about, I feel it was targeted at me."

"It could have been a joke," Edward said.

"A lion that is about to pounce and maul two men is not something you joke about," Lance spat. "Someone was messing with me—or us. I don't even know what to believe anymore."

"I think you should watch your back closely," Edward said. "If other weird things have happened to you, your mom, and even Amy…well…I mean to say…"

Edward struggled with words. He was not sure how to tell Lance to be cautious. Then he added, "Jill did get this strange email a while back from an anonymous person asking her to make sure you don't marry Amy. We did not want to bring it up because we felt it was just a joke, but I guess there are some strange things happening to you."

"See! Someone is trying to infiltrate my social circles too," Lance replied.

"Well, you know that Claire is not physically here to cause you hell," Edward said. "You did place a restraining order and you now have proof that she's following it. We can't prove who the email came from. The sender's email address seemed random. However, maybe this is someone else? Does Amy have a crazy ex by chance? "

"I don't think she does," Lance said.

"You don't think this could be the work of Victoria Price?" Edward suggested. "Who else would hate your family so much?"

Lance mulled over what Edward had said. Even though Lance had a visit with Victoria and came to the conclusion that she was innocent, there was always the possibility that it was an act. Then Lance realized something else.

"The woman I saw at the cemetery and yesterday at the cave was slim and slender. Victoria Price has gained serious weight. There's no way it was her."

"How do you know she gained weight?" Edward asked, and Lance finally divulged his recent visit with Victoria Price.

"I think she is more than done with that part of her life," Lance finished. "Maybe my father's death really was an accident. There isn't much proof on both regards."

"I can't believe you went to see that lady," Edward exclaimed. "That woman caused your family so much grief—even if she didn't kill your dad, she still ruined your parent's marriage."

145

"I know. I don't ever want to see that woman again," Lance explained. "I found my closure. She has been punished enough, and her life is not what it once was. She's had her hell and price to pay. Anyways, we better get going. We have to work today."

The rest of Lance's week slipped by faster than he would have thought considering he was anxious to head to Las Vegas for his bachelor party. The night before the flight to Vegas, Lance had a scheduled session with Rose. He had not seen her since the night they ended up drinking together and kissed.

Lance was thumbing through a gossip magazine in Rose's waiting room and tapping his foot nervously on the shag rug on the floor. His eyes kept darting to the clock that was ticking lazily on the wall. He had a water bottle with him that he kept absent-mindedly taking sips from even though he was not thirsty.

"Lance," Rose called from her office. "I'm ready."

Lance walked into Rose's office. She was seated at her desk and typing on her computer. She saw Lance and smiled. Then she got up off her desk chair and sat herself in her swivel leather seat that was directly in front of her patient's couch.

Lance took a seat and rolled up his long sleeve shirt because he was beginning to feel stuffy in the office room. It could have been his nerves that were making him sweat and his heart beat fast.

"How are you today?" Rose asked.

"I'm…fine," Lance replied. "You?"

"Not bad," Rose said while flipping through a notepad she had on her lap. "So, what should we discuss today?"

Lance thought about telling Rose what had happened to him the week before at the old abandoned zoo, but decided he was tired of talking about the weird experiences he had encountered without knowing who or what was behind them. Lance was silent for half a minute before he spoke.

"I have my bachelor party this weekend," Lance said. "I leave tomorrow for a long weekend. I took some time off work. My groomsmen and I are flying out tomorrow morning."

"Oh, that should be fun," Rose replied automatically. "How many in your party?"

"With me, there will be six of us," Lance said counting off his party on his fingers. "Me, my best man Edward, my brother Dylan, and three other friends of mine from college who live in different parts of the country. They are meeting us in Vegas."

"I see," Rose said. "How about we talk more about your last relationship? I think it would be best to cover some more grounds on that as we get closer to your wedding so that we can help you get through some of those dark memories."

"That's fine," Lance said. "I never talked about our first big fight. Let's start there…"

Lance walked a block down the street from his Seattle apartment to arrive at the doorstep of Claire's apartment. Her roommate answered and looked scared.

"Hey Jane," Lance greeted Claire's roommate.

"She's locked herself in her room," Jane replied.

Lance walked into Claire's apartment, which was very clean and neat. Her furniture was modern and very minimalist.

"Has she said anything?" Lance asked.

"No," Jane said. "She came in bawling. What happened?"

"She was supposed to stay over at my apartment tonight, but she got very drunk and became angry with me," Lance explained. "All because I told her she should get rest at home and was too drunk to stay with me. I did not want to babysit her. She went into hysterics, and then she sent me a text saying she was going to hurt herself and take some pills. I'm scared."

"Yeah, she told me the same thing," Jane said. "Should I dial 911? I'm freaking out."

"Let me try to comfort her," Lance suggested.

"Did Claire's moment of drunken lapse in judgment scare you because you almost overdosed on pills as a teenager?" Rose interrupted Lance's story.

"Well, yes," Lance admitted. "The next day after she calmed down I told her I couldn't do it anymore. We had only been together for four months and she had a huge freak out. I was threatening to move back to Austin, and she got scared and sent me long text messages to convince me to stay. I should have left then, looking back at this whole relationship. But I gave in. I took her back and we patched things up with our relationship. She said she would spend more time helping me find a job. It comforted me to know she was so caring and really wanted me. Even though she showed me a side of her that was very scary, I was in love."

"She showed her true colors though," Rose said. "That was your first red flag that Claire had issues. But of course, love makes us do many crazy things. Love is beautiful and love is ugly."

Rose looked out of her window for a few seconds and then turned back to Lance who was staring at his hands on his lap. Lance struggled with a thought for a second before looking up at Rose.

"About the other night…" Lance began.

"It's nothing," Rose said automatically. "I mean to say, it is water under the bridge. We had been drinking. It was quite the accident. I hope we can continue to be professional."

"I, um," Lance struggled to find the right words to say. "Amy cannot ever know about this."

"Doctor-patient confidentiality," Rose said. "We can forget it ever happened."

"I'm sorry," Lance said. "I'm not sure what I was thinking. Maybe this wedding planning is making me nervous."

"It happens," Rose said. "Don't stress about it. You have a very fun trip ahead of you. That will be so much fun."

"Does Dana know about us?" Lance asked.

"I did not tell her anything," Rose said. "Only you and I know what happened, and it will stay that way."

"Thanks for the discretion," Lance said. "It did not mean anything of course."

Rose had a hurt look on her face for a fleeting second before she smiled and nodded.

"Not to say...I mean...you're a beautiful...great person...I just..." Lance fumbled for an explanation.

"No need to explain," Rose added. "Honestly, we all have our moments of weakness. Mistakes are made. Rules are broken. We are only human and these are our weaknesses."

"Right," Lance said while not feeling as if he agreed with that statement. "Well, I guess I'll see you next week."

"Have a good time in Las Vegas," Rose said cheerfully.

"I will," Lance replied.

Lance walked out of Rose's office. Once he was outside, he dialed Amy on her cell.

"Hey babe," Lance said. "Want to come over and help me pack?"

"Sure," Amy replied. "I'll be over in an hour."

Amy helped Lance pack his various outfits for his five-day trip to Las Vegas. They ordered Chinese food for delivery and watched a movie after the packing was done. Halfway through the movie, Amy jumped up suddenly from the couch and ran to her purse that was on the kitchen counter.

"I forgot to show you the wedding invitation cards!" Amy said excitedly. "My mother helped me send them out."

"Awesome," Lance said. "Let me see."

"Here you go!" Amy said excitedly, and she handed Lance a white card with gold fancy lettering and black filigree on the top of the invitation.

Lance read the card aloud, "Ahem...'You're invited to celebrate the union of two souls in holy matrimony at the wedding of Lance Avery and Amy Aberdeen. Please join us in a celebration of their vows and a wonderful evening of merriment and marriage. We request the honor of your presence at their marriage on Saturday, the seventeenth of June two thousand and fourteen at six o' clock in the evening.'"

"What do you think?" Amy asked.

"I like it," Lance said. "It's very simple, yet classy looking. Good job. It even has the address of St. Austin Church—the location where we'll become husband and wife."

"Glad to hear! My mother and Jill have been very helpful," she said. "Now, if only you were excited about helping me with more of the wedding logistics."

"It's all you baby," Lance replied. "You know you want full creative freedom on it, and I've agreed to let you do that."

"Well, helping lick envelopes would have been nice," Amy added sarcastically.

"Fine," Lance groaned. "When I get back I'll help you with any mundane tasks you might have for me."

"Perfect," Amy said.

After they finished watching the movie, Amy kissed Lance goodbye and left his apartment. Lance took off his contacts and slipped into his pajamas. With the help of an anti-anxiety pill, he fell straight to sleep.

Chapter Thirteen

Lance, Edward, and Dylan were seated in first class by each other on their flight to Las Vegas. Dylan had his sunglasses on and was fast asleep on the three-hour flight to Las Vegas from Austin. They arrived at the airport at the crack of dawn to catch their flight. Lance was struggling to fall asleep. He was unable to find a comfortable position to sleep. Edward was deeply immersed in reading a book.

"Any drinks for you today?" a female flight attendant asked Lance and Edward.

"I'll take a diet coke," Edward replied.

"Can I do a glass of red wine?" Lance asked.

"Certainly," the flight attendant smiled. "I'll be back with your orders shortly."

"Starting early?" Edward teased when the flight attendant walked away.

"Why not?" Lance replied.

"What time is the rest of the crew landing?" Edward asked.

Dylan had awoken from his sleep and pulled off his sunglasses.

"Yeah, I haven't met these guys," Dylan said. "But I've been emailing them to plan this weekend in Vegas so it'll be nice to put a face to their names."

"Right," Lance said. "So Brad Barber was in my fraternity. He was the president of the frat the year I graduated. He lives in New York City now. Then there's Wes Parsons. Wes and I were in business school together. He was my freshman year dorm roommate. Wes resides in D.C. I lucked out having him as a roommate. We got along well. Last, but not least, is good 'ole Patrick Wheeler. Patrick went to high school with me. He lives in Houston."

"Oh, I think I vaguely remember Patrick," Dylan said. "He was kind of chubby, right?"

"Yeah," Lance laughed. "He still is, and you know what, it makes him who he is. He's hilarious. That guy needs to be a comedian."

"I'm looking forward to meeting your other close friends," Edward said. "Of course I've known you the longest."

"Hey buddy," Dylan piped in. "I knew him since he was born. We used to share a room."

"Well you're brothers," Edward added. "That doesn't count."

A woman wearing a purple shawl over a black business suit with large sunglasses and a hat, walked out of the restroom in first class. She was carrying a designer handbag that she dropped right at Lance's feet.

"I'm so sorry," she apologized.

"It's ok," Lance assured the woman.

Lance reached down to help her, but the woman insisted she could handle it on her own.

"Thank you sir," she said. "I have it."

The woman picked up her purse in a hurry and walked off to the coach section of the plane. They could hear a flight attendant arguing with her because she was not a first class passenger and was not allowed to use the lavatory up front.

"It looks like she dropped her coin purse," Edward said while noticing there was a small designer coin purse on the ground.

Lance reached for it and unbuckled himself.

"I'm going to go give it to her," Lance said, but Dylan snatched the purse out of his hand. "Dylan—give that back."

Dylan opened the purse and was shocked to see several casino chips marked in various denominations. Most of them were labeled as "$100."

"Whoa!" Dylan gasped. "There is easily more than five grand in this coin purse."

"We need to give it back to her," Lance said.

"She lost it," Dylan joked. "Finders keepers."

"We can't keep that," Edward added. "She'll realize she lost it and come searching for it."

"I think we should have ourselves an amazing night tonight boys," Dylan said pocketing the coin purse.

"Are you serious?" Lance whispered, and he looked around to check that they were not being watched or listened in on.

"You can't do that," Edward said. "That's stealing."

"Dylan, give it to me," Lance threatened.

"Or what brother?" Dylan taunted.

It was then that Lance realized Dylan's eyes looked bloodshot. He was high on something. Lance could tell Dylan was getting worked up and knew he would make a scene because he was neither sober nor thinking clearly. Lance decided to back off and shrugged his shoulders. He turned to Edward and whispered in his ear.

"He's high right now. We'll draw attention to ourselves and he could get in trouble with the law for being under the influence of an illegal substance," Lance said.

"What did you say?" Dylan snapped loudly.

"Nothing...*brother*," Lance said through gritted teeth. "Rest. We have a long night ahead."

"We do," Dylan agreed while putting his glasses back on, "and a long night of gambling and paying for strippers ahead."

The woman who dropped her coin purse did not come back to first class for the duration of the flight. Once they had landed and docked, Dylan quickly got out of his seat, pulled out his luggage from the overhead bin, and ran out of the plane as if he had to use the restroom.

"Shit," Edward said. "We better go too. What if that lady comes back to us?"

Lance nodded in agreement, and they walked out of the plane as swiftly and inconspicuously as possible. They saw Dylan waiting in line for a coffee at one of the airport terminal bakeries. Lance was about to open his mouth to say something when they were within earshot of Dylan, but Dylan spoke first.

"I see her walking to baggage claim," Dylan said. "We are in the clear."

"I can't believe you did that," Lance said angrily. "That poor woman!"

"She didn't look poor," Dylan said matter-of-factly.

"That doesn't matter," Lance spat. "This money is not ours. It's going to bite us in the ass."

"That's my problem," Dylan said. "As one of your groomsmen, let me plan out the rest of the night. I'll get us reservations at a swanky place for dinner, and we'll make some serious dough tonight playing blackjack."

Lance and Dylan argued during the entire cab ride to their hotel. Edward plugged in his earphones to ignore their bickering. At the end of the ride, Lance gave up and decided he was not going to babysit his older brother as it was his own special weekend. They arrived at their hotel lobby and found Lance's three friends waiting for them.

"Guys!" Lance said excitedly as he gave Brad, Wes, and Patrick a group hug.

Brad had blond hair and was wearing slacks and a blazer. He looked very business-like. Wes was black with short dark hair and a well-toned physique. It was apparent that he spent lots of time at the gym. He was also dressed in a suit, but had the top two buttons of his undershirt left open for a casual look. Patrick was completely different from Brad and Wes. He was wearing flip-flops and cargo shorts with a button down shirt that had palm trees all over it. He had long brown hair that fell to his chin, and was on the hefty side with a round face. His eyes were piercing blue, and he had a friendly smile.

"Gents," Lance said gesturing to Edward and Dylan, "meet Edward and my brother Dylan."

Edward and Dylan exchanged handshakes with Brad, Wes, and Patrick. They all hovered around the entrance to their hotel and caught up for about fifteen minutes before Lance urged everyone to check in. Once they all had their room keys, they proceeded down the lobby and into a foyer where the elevators were stationed. Lance pushed the up button to call the elevator. It arrived and all six of them squeezed into it. As the door closed, Lance and Dylan both noticed a familiar woman getting off another elevator across the hall. She was wearing a purple shawl and she looked distressed.

Lance and Dylan made eye contact but did not say a word until they both arrived at their hotel room, which they were sharing.

"She's staying in our hotel," Lance said as soon as they closed their hotel room door behind them.

"What are the odds?" Dylan said nervously.

"What if she sees us?" Lance asked. "She may remember us and ask questions."

"That's a big 'what if,'" Dylan said. "We'll be fine. She'll have no proof."

Lance decided that fighting with his brother was not how he wanted to start off his bachelor party, so he gave in and pretended he had no idea where he found the casino chips.

Later that evening, the six men met at the hotel's five star restaurant. Dylan had made the reservations and an expensive bottle of champagne was waiting for them once the hostess led them to their table. They all took a seat and a waiter began to fill everyone's glasses with champagne.

"Nice choice," Brad said to Dylan.

"I'm starving," Patrick added.

Lance leaned over to Dylan's ear and whispered, "Did you cash some of those chips in then?"

"Sure did," Dylan grinned. "Get the most expensive thing on the menu. Dinner is on me."

"Karma is going to bite you in the ass," Lance said with a bad feeling in the pit of his stomach.

"Stop worrying," Dylan replied with annoyance. "Now, let's get a round of oysters. Actually, let's make it two rounds."

The waiter brought two dozen oysters to the table. Dylan grabbed two at once as soon as they were placed on the table. Patrick had ordered a side of fried calamari and had begun to devour them as if he had not eaten in days. Wes and Edward were carrying on their own conversation. Brad picked at a salad he ordered and spent the early part of the meal catching up with Lance.

"The big day is less than two months away," Brad said. "Are you ready?"

"I just want this to be over," Lance said. "Planning a wedding is stressful and my fiancé is being very picky about all the details. It is exhausting."

"I'm sure it will be wonderful," Brad said.

"How's New York treating you?" Lance asked after consuming an oyster.

"The weather is great, now that it is finally warming up," Brad answered. "The winter was brutal. Makes me miss the Texas weather."

"Well we've had a couple heat waves in Texas and random rainstorms," Lance said, "but definitely not those brutal snowstorms you've been having."

The waiter arrived at the table with another bottle of their finest champagne. The waiter pulled out a pen and pad and asked everyone for their order. Everyone in the party ordered some of the most expensive items on the menu from lobster to fine steaks. Patrick even ordered two entrees because he insisted that his steak was not big enough to fill him up.

"That guy needs to lose some weight, don't you think?" Dylan joked with Lance in a whisper.

Lance rolled his eyes and gave his order to the waiter.

"I'll do the whole lobster with a baked potato. Thank you," he said.

"So, who is ready to thrown down some bills tonight," Wes said to the table.

"I sure as hell am!" Dylan said. "Do you guys want to...*party?*"

"What—are we in college again?" Brad joked, but his eyes flashed in shock when Dylan pulled out a small container with white powder in it.

"Is that what I think it is?" Patrick asked with a smile.

"Dude, put that away!" Lance snapped. "We are at a fine dining establishment. Not some rave."

Dylan waved his hands at Lance to silence him. He poured the white substance on a butter knife and looked around the restaurant. When he made sure that other tables or the restaurant staff were not watching him, he pulled the butter knife up to his nose and took a hit of his cocaine.

"Oh my God!" Lance hissed. "Are you out of your mind?"

"Not yet, but I hope to be! Wooo!" Dylan said, and he punched the air in victory causing other tables to look in his direction and scowl.

Patrick whispered into Dylan's ear, and Dylan smiled. He pulled out his container and poured the substance onto the butter

157

knife again and passed it to Patrick who sniffed it within a few seconds.

"Dude," Wes gasped. "We're not kids anymore. We can drink heavily while we are here, but coke is not a good idea."

"Thank you Wes for agreeing," Lance said.

"Yes, thank you Wes for trying to rain on our parade," Dylan said, and he put his arm around Patrick.

"I'm going to run to the bathroom," Lance said with irritation. "I'll be back."

Lance left the table and put the napkin that was on his lap on his chair. He headed to the bathroom and sent a text to Amy telling her how his bachelor party was turning into a frat party with Dylan's incessant drug use.

Amy called Lance right after receiving his text message.

"Are you ok?" she asked sounding very concerned and worried. "I don't want you to take anything. Please."

"Babe," Lance replied. "I'm not. My brother is acting immature and trying to be the center of attention again. I can't deal with his behavior. Did I mention a woman dropped five k in casino chips, and he's been cashing some of it in to pay for our outrageous dinner?"

"What the hell?" Amy sounded worried. "He can go to jail!"

"That woman is staying at our hotel," Lance added. "If she recognizes him, this could be a bad, bad thing."

"It puts you in jeopardy," Amy pleaded.

"I know," Lance replied. "I want to remain low key but the entire restaurant has our attention. It's rather annoying."

Lance finished his conversation with Amy, and then used the restroom. When he returned to the dinner table, he found his groomsmen looking red in the face. Patrick and Dylan exploded in laughter.

"We took shots," Patrick said while panting. "We couldn't wait for you. You took too long. Drink up!"

Dylan passed a shot glass to Lance and said, "It's tequila." Lance took it and drank it.

"Might as well join you," Lance said sarcastically after shivering from head to toe from the harsh taste of his tequila shot.

"Good job!" Patrick cheered and gave Dylan a playful punch in the shoulder.

Lance had to admit that his dinner was one of the best he had ever had. The food was made from high quality and fresh ingredients. His dinner party was laughing and telling each other college anecdotes. The waiter was even enjoying the table and jumped in on some of the jokes that they shared. Lance found himself feeling the effects of the alcohol hitting him once the bill for the dinner arrived at the table. He felt slightly light-headed and dizzy, but it passed.

"You ok?" Edward whispered to Lance.

"Fine," Lance said. "I'm actually feeling good...and relaxed."

"Great!" Edward cheered. "Then let's go hit the tables!"

Dylan paid the bill and left a two hundred dollar tip for the waiter. The party then filed into the casino downstairs and found the first open blackjack table. Dylan pulled out some of his casino chips and began betting.

"Can we have a round of beers for my boys," Dylan drunkenly asked a cocktail waitress who was handing out cocktails to a nearby table.

The waitress nodded and returned a few minutes later with six bottles of beers for the group.

"Cheers," Wes said to the group while raising his beer. "Let's toast to the groom!"

159

The men all raised their bottles in honor of Lance. Lance smiled and quickly chugged his beer as if it were a contest to finish first. One beer became two and two beers became three. The night continued around the same table. It was almost three o' clock in the morning when a group of two tall security men arrived at their table.

"Is there a problem?" Dylan asked one of the men who had placed his hands on Dylan's shoulder.

"We need to take you to our back office for some questioning," one of the men said.

"Why?" Dylan asked in an agitated tone while turning red.

Lance's heart sank, and he began to sober up fast. At the entrance of the casino, he could see two more security officers speaking on a two-way radio beside a woman with a large hat and a purple shawl. The woman was still wearing sunglasses over her face even though she was indoors and it was three in the morning.

"Oh my God," Lance said aloud.

Dylan looked at him with confusion then followed his gaze to where he saw the woman in the purple shawl staring at them with what appeared to be an angry face.

"Shit," Dylan said to himself, and he let the security officers grab him by the shoulders and forcefully escort him to a back room.

"Wait," Lance said to the security guards as he felt himself turn completely sober from the adrenaline rush he was experiencing.

"I'll handle this," Dylan said to Lance, and he threw a plastic bag under a table that only Lance saw.

Dylan had been escorted into a back holding room with the doors closed. The woman in the purple shawl was waiting outside with two officers. Lance ran to the table and picked up the bag Dylan dropped. Lance fell to his knees as if tying his shoe. He found the bag, and put it in his suit pocket. It was Dylan's bag of cocaine.

"What are we going to do now?" Edward asked nervously.

"Why was he arrested?" Wes added to the worry.

"It's a long story," Lance said. "I need to go help him. How about you guys take refuge in our room. Here's our key."

Lance handed Brad his key, and they all nodded in agreement.

"I can come with," Wes said. "I am a lawyer after all."

"Right—sure," Lance agreed.

Lance and Wes walked up to the door. The woman in the purple shawl saw them and pushed her glasses up to her face. She shifted awkwardly at the sight of them.

"Hi," Lance said to one of the security officers. "My brother was pulled in there. He's been drinking. This is his lawyer. I think we should be with him."

"No can do," one of the security men replied in a deep voice. "He's being held for questioning."

"Those men are not the police," Wes chimed in. "By law, they cannot detain him. And why is he even being detained? He's been with us the whole night and we've been *spending* money on a table."

"I cannot discuss this with you," the guard said.

The woman in the purple shawl fixed her hat and dusted lint off her black business blazer before speaking up.

"He stole my casino chips," she said in a small, shy voice. "You...you were on the airplane next to him when I dropped my coin purse."

"I don't know—" Lance began.

"Do you have proof?" Wes cut off Lance.

"I saw him walking around the casino and I told security about my suspicions," she replied. "They looked at camera footage of you at the restaurant upstairs and at the blackjack table. I saw him pull all those chips—*my chips*. They used facial recognition technology in this hotel to find him, and the footage of him does not show him pulling out money from an ATM or by any other means. He came to the hotel with this money already. They are going to question him, and if they find inconsistencies with the recorded footage, they will know he stole it."

161

"Did he have the coin purse on him?" Wes asked.

"Well, no," the woman replied angrily, "but that could mean he left it in his room."

Lance slowly pulled out his phone and texted Edward to search Dylan's bags for a designer female coin purse. He wrote: "If you find a designer coin purse in Dylan's bag, throw it in a trashcan outside of our room. I'll explain later. Important. NOW."

The door to the holding room opened and the security guard asked Lance to step in.

"You wait outside," the security guard told Wes who was about to follow Lance into the room.

"I'm their lawyer," Wes demanded. "You have no right to hold them here."

The guard closed the door on Wes' face, and locked it. Lance sat at a table by Dylan. There were three other men in there standing behind Dylan with their arms crossed.

"The woman outside," one of the guards explained, "says she lost her money on her flight here. She said she saw you both here and recognized you from the flight. We looked at camera footage of you in the hotel and saw that you were spending a large sum of money...spending a large sum as if it was not yours."

"Prove it," Dylan snarled. "We come from money asshole."

"Shut up," Lance kicked Dylan under the table.

"We're here for my brother's bachelor party," Dylan snarled. "No need to waste our time with your pathetic excuse to find something to do because you're bored of standing out there and watching drunk people. I'm sure this is more enthralling."

Dylan had touched a nerve. One of the security guards whispered something into his two-way radio. Another guard lifted Dylan up with ease by his armpits, and the last guard looked through his blazer coat and pulled out a few chips that were in his inside pocket. They were all marked with hundreds.

"Can you prove you pulled this money out?" the security guard asked.

"If I wanted to, yes, but I did not do anything wrong," Dylan replied stubbornly.

Lance started to sweat heavily from his forehead. The fluorescent lights in the room were making his head throb. He could feel his heart racing faster than normal. His vision began to cloud, and he felt light-headed again. Lance gripped his hands on the edge of the table.

"I'm not feeling—" Lance began to mumble, and then he fell over backwards on his chair and hit the concrete floor.

Chapter Fourteen

Lance woke up around noon in a hospital bed. He looked around the room and darted upright quickly in shock. He had no recollection as to how he had ended up there. Edward was asleep sitting up on a chair in the room.

"Ed!" Lance called to him making him wake up suddenly.

"You're ok!" Edward said with a smile and bags under his eyes. "I was worried sick."

"What happened to me?" Lance asked.

"It turns out that you were rufied," Edward said. "Did you take anything?"

"What?" Lance said in shock. "I did not!"

"I didn't think so," Edward replied. "The doctor says someone may have slipped it in your drink."

"How? Who?" Lance said, but his memory was not clear and he could barely remember his last moment of sobriety from the evening before.

"You drank heavily too," Edward said. "Are you sure you're ok? I found this in your blazer when they brought you in. I pocketed it so as not to cause alarm to the cops. Your brother is already in a mess."

"What?" Lance said and Edward pulled out Dylan's bag of cocaine that he had dropped. "It's Dylan's. He dropped it before those security guys apprehended him. I remember now. Wait, where is Dylan?"

"Jail," Edward said sadly. "Wes is at the police station working out bail for him. Patrick is passed out in his hotel room. He had had too much to drink and some of Dylan's drugs too. I don't know where Brad went. He was here this morning, but he must have left after I fell asleep."

"How could this have happened?" Lance said. "It's only been one day into my bachelor party trip."

The doctor walked into the room after knocking. A female nurse accompanied him. The doctor appeared to be in his sixties and was bald with square-rimmed reading glasses. He glanced over a chart that he was holding on a clipboard then looked at Lance.

"You're very lucky," he said. "With the amount of alcohol in your system and the drug we found in your system…well, be thankful you woke up today."

"I didn't take any drugs," Lance said.

"It happens a lot in this city," the doctor replied. "Sometimes people slip things into others' drinks. Whether it is for date rape purposes or to steal from someone, it is a common issue here in town."

"Damn," Edward sighed.

"Can I be released?" Lance asked.

"Yes," the doctor replied. "I can clear you. I would take it easy on the drinking for the rest of your stay. People tend to get drugged when they are drunk and not aware of their surroundings. Be cautious."

"Right," Lance said while rubbing his head as it felt like it was going to explode.

Lance and Edward arrived at the hotel half an hour later. Patrick and Brad were waiting for them outside of Lance's room.

"Any word from Wes or Dylan?" Lance asked Brad.

"Yes," Brad replied. "They are working with a bail bond. Your brother should be free and clear within the hour. The money was returned to the woman. Dylan will still have to go to court, but the woman is surprisingly not pressing charges. She did not stick around long last night after the money was taken out of your brother's hands."

"I'm sorry for my behavior too," Patrick said. "I feel like maybe I encouraged Dylan to go hard."

"I think it is best we try to have a clean stay," Lance said. "Drinking is fine, but nothing harder than that."

"Agreed," Edward said. "It is his weekend. We can't screw that up."

"I kind of want Dylan to fly home," Lance said. "He's due for rehab and coming here before he checks in was not a good idea. My mom will be pissed. There's no doubt she'll be footing his bail."

"Here," Edward whispered and he passed Dylan's cocaine to Lance in secret.

Lance pocketed the bag and cleared his throat.

"I need to use the restroom gents," he said. "I'll be right back."

Lance entered the restroom of his room and placed the bag of Dylan's drugs on the counter. He turned on the sink and poured warm water on his face to wash away the previous night's sweat. He looked at himself in the mirror and tried to angle his head so he could see the side where he fell. He had a small bandage over where his skin tore open, but the wound was shallow.

Lucky me, he thought. *I could have split my head open.*

Lance looked at the bag of white powder and opened it. He pinched a small bit of it with his fingers and put it close to his nose. He gave a very tiny whiff and then poured some of the drug on the bathroom counter. Lance pulled out a credit card and shaped the clump of dust into two thin lines. He moved his face and nose closer to the counter and right over the lines. He took in a deep breath and in less than ten seconds he had inhaled both lines to a feeling of euphoria tingling throughout his entire body.

Lance felt alive and invincible for the first time on that trip. He held the bag over the toilet in an attempt to flush it down, but then decided to keep it in his blazer pocket. He looked at himself in the mirror and smiled.

"This is *my* trip," he said to his reflection.

For the next hour, Lance was on an adrenaline rush and was playing the penny slots as if he had an endless supply of change. He kept forcing hundred dollar bills into the machine in his feeble attempt to win money, but the credit keeper kept dwindling down to zero.

Wes and Dylan arrived back at the hotel later that afternoon. Dylan looked like he had not had any sleep and decided he was going to take a sleeping pill to sleep for the rest of the evening.

"I'm not hungry either," he said. "I'm sorry again for screwing up last night. It won't happen again."

"You are an adult," Lance said. "You can deal with that on your own and if mom wants to make it her business, well, that is between you two. I'm getting myself out of that mess."

"Fair enough," Dylan said. "Good night bro. Good night gentlemen."

"Well at least he's out of your hair," Edward sighed with relief after Dylan disappeared onto an elevator.

"For now," Lance said, but he was on such a high that he did not care about his brother or his mistakes at that moment. "Let's go to a strip club tonight!"

"YES!" Patrick and Brad yelled in unison.

After dinner, they took a cab out of the Las Vegas strip to hit up a strip club that was located in a warehouse-looking building. There were purple velvet ropes at the entrance and two sleazy looking large bodyguards. Lance and his party all showed their IDs to the bouncers, and then were admitted into the venue. There was hundreds of men and a few woman dancing and drinking the night away with about ten female models dancing on the tables in underwear and completely topless.

"Hot," Patrick called out over the loud music when they got to the bar. "Boobs everywhere! Have I died and gone to heaven?"

"Yes," Lance said. "Be right back. Bathroom."

Lance went to the restroom and found a vacant stall. He walked into it and pulled out the leftover bag of cocaine. He poured a line of the powder on top of the toilet paper dispenser and shaped it with his credit card. Then he took a quick huff of it and felt the tingling sensation hit every inch of his body. He smiled and left the restroom with a feeling of giddiness.

"Drinks!" Lance demanded when he found Patrick, Wes, Brad, and Edward at the bar. "And we need dollars for the ladies!"

"Are you drunk already?" Edward asked sarcastically.

"What? No!" Lance lied and he took a shot out of Patrick's hands and drank it.

"That was mine!" Patrick snapped. "Get your own!"

"I'm the bachelor!" Lance retorted.

Patrick rolled his eyes and ordered another drink from the bartender. Brad and Wes were at a nearby table where a blonde woman was dancing around in a red bikini with tassels on her breasts. Wes pulled out a few dollar bills and started throwing them at her heels. She got on her knees and blew flirtatious kisses at them.

Lance continued to drink throughout the night. He was at a point where he had forgotten he had woken up in a hospital earlier that day. He was finally in the element of partying for his own cause. Edward was the first one to get kicked out of the bar for falling asleep at his table. He had had too much to drink and was passing out. Brad walked Edward out and paid for a taxi to drive him back to his room.

Brad returned with more dollar bills in his hands, and he proceeded to fan himself in front of two dancers with the bills. Patrick was getting a lap dance by a very petite brunette Asian woman who kept slapping his face with her ponytail in a flirtatious manner. She kept giggling and kicking her feet in the air. When Patrick reached for her backside, she slapped his hands off and used her finger to signal "no" to him.

"I'm hungry," Wes slurred later that night. "What's open late? I could go for a burger and fries."

"Me too," Patrick exclaimed. "Let's get some food!"

"I'm gonna stay a little longer," Lance said while he fed a dollar to a dancer's mouth.

Brad, Wes, and Patrick stumbled out of the strip club and called a taxi to pick them up. Lance realized that all of his friends had actually left him and he began to panic. He left his table and waved the dancer goodbye, then blew an air kiss at her. When he stumbled outside, he realized his friends had already been picked up.

"Shit," he mumbled.

"You ok solider?" a scantily clad woman with blonde hair said to him.

"Do you work here?" Lance said drunkenly, and he found it difficult to focus on the woman's features because his vision kept blurring from the alcohol and fatigue.

"Maybe," she said in a raspy voice. "Have any plans for the rest of the evening?"

"I need to go home," Lance slurred. "Can you help me find a cab?"

"Sure thing honey," she said politely.

Miraculously, Lance found his way back to his hotel room. He felt as if he had been escorted safely because he ran into no problems on his elevator ride up to the floor he was staying on. When he entered the room, he found a note on the side table of his bed. It read: "Lance, I went down to gamble. Don't worry. I'm not drinking or taking anything. I might be out late."

Lance dropped the note onto the floor and sank onto his bed with all of his clothes still on. He pulled out the covers and put them over his body. He could feel his body sink into the sheets as if he was a part of his bed. His head felt like air, and for a fleeting moment he thought he could fly. His vision blurred and within seconds he fell asleep.

Lance felt warm hands touching his cold body. He felt the tie he was wearing become undone. It was pulled off him so fast, he thought he was being strangled at first. He opened his eyes, but he could not see well. His vision was foggy. He looked down at his chest and saw a pair of soft hands slowly unbutton his dress shirt. Once his skin was exposed to the open air, he felt a shiver of cold drop down to his spine. Then, the button of his slacks was unbuttoned and in the distance he could hear his zipper being opened.

Lance looked above him and saw a beautiful blonde girl smiling back at him flashing her white teeth. She whispered into the night.

"Hello my love," she said sweetly before kissing his cheek and making her way to his lips.

Lance kissed the woman passionately and put his hands around her waist and began to unzip the lace dress she was wearing. The woman took Lance's arms and put them behind his head. She was dominating him, and he was enjoying every second of it. Lance felt as if all he had to do was lay there.

"We'll be together forever…soon," she whispered into his ear, then blew her hot breath into it. "I love you."

"I love you too," Lance said automatically. "You make me feel good."

"This feels just like the first time," she replied. "Like when we were at that pasture in the sheep's meadow."

"Yes," Lance's mind flashed to that memory.

"We'll have kids one day," she said. "You'll be an amazing father."

"Claire…" Lance gasped into the night as they shared a very passionate exchange.

"Lance," she moaned back. "You're so gorgeous."

"*You* are gorgeous," Lance said, and he put his hands on her cheeks.

"Be mine," Claire said. "Just mine. Nobody else's. I want our lives to be one—together."

"Yeah..." Lance replied automatically.

"The stars aligned for us," Claire said. "I want you to remember that. We are meant for each other. We both have issues. We will work them out with therapy. Nobody is perfect."

"I know," Lance responded.

"Do you love me Lance Avery?" Claire asked.

"I do," Lance replied.

"Would you want to marry me?" Claire asked in a seductive voice.

"But I'm..." Lance struggled for words. He felt confused. "I mean, yes I will get married. I am getting married. Are we getting married?"

"Eternal love will marry our fates together forever," Claire teased. "Our anniversary is approaching fast on June 17. That will be the day we will bind our love and marriage of our union forever. Do you want that?"

"I do," Lance said. "I want that so much Claire Carpenter."

"Then let's do it," Claire insisted. "Let's run away from the world and your crazy mother. No rules. Just us. Maybe we can go to an island and live on our own and walk around naked every day and get golden tans."

"Ok," Lance uttered.

"I love, love, love you," Claire whispered into his ear.

Lance was overwhelmed with emotion. He could not feel his body. It was as if his joints were paralyzed. He could not feel his feet or fingers. His vision kept blurring. He saw a flash of violet fly before his eyes into darkness.

"Just lay there," Claire whispered into Lance's ear. "Let me take care of you. That's what I'm here for."

Lance lost feeling in his body as it went numb. His mind went blank, and his eyelids were too heavy to open. He tried to gain control of his body, but was unsuccessful. He felt someone on top of him, and while it felt beautiful and friendly at first, he began to experience a forced pressure. He felt two hands on his wrists tighten. He heard moaning and heavy breathing. He felt his bed shake as if he was in an earthquake. His skin went from feeling cold to warm to feeling hot. He began to sweat from pores all over his body. He felt the sheets beneath him turn damp from the perspiration.

Lance groaned for moment when he realized there was nothing on top of him. He felt cold. He looked down at his body and realized he was naked. He looked over at the window of his hotel room and saw that the sun was rising. It was six in the morning. Lance tried to get up, but his body felt like it was full of rocks. He could not move. He felt a sensation in his stomach in time to realize what was about to happen. He turned his head to the side with all the force he could muster, and he vomited onto the hotel floor while staining the white linen sheets of the bed.

Lance wiped his mouth clean and struggled to get up. He felt nauseous and as if he were about to throw up everything he consumed the previous evening. Lance ran to the bathroom toilet and spent the next twenty minutes emptying his stomach while feeling pain all over his body.

Dylan came into the room around seven and found Lance passed out by the toilet. Dylan shook him awake and sighed with relief when he saw that he was breathing.

"I take it you didn't take it easy?" Dylan asked. "You might want to put on some clothes."

Lance got dressed into a pair of sweats and a hoodie. He looked at himself in the mirror and the reflection staring back at him was pale and scared looking.

"What happened?" Dylan asked.

"I don't know," Lance answered. "I remember getting back to the room after the strip club…"

"You went to a strip club?" Dylan asked. "Jealous."

"I passed out and had the craziest dream," Lance said. "It's been a while since I've..."

"Since you've what?" Dylan asked after a couple seconds of awkward silence from Lance.

"Since I've done cocaine," Lance said. "I used your bag. I think I used it all."

"Well, look who is the druggie now?" Dylan teased. "Well, at least it went to good use I hope?"

"I feel like shit," Lance said. "I think I was hallucinating. I had the craziest dream about my ex...*Claire*."

"Did you get a kiss from a stripper?" Dylan asked.

"No, why?" Lance asked curiously.

"You have lipstick on your cheek near your ear," Dylan said.

Lance looked at himself in the mirror and saw a small lipstick imprint on his cheek.

"Ha," Lance said. "I probably did come to think of it."

Chapter Fifteen

Lance spent the rest of the afternoon by the hotel pool recovering from his wild evening. He felt like every inch of his body had been hit by a hammer, and he was not able to eat anything without the feeling of wanting to throw up.

"How are you feeling there?" Edward asked from the pool chair next to Lance.

"Shitty," Lance replied. "We still have three more days left on this trip. I don't think I can survive another night."

Wes and Brad walked over to them with drinks at hand. Lance took one look at their cocktails and then covered his eyes in disgust.

"I guess Patrick can drink the extra one," Wes said while passing a drink over to Patrick who was sitting in the hotel's hot tub.

"Hair the dog," Brad joked while raising his glass to Edward who had taken a margarita off the tray Brad was holding.

"No," Lance mumbled and put a towel over his face.

"What are the plans for tonight?" Patrick called.

"Not sure," Edward said. "Mister bachelor...what do you want to do?"

"Not drink," Lance said. "Not take any illegal substances."

"Should we do a show?" Brad asked. "Maybe a magic show or something?"

"That sounds absolutely lame!" Patrick laughed.

"Where's Dylan?" Edward asked looking around.

Lance came out from under his towel and looked around the courtyard.

"Up to no good I'm sure," Lance muttered sarcastically, and he put the towel over his head. "I think I might have been drugged again last night."

"Really?" Edward asked.

"I think so," Lance said. "I feel the same as I did after leaving the hospital yesterday. This town sucks."

"You don't know that happened to you?" Wes questioned.

"I blacked out!" Lance said finally and sat up. "I never black out and then twice in a row I have no recollection of the night before."

Dylan came running into the pool area with a beer bottle in hand. His shirt was half tucked in and his sunglasses were askew. He had sweat stains on his shirt and sweat pouring from his forehead.

"What's up?" Lance asked Dylan curiously.

"I just met a fascinating woman at the casino who's a fortune teller—psychic—whatever you want to call it," he replied.

"Ok." Lance replied sarcastically.

"She wants to read our energies!" Dylan said. "I got us a great deal. We can meet with her tonight. We can all do a reading, one by one."

"I've always wanted to do something like that," Patrick said excitedly. "Nice job finding us something cool to do, dude."

"Not interested," Lance replied. "My energy is worn out. But you can have fun with that."

"I'm going to pass too," Wes replied. "I want to check out this hip nightclub tonight at the hotel across the street. I got us on the list."

"Yeah," Brad agreed. "I want to check it out too."

"Same," Edward said.

"Fine," Dylan sounded flustered. "Then I guess it's just you and me Patrick."

Later that evening after dinner, the group dispersed into different festivities for the evening. Wes, Brad, and Edward went to the nightclub. Patrick, Dylan, and a reluctant Lance left the hotel in a cab to the outskirts of the strip to a shady looking strip mall.

They paid the cab driver and got off at the mall. There was a neon green sign that read "Psychic." Dylan clapped his hands in excitement.

"This will be fun," he said.

"I can't believe you persuaded me to do this," Lance said.

"Well it's Vegas!" Dylan said. "It's fun to do out of the ordinary things."

"I feel this whole weekend has been anything but ordinary," Lance grunted.

"It'll be fun dude," Patrick playfully slapped Lance on the back. "Come on!"

When they opened the door to the psychic's place of business, a bell chimed to announce them. A beautiful Asian woman with long jet-black hair came out to greet them. She had a gold headband and lots of dangling jewelry on her wrists.

"Dylan," she said smoothly, "so lovely to see you again."

"Thank you for having us," Dylan said. "This is my brother Lance...the bachelor...and his friend Patrick. Guys...this is Lucy."

"Pleased to meet you both," Lucy replied. "There is a lot of energy coming from you three. I think each session will be worthwhile. I have a few other psychics and healers in the house today. Sara will work with you—Patrick. Tanya will work on you Dylan. I will work on Lance. I feel his presence is very interesting."

Lance stared at Lucy as if she was insane. Dylan looked disappointed that Lucy was not going to do his reading.

"This way Lance," Lucy said, and she grabbed him gently by his wrist. She led him to a room in the very back.

Lanced walked into the room, which was lit by a red dim light bulb. He sat down on a cozy velvet chair. There was a crystal ball on Lucy's table and across from him was her chair, which was regal looking.

"Is this your first time ever having a reading done?" Lucy asked.

"Yes," Lance said, and in his mind he thought: *If you could read my mind and are a real psychic you would know that.*

"Excellent!" she said. "Your mind has not been exercised much. It will be fresh for me to read."

Lucy pulled out several tarot cards and began to place them in front of her faced down. She rubbed her chin and stared into her crystal ball in thought. Lance's foot began to tap nervously underneath the table.

Lucy began to flip over the cards to reveal strange characters in various situations. Lance looked into Lucy's eyes and saw that she looked upset by what she was seeing.

"What is it?" Lance asked skeptically.

"This," Lucy said pointing to a card of a black hooded skeleton with a scythe, "is the death card. That is the grim reaper."

"Ok..." Lance was unsure how to respond.

"It's so weird that we have come across this tarot card at the beginning of our session," Lucy said in a somber tone that Lance figured was only an act. "There will be a death in your life...soon. Judging by these other cards, it will happen this year. It could be someone close like a family member...or *you.*"

"Right," Lance muttered.

"I do not always like to be so blunt," Lucy said. "But I don't want to lie to you either. This reading has started off so grim."

Lance rolled his eyes when Lucy was not looking. She pulled out another set of cards and placed them next to the ones she had first picked. She began to flip them over. Her expression of sorrow had remained intact.

"The hanged man..." Lucy said. "Don't worry—it does not necessarily mean death. It does signify that there will be a suspended action in your life. A decision or life event will need to be or will be postponed. Do you have a big life event coming up? A wedding perhaps? This is the lover's card right here as well."

"My brother told you I was getting married," Lance said while not trying to conceal his annoyance with the reading.

"I'm sorry," Lucy said. "When I enter my element, the physical world outside and the experiences I have had in it are eliminated from my mind. Therefore, I apologize, but I did not recall that right away."

"I see," Lance said automatically. "I am to be wed in June."

"Perhaps the cards are saying that you need to wait longer," Lucy said.

"I'm not going to change the date," Lance said flatly. "It would be costly and the date is very significant."

"June 17 comes once a year," Lucy said. "But it comes again as the world revolves."

"Yes but..." Lance began, and then he furrowed his eyebrows. "I never said when my wedding date was."

Lucy smiled and flashed her pearly white teeth. She stood up from her chair and picked up the crystal ball. She placed the ball on a side table near the door.

"I'm a psychic. I'm a healer. That date came to my mind," Lucy replied.

"Or did my brother tell you that too?" Lance asked.

"No," Lucy replied, and her voice began to sound agitated and no longer smooth and calming. "I sense something is bothering you. Something that you don't feel you have control of."

Lance remained silent.

"I see a dark energy clouding you," Lucy continued while examining his entire body from head to toe with her eyes. "The moment you walked in, I felt it. I need to cleanse you of your past. You need to rebuild. You need a new carpenter. *Carpenter...*"

Lucy closed her eyes and put her fingers to her temple. She took a deep breath before opening them. She stared into Lance's eyes, and then she took her seat again.

"Carpenter. Does that word mean anything to you? Are you a builder? It keeps popping up in my head," Lucy said.

"Um," Lance appeared puzzled. "My ex girlfriend's last name was Carpenter."

"Her memory resides in your head," Lucy said. "I can tell. That is where there is a heavy burden. May I ask what happened to end that relationship?"

"You should know," Lance said. "If you're *psychic.*"

"I do not expect most people to come in here and believe a word I say," Lucy said. "But I usually am respected. Your mockery is not going unnoticed, and if you want me to help you, then you best change your attitude to get the most out of this session."

"I'm done here," Lance said angrily.

"Trust," Lucy said. "You find it hard to trust. You cheated on her, didn't you? She lost her trust in you. Then you shut her out. You blocked her out of your life. There's darkness in you. Drugs. Suicide. Child molestation. Yet, you think that moving on in the route you are going, is by far the answer to living a normal life?"

"What the hell?" Lance sounded nervous.

"Sometimes I like to wean into sessions," Lucy said, and she got up from her chair again to pace around the room. "Sometimes I start slow so as not to scare off people. But you made me go there. You made me pull out my big guns. I see you very clearly Lance. I see the horrors of your past and how you are working hard to become normal again. Your mistakes will catch up to you and you will surely pay the *price.*"

Lance was dumbfounded. He felt a mix between being offended and outraged at Lucy's statements. Lucy took her gaze off Lance and reached for the card on the top of her deck. She pulled it out and showed Lance the face of the card before she looked at it. Lance's face gave Lucy satisfaction. She turned the card over to look at it and gave a soft laugh.

"The devil's card," she said. "Here is a picture of the winged devil. He has a naked man and woman at his feet with shackles on their necks. They are his prisoners and the tails on their human bodies signify that they are becoming more and more like the devil himself."

"What the hell does that even mean?" Lance demanded.

"It can mean several things," Lucy said. "Cheating between two lovers. Addiction. Loss of control...."

Lance felt as though a part of him could believe the woman before him had some kind of supernatural vision because some of the things she spoke of were things that Lance had not shared with anyone else, except his therapist Rose.

"I..." Lance began. "I am at loss for words."

Lucy seemed satisfied with his response because she gave him a friendly smile.

"Make sure to give yourself as much closure as possible to things from your past," Lucy said. "Going into a marriage can be a burden on one's soul if he or she has a dark past. If you want the marriage to live on until death do you part, then you should find closure in the darkness I see in your energy."

"How?" Lance asked.

"That's for you to self discover," Lucy replied. "Well, our time is up. We take cash or card. This session will be fifty dollars."

"That was complete bullshit," Lance said angrily to Dylan on their cab ride back to the hotel.

"Mine was pretty good," Patrick added.

"Mine too," Dylan said. "What was wrong? Lucy is awesome."

"She's a fraud," Lance said angrily, although he was disturbed by much of what Lucy had told him. "I'm ready for bed."

Lance spent the rest of his stay in Vegas sober. He was paranoid about getting drugged or using again. His body was yearning for a release, but he knew that the consequences of addiction would be detrimental. When Sunday morning arrived, Lance had to throw water on Dylan to wake him up from his late night of partying.

Lance bid farewell to Patrick, Brad, and Wes who were all traveling back to their prospective cities. Lance, Dylan, and Edward boarded their flight back to Austin looking much more tired than when they arrived.

They took their seats in first class and Dylan immediately asked the flight attendant for a vodka soda.

"Your liver is going to shit," Lance muttered.

"You only live once," Dylan teased.

"I'm going on a cleanse," Edward said. "This weekend in Vegas was killer."

"Are you checking in soon?" Lance whispered to Dylan.

Dylan gave Lance an angry glare before whispering back, "To make you and mommy happy I suppose."

"You really need rehab," Lance said. "You were crazy this weekend. You got arrested for heaven's sake."

"Ok little brother," Dylan snapped. "Are you trying to be dad now?"

"No," Lance retorted. "Dad's dead. Can you not joke about him?"

"Are you guys going to fight the whole way?" Edward asked. "If so, I'm putting on my headphones for the rest of the way."

A few hours later, they landed in Austin. The flight attendant came onto the speaker and said, "You may now use your portable electronic devices."

Lance turned on his cell phone and watched as the signal bar icon on his phone went from "searching" to "in service." A voicemail from Amy popped up on his phone's screen. Lance pressed his phone to his ear.

"When you land back in Austin, call me," said the rushed voice of Amy. "It's about my dad."

Chapter Sixteen

Amy answered her phone after two short rings.

"Hello?" she answered in a hoarse voice.

"I just landed," Lance said. "What's the matter with your dad?"

"He got home from China a few days ago and everything was fine…" Amy spoke quickly and sounded as if she was about to cry. "Then he collapsed right before breakfast. He was showering. He hit his head on the side of the tub. He had a heart attack. He's in the hospital with a concussion. He's ok…I think. The doctors say he'll recover from the heart attack, but they are monitoring his head injuries because he's in his sixties."

"Oh my goodness," Lance gasped. "I'll get a cab to take me straight to the hospital. I'll be there soon."

Lance hung up on Amy and addressed Dylan and Edward with his plans.

"I'll have to get the next cab and head straight there," Lance told them. "She needs me."

"Of course," Edward said.

"Yeah, go see your girl," Dylan replied.

Lance arrived at the hospital where Amy's father was being cared for. He met Amy in the lobby. She was wearing yoga pants and a grey fleece hoodie. Her hair was in a ponytail and her eyes looked bloodshot with shadows underneath them.

"Lance," she cried while giving him a hug. "Come. Upstairs."

They entered an elevator and rode up to the third floor. They walked out, and Lance spotted Amy's mother Grace at the end of the hall pacing back and forth on her cell phone. It appeared as if she was having a heated conversation.

"She's on the phone with my grandmother," Amy said. "My dad's mom. She's handicapped and cannot make it down here so my mom is filling her in on the details even though they don't get along."

Grace ended her call when she saw Amy and Lance walking towards her.

"Lance, dear," she said frantically. "Welcome home. I'm sorry you had to be dragged here right after your bachelor party."

"Nonsense," Lance said. "Family is important."

Amy grabbed Lance's hand before they walked into the room where her father was. Grace followed behind them.

"Simon is expected to recover," Grace sighed. "He's resting. His head is fine. Nothing serious. He had a slight concussion, but he's cleared to rest now. I think he'll have to do less traveling now. I'm hoping he can retire soon."

"It's my fault," Amy sniffed. "I feel like he's working more so that we can have money for the wedding."

"Shush," Grace said. "We have plenty of money. He does not need to work. He only does it because he's a stubborn old man."

Grace put her hand on Simon's shoulder. She had tears streaming down her face, but she was smiling, and the look in her eyes was pure love. Lance found it comforting to know that after decades of being wed, the Aberdeen's could still show so much affection and love with each other. Lance always envied Amy's relationship with her parents and even the fact that she had a father, while his was deceased. He had always wished his father was alive and both his parents still happily married. He never told her he was envious, but he was reminded of those feelings he had locked away at that moment.

"If something happened," Amy said. "I don't know what I would do without dad around."

"You get used to it with time," Lance said automatically.

"Oh," Amy turned red. "I'm so sorry Lance. I didn't mean—I forgot..."

"It's fine," Lance said, and he gave her a kiss on her forehead. "Your dad will be there to walk you down the aisle."

"Yours will be watching from heaven, dear," Grace said giving Lance a hug.

"Mrs. Aberdeen," a female nurse walked into the room. "Someone delivered these roses in a vase. Should I leave them on the table?"

"Yes," Grace replied. "Leave them right there."

Grace continued to hug her daughter and cried softly onto her shoulder.

"The doctor said he might have some short term memory loss," the nurse continued, "but it will be temporary. He'll be back to normal in a few days. When he wakes up from his rest, we should have a good idea of when to clear him for release."

"Thank you dear," Grace told the nurse. "Does anyone hear a strange buzzing noise?

"Could be the intercom by the bed," the nurse replied. "It's faulty."

Lance and Amy went for a walk around the block outside of the hospital to escape the odd smells and cries coming from various rooms. They found a coffee shop nearby to sit down at.

"How was Vegas?" Amy asked. "Anything crazy?"

Lance considered being truthful about Dylan's arrest and his experience of being drugged, which led him to wake up at a hospital, but he decided that she had enough heavy burdens on her plate.

"Vegas was fun," Lance manipulated the story of his trip. "Dylan was boozing like crazy. Patrick was eating at all the buffets. Wes and Brad were being their typical playboy selves and going to various nightclubs. I admit they dragged me to a strip club, but I was good."

Amy rolled her eyes and laughed, "Of course you are good. That's why I'm marrying you. My bachelorette party is supposed to be next weekend, but after what happened with dad, I think I want to postpone it."

"You know he'll say you are being ridiculous," Lance said. "He will want you to enjoy time with your girls."

"Well our trip is to Cancun," she said. "It's not far away, and it is really easy to reschedule."

"Listen," Lance said. "Go! Jill has been working hard to help plan it with you and your bridesmaids. Your dad will make a full recovery. He has your loving mother to help take care of him."

Amy smiled at Lance's words. She nodded and replied, "Ok."

"I wish my family was not dysfunctional," Lance blurted out.

"What do you mean?" Amy asked.

"Well," Lance explained, "your parents get along. When my dad was alive, it was business before pleasure and my mother and he fought every other day. And of course Dylan always got the attention. I don't know what happened to him. He had honors in college, nabbed a big boy job right out of graduation, and yet he keeps screwing up and dabbling into hard drugs. My mom is forcing him to go to rehab. He's supposed to check in some time this week."

"That's a lot," Amy said. "You've been dealing with so much."

Lance looked over Amy's shoulder and saw a man and woman leaving the hospital while pushing a stroller with a newborn baby. He turned his attention and looked into Amy's eyes. His heart began to beat with guilt, and he felt remorse with every beat it made. For a fleeting second, he considered telling her about his lapse in judgment with drugs and kissing Rose. Then his mind raced to that night with Rose and he felt another surge of excitement in the pit of his stomach that was misplaced with his current mood. He shook off that feeling and tried to force it into guilt and shame. Then, his mind raced back to his vivid dream about Claire. It was so real and exhilarating for him to relive the sexual feelings he shared with Claire that were much stronger than his sexual feelings with Amy.

Lance looked over at the happy couple with their newborn child, and realized he was not even sure he would ever make a good father. His father had died when he was a teen, and he never had an adult male figure to help him become a man. He became a man on his own accord, but he felt like only a fraction of a man missing several pieces of the puzzle of his growth.

"I should probably get back home," Lance said suddenly. "I'll go back up to the hospital and get my luggage. I need to unpack and prepare for work. Will it be ok if I leave you?"

"Yes…yes of course baby," Amy said.

Lance sat in his living room with the lights off later that night. He was shining the black light that had been left at his doorstep by an anonymous person. He read and reread the invisible messages on the wall that were quotes from *The Scarlet Letter*.

"To the untrue man, the whole universe is false- it is impalpable- it shrinks to nothing within his grasp. And he himself is in so far as he shows himself in a false light, becomes a shadow, or, indeed, ceases to exist."

"…if truth were everywhere to be shown, a scarlet letter would blaze forth on many a bosom…"

"Like father, like son."

187

"If you are not in Austin," Lance said to himself, "then how are you coming back into my life. Regardless of what my lawyer learned, there's no way this isn't your work. Why do you keep haunting me?"

Lance turned his lights back on and spent the rest of the night painting over the written messages. He worked quietly to himself, until someone knocked at the door.

"Hello," Lance answered the door.

Dana was standing at the doorway. She gave Lance a smile and asked to come in.

"Sorry to bother you on your Sunday night," Dana said. "I know this sounds silly, but have you heard from Josh lately?"

"No, I've been out of town in Vegas," Lance said.

"Oh—right," Dana said. "He hasn't returned my calls and I guess...well...after that crazy night we had at his place...well I thought maybe he and I could try to get to know each other. I was hoping it would be more than a one night thing."

"Right," Lance said. "Well, I really don't know what is up with him. I mean, we aren't that close. We hung out that night for the first time in years. I met my ex through him, so after we broke up, our relationship was strained and awkward because he was kind of put in the middle of it. My ex reached out to him to vent about me, and I ended up doing the same thing."

"Well, I'm sorry to have bothered you," Dana said sounding defeated. "I guess being new in town makes you more vulnerable to hopeful romantic flings."

"If I do talk to Josh," Lance added, "I'll make sure to remind him to hit you up."

"Thanks," Dana said, and she left Lance's apartment.

Lance had been dreading his next appointment with Rose. However, after the crazy events that had happened to him in Las Vegas, he knew he had to talk about it to get it off his chest. The guilt of keeping it from Amy was haunting him, and the irony of that was the guilt of his kiss with Rose made matters even more worrisome for him.

"Good to see you again," Rose greeted Lance with a friendly smile.

"Hi Rose," Lance said awkwardly while hanging up is blazer on a coat hanger near the entrance to the office.

"Take a seat," Rose said. "Did you enjoy your bachelor party?"

"It was ok," Lance said.

"Just ok?" Rose said with a raised eyebrow of curiosity.

Lance dived into everything that happened to him in Las Vegas. He began with the story of Dylan stealing money from a woman that led to his arrest, to having his drink drugged behind his back, which led him to wake up at a hospital. Then Lance divulged the details of his vivid, drug-induced dream about Claire and his encounter with Lucy the psychic.

Rose was silent for a few minutes when Lance completed telling his story. She sighed heavily and then looked at Lance seriously.

"You've had quite an adventure," Rose said. "I trust that the cocaine use was only a one time thing?"

"I do not plan to use it again," Lance said truthfully. "It really messed with my head and made me feel horrible."

"Good," Rose said placing her hands together. "That dream irks me. It sounds like you have a lot of issues that are still unresolved with Claire. May I ask what that may be?"

"I was wondering what it was myself," Lance said. "But I had a moment when I woke up from the dream where I realized that it all has to do with closure. I never gave Claire a real apology. I left her cut and dry when we broke up and blocked her off all my social media accounts, emails, and my phone numbers. She tried to communicate with me to find her closure, yet I did not reciprocate. She sent me about five long emails after our breakup begging for me to talk to her, but I chose not to."

"And why did you let that pass without saying anything?" Rose asked.

"I was scared," Lance admitted. "I knew she was mad when she had learned of my dark skeletons. I was afraid she would reveal those secrets to the world. She hacked into my email and found a word document I created that listed all my issues. I wrote it down one night so that I could focus on what I needed therapy to help me with. Of course, it wasn't until a few months ago that I finally came to therapy...here I am."

"She found this document?" Rose asked. "Did she do anything with it?"

"I started dating this one girl," Lance said. "Briefly. Somehow, Claire found out about her and sent her an email with that document attached. It scared her away and Claire managed to do what she wanted—scare someone else away from dating crazy *me*."

"Well, she should not have done that," Rose stated, "but I imagine she was very upset with you."

"To say the least," Lance said. "That was the last straw."

"Then came the restraining order I presume?" Rose asked.

"Yes," Lance nodded.

"Do you still think she's behind the strange occurrences that have been happening to you?" Rose asked.

"Well a private investigator said she's still in Seattle going about her every day life," Lance said. "But the messages on my wall sounded like her. Someone broke into my apartment to taunt me. Not to steal anything."

"Right," Rose said, and she looked deep in thought.

"And then there is that woman in black," Lance continued. "She's dressed up like she attended a funeral. I keep seeing her, but then sometimes I think, maybe I'm seeing things."

"Perhaps the wedding planning stress has overwhelmed you?" Rose suggested.

"Maybe," Lance said.

"Do you think you would ever speak to her again?" Rose asked.

"No," Lance replied. "It would be against my restraining order on her. There's no way I can ever confront her again. The damage is done—on both ends. We both made several mistakes, and we paid for them. All I can do now is move forward and not think about this anymore. I have a future to plan with my soon to be wife."

Lance considered talking to Rose about their kiss. It had been troubling him throughout his bachelor party trip. The only downside to talking about it was that Rose herself was on the receiving end of the kiss.

"Is something else troubling you?" Rose asked seriously.

"No," Lance lied in a small voice.

"Well then, how about we pick up next week?" she said pulling out her pad and pen. "Same time next Tuesday?"

"Sure," Lance said.

"I'll see you then," she smiled.

Lance walked out of Rose's office and onto the sidewalk where his car was parked a few meters down. As he was about to get into his car, he realized he had left his blazer jacket in Rose's office. Lance doubled back to the office and knocked on the door. Rose answered.

"Forget something?" she asked.

"My blazer," Lance said. "I left it on the coat hanger."

"Come back in," Rose said. "I'll get it for you."

Lance walked into the lobby of her office and thumbed through the magazines on the coffee table while he waited for Rose to return.

"Here it is," she said.

"Ah, thanks," Lance reached for his blazer and put it back on.

"It fits you well," Rose said.

191

"Thanks," Lance said, and his heart began to race.

He looked at Rose's eyes intently. He clenched his fists and felt his palms sweat. Rose kept staring back at Lance as if their quiet interaction was normal. Lance opened his mouth to say something but no words escaped them. Rose ran her hand through her blonde hair and absent-mindedly fixed the skirt she was wearing.

Lance backed away from her in the direction of the exit. He turned around without saying a word and closed his eyes to fight a temptation. Lance reached for the doorknob and decided not to open the door. Rose walked over to his side and reached for the doorknob herself. Instead of opening it, she turned the lock on the door and pulled down the blinds of her windows.

Lance began to breathe heavily and nervously as Rose put her hand on his arm. She smiled and flashed her pearly white teeth.

"Should we talk about the other night?" Rose asked. "I feel like it has been on your mind. I mean...I know it has. I can tell."

"I..." Lance had nothing to say.

He stared at her as if only seeing her for the first time. He knew in his heart he was attracted to her and the taboo of her being his therapist only excited him. It was wrong, and that was the style that turned him on, even though he was engaged.

"Screw it," he sighed and he reached for Rose's face and began to kiss her.

Rose reciprocated willingly and put her arms around him as if they had been lovers for a long time. Lance reached for the zipper on her skirt and began to undress her.

"Follow me," Rose breathed heavily into Lance's ear.

She grabbed his hands and walked him into her office. She undressed to her underwear. Lance's reaction to what she was wearing caught him off guard. For such a professional looking woman, her underwear revealed a different story. She was wearing red lace and a very revealing bra and panties. She got on her desk with her heels still on and laid her back flat on it while pushing her paperwork off it onto the ground.

"Take me," she whispered.

It was a moment of intense heat with the friction caused by both of their bodies intertwining. He felt a sense of comfort and familiarity as he caressed Rose's body. His sweat fell onto her skin and hers rubbed into his. Rose blew hot air into Lance's ear, making him shiver from head to toe. His mind never escaped to any flashbacks of Claire like it had when he was intimate with Amy. He gave his undivided attention to Rose and it never wavered.

An hour later, Lance found himself scrambling Rose's office for his underwear. Rose was buttoning up her blouse while still seated on top of her desk.

"That was fun," she said.

"Yeah," Lance said awkwardly with feelings of guilt beginning to sink into his heart.

"What happens now?" she asked.

"I don't know," Lance said. "You're my therapist. We...we crossed that line."

"I don't mind that we did," Rose said. "And I'm willing to still work with you. Maybe we only needed to get that off our chests. I see the way you look at me."

"Yes, but..." Lance sounded hoarse. "I'm getting married soon. I can't screw this up."

"It seems to be a pattern," Rose said. "You did the same to Claire. Cheated..."

"Ok," Lance snapped. "That's not fair. You can't use your psychological methods on me regarding this."

"Sorry," Rose blushed.

"I think it is best if we discontinue our sessions," Lance said.

"I agree," Rose said with hurt clearly visible in her eyes.

"I can't live a lie," Lance began to cry, and he sat on Rose's couch. "I can't do this. I want to marry Amy, but maybe I'm not ready for the commitment."

Rose shifted uncomfortably on her desk. She walked over to Lance and put her hands on his shoulders. She gave him a gentle rub. Lance wanted to move her hands, but they felt nice on him. He turned around to her and gave her a kiss on the lips before quickly getting up and heading for the door.

A stunned Rose looked at him as he was about to exit her office.

"Will I see you again?" she asked.

"I think you know the answer to that," Lance replied.

Rose nodded in agreement. Tears began to form in her eyes. She looked over at Lance as if it were for the last time.

"I do know the answer," she said sadly.

Lance turned on the ignition of his BMW and sat in silence for a few minutes. Through his rearview mirror, he saw Rose lock up her office and walk to her car while on her cell phone. When she had driven off and was out of sight, Lance called Amy on his phone.

"Amy, are you at home?" Lance asked. "We need to talk."

Chapter Seventeen

Lance was seated at Amy's apartment dining room table. He was tapping his foot nervously against one of the table's legs. Amy had her head down on the table with her hands over them. She was crying.

"Baby..." Lance whispered trying to calm her down.

"Stop," her muffled voice replied.

"I'm very sorry," Lance said. "I couldn't keep it inside me. I wanted to be honest with you. As your fiancé, I felt I could no longer hide this secret."

"I mean," Amy's head jolted up, and she sat back upright on her chair. "...how could you?"

Her face was red and wet from her tears.

"I'm sorry," Lance said while hanging his head down.

"I trusted you," Amy responded angrily. "And you couldn't tell me when you got back from Vegas?"

"I didn't want you to worry," Lance replied. "Especially because my brother checked into rehab yesterday. Officially."

"Drugs, Lance?" Amy spat. "You were doing drugs in Vegas. You got drugged and ended up in a hospital. You didn't even care to tell me?"

"Well, when I returned I went to see your dad in the hospital," Lance said. "The timing wasn't right."

"You waited forty eight hours to tell me?" Amy spat angrily.

"Like I said," Lance retorted, "you were preoccupied with your dad. I did not want to burden you."

"You're my future husband," Amy replied. "It is my duty to be there for you too and make sure you are well. This scares me. You need to always be one hundred percent honest with me."

Lance shifted uncomfortable in his seat. He had arrived an hour earlier at Amy's apartment with the intention of telling her he had hooked up with his therapist, but he could not muster the courage. He was afraid she would go crazy like Claire. He could not bear to share his shame and guilt, so he decided to confess about what happened in Vegas with Dylan's arrest and then his own drug use to get some of the remorse out of his system.

"I'm disappointed," Amy said. "Now I question if we should even get married."

"Baby," Lance pleaded. "I love you. C'mon."

"I need space," Amy said.

Those words resonated with Lance because he had once said them to Claire when they had a heated fight in the middle of their relationship.

"Ok," Lance said sounding defeated. "I'll give you space."

"Starting now," Amy insisted. "I'll call you when I'm ready. You need to make sure you stay clean. Maybe talk to your therapist about this."

"I have," Lance said.

He was about to tell her that he parted ways with his therapist, but he had already given her enough bad news for one night. He decided to keep that to himself for the time being. Lance attempted to hug Amy, but she pushed him away and gestured for him to leave. Lance hung his head and walked out of her apartment without a glance back.

The week went on and he had not heard from Amy. He debated on sending her a text or email, but he knew that giving her the space she wanted was key to surviving the fight they were in. Lance decided to drive to the north part of town to visit his brother at the rehabilitation center.

Lance called his mother from his car before arriving at the center.

"Hello?" said George's voice through Lance's car audio speakers.

"Hi…George," Lance replied. "You answered my mom's cell?"

"Yes," George said. "Your mom went out for a walk because she's been stressed out lately. Mostly because of the hell your brother has put her through with his arrest and now going to rehab."

"Understandable," Lance replied.

"And she keeps nagging about her missing book as if it was an expensive diamond ring she lost or something," George vented. "It's driving me crazy."

"Sorry to hear," Lance said not really feeling sorry at all. "Can you tell her to call me later?"

"Sure," George said. "Anything important?"

"I wanted to see how she was doing and to let her know that I'm going to pay a visit to Dylan. He can have visitors on weekends," Lance replied.

"Well, give him our love," George said before Lance ended the call.

Lance arrived at the rehabilitation center in the hill country a few miles north of Austin. A counselor greeted him at the entrance.

"Follow me," the female counselor said. "Dylan is waiting for you in the guest common room."

They arrived at the common room, which had several various groups of people spaced out around the large room. Dylan was seated on a rocking chair and waved at Lance upon eye contact.

"Hello big brother," Lance said giving Dylan a hug. "How are you feeling?"

"I've been getting so much sleep," Dylan said. "It feels amazing."

"I'll let you two be," the counselor told them and she left the common room.

"Let's go for a walk outside in the courtyard. There's a view of the lake from there," Dylan suggested.

Lance and Dylan took a stroll down a winding path in the back courtyard of the center. There were beautiful gardens full of flowers and plants that were growing fruit.

"We do horticulture for fun," Dylan explained. "I hated it at first, but it's very rewarding to see what you plant begin to grow."

"So it's been one week," Lance said. "One week sober. One week here. Are you feeling any withdrawals?"

"None," Dylan said. "I think I'll be fine. I have to do forty-five days as part of the program, but I really think that once I do it, I'll be good to get back to normal. The bank has me on a leave of absence. At least I'll go back to the real world with a job still."

"I'm proud of you," Lance said. "You had me worried. Vegas was a very crazy trip."

"I'm sorry for that crap," Dylan said with his head hanging low. "I really messed up."

"It's fine," Lance said. "You were not well. Addiction is a disease."

"I'll be well for your wedding," Dylan replied. "I will not let you down."

Lance smiled and put his arm around Dylan's shoulder. For the first time in a long time he felt he was truly bonding with his brother. He had always felt he was hidden in his brother's shadow, but his recent arrest and drug addiction made him realize that his brother was not the picture perfect sibling who could do no wrong. He had always thought this.

"How's Amy?" Dylan asked.

Lance struggled for a while before he decided to be truthful.

"We're not speaking right now," he said. "We had a fight about something and right now she needs space."

"What?" Dylan gasped. "The wedding is almost a month away!"

"I know," Lance said. "We'll be fine. She'll reach out to me when she's ready. She needs space. I learned in therapy that giving space to your partner is key to a good relationship."

Lance's thoughts fell on Rose and how he had cheated on Amy with her recently. Then he remembered how he would always ask Claire for space when they had difficult fights.

"Is there something else bothering you?" Dylan asked.

"No," Lance lied. "Why do you ask?"

"You look deep in thought," Dylan said. "Positive?"

"I guess the thought of the wedding nearly a month away is stressing me out," Lance said.

"I don't blame you," Dylan said. "Luckily I'll be fresh out of rehab a few days before June 17th."

"Good," Lance said.

"Have you spoken to mom lately?" Dylan asked.

"I tried to call her before coming to see you," Lance replied, "but George answered her cell. He told me that she was stressed out over some book she lost."

"Is she still crying over that?" Dylan asked sarcastically.

"I wouldn't say she's crying over it per say..." Lance said. "It sounds more like she's upset and angry about it. I've never seen her be that bothered by something before. She once lost a diamond bracelet and she shrugged her shoulders and bought a new one."

"Maybe this book is irreplaceable," Dylan said. "I'm sure it has sentimental value."

"I guess," Lance replied. "I do want to make it a point to go see her at the condo."

"I wish I could go over," Dylan said. "She has yet to come visit me here. I'm glad you came though."

"Of course," Lance said. "What are brothers for?"

"Thanks," Dylan smiled. "You were at her condo not too long ago. How did her carpets turn out?"

"Huh?" Lance asked while staring at a butterfly landing on a flower in the garden.

"The last time I was there," Dylan said, "I let a carpet cleaning team in. I went to visit mom and George a few weeks ago for dinner. Afterwards, they had to run out for some show. I stayed and helped myself to some dessert. Before I was about to leave and lock the door, a carpet cleaning man and woman showed up saying mom had an appointment. I figured she forgot to tell me they were coming."

"Oh," Lance said. "Yeah, her carpets looked clean. Immaculate even. She—well her help, I should say—does a good job of keeping her penthouse in tip top shape."

"That sounds like mother alright," Dylan laughed.

"Get well here," Lance said. "I mean it. I want you to get cleaned up. We've all had a crazy last few weeks, but we should make sure our health is a priority in our lives."

"I know brother," Dylan said. "I will focus on getting better. I know I will be fine."

Lance felt his phone vibrate in his pocket. He pulled it out and saw Amy's name flashing on the screen. His heart skipped in excitement because it was the first message he had from her in a few days.

"Who is it?" Dylan asked.

"It's Amy," Lance responded. "She texted saying that her dad is going to be released from the hospital tonight. He's recovering well and his memory seems to be back. She wants me there with her when he's wheeled out of the hospital."

"Well I guess she's done being upset with you," Dylan said happily.

Lance left the rehabilitation center happier than when he had arrived. He was racing down the highway to get back into the city to meet up with Amy at the hospital where her dad was still a patient.

"Glad you could come," Amy said to Lance in the lobby of the hospital. "I'm sorry about our fight."

"It's ok," Lance said giving her a tight hug. "No more craziness from here on out. I promise."

"It's water under the bridge," Amy said. "I really love you and there's no one else I want to exchange vows with. I'm looking forward to our big day in a few weeks."

"I'm so happy to hear you say that," Lance said with relief. "I've been waiting to hear from you."

"Dad's awake and talking," Amy said. "Come say hi."

They went up the elevator to the floor her dad was on, and entered his room. Simon Aberdeen was eating yogurt from a bowl while still in his patient gown. His room looked like a flower shop. There were several bouquets of flowers and get-well baskets that had been sent to Simon during his recovery in the hospital.

"You're quite popular Mr. Aberdeen," Lance joked.

"Lance!" he yelled excitedly. "I was wondering if I was going to see you before I left this prison."

"You were asleep the last time I was here," Lance said.

"Amy told me," Simon replied. "She mentioned you don't like hospitals too much."

"She's right," Lance said softly and he closed his eyes to remember the reason he had once told Amy that hospitals were not his favorite place to visit.

A fourteen-year-old Lance was sitting in the backseat of his mother's Mercedes SUV. His mother was in the passenger's seat

201

and his brother Dylan was seated beside him in the back. George was driving the vehicle as fast as he could through traffic.

The car ride to the hospital was silent, except for the soft cries coming from Marissa. She was sobbing silently into her handkerchief. She looked pale and had shadows under her eyes that looked as if she had not slept well in days. That morning she was notified that her husband was found dead in a pool at a house they were planning to sell. Lance had silent tears slipping out of the corners of his eyes. The family had been in shock since they had all learned he was found dead while they were having breakfast that morning.

"Thanks for driving," Marissa said softly to George, and she patted his shoulder.

"Of course," George said somberly. "My brother…"

Jeremy Avery's body was taken to a nearby hospital in hopes that he could be revived as a standard protocol. He was pronounced dead shortly after arriving. Lance, Dylan, Marissa, and George were told they could see his body at the hospital before it was moved to the morgue. Dylan had protested going because he was afraid to see his father dead. Lance was not sure how to process how he felt. He was very close to his father, and he could not believe that it was all over. His life had ended and theirs would go on without him.

They arrived at the hospital room where Jeremy's body was being held. His clothing had been removed and a robe had been placed on him. Marissa looked at her husband's body with a look that appeared to be struggling with many emotions. She did not cry for a whole minute, but her eyelids twitched and her hands shook occasionally. It was as if Dylan and Lance were waiting for their mother's emotions to take effect before their own could overwhelm them.

Marissa sat on a chair and crossed her arms. She began to cry onto her shoulder. Lance and Dylan joined her in tears of sorrow, and they both embraced her. Together they mourned their loss. George sat on an opposite corner of the room with his head against the wall and his fists clenched in anger.

"Who would do this?" he said angrily. "Who would kill such an amazing man?"

Marissa looked up at George and stopped crying. Her eyebrows narrowed in anger and she spoke with restrained calmness, "That slutty bitch he's been sleeping with. His assistant Victoria. I know she was the last one to see him."

"Mom," Dylan said, "are you sure it was her? Maybe it was an accident."

"Yeah," Lance said. "She's always been so nice."

"You know your father was having an affair with her, and we were in the process of getting divorced," Marissa said hysterically. "If he had been faithful, that crazy jealous bitch would not have done this!"

"You can't be saying that," George said suddenly. "Let the police find clues. It's not smart to be making accusations out loud like that. They'll think you did it."

Marissa looked at George as if he had slapped her in the face. She began to cry so loud that a nurse from a next-door room, accompanied by a doctor, had to come in and check on them.

"Mrs. Avery," the doctor spoke up, "Ma'am. We'll need you all to clear the room shortly so that we can move his body to the morgue."

There was a few seconds of silence before Simon spoke up.

"So when do I get my wheelchair?" he asked.

"Shortly, dear," Amy's mother Grace said as she walked into the room along with Jill.

"Hey Lance," Jill said.

"Hi there," Lance said back to her.

"Can you three help carry these flowers and baskets to the car?" Grace asked Lance, Jill, and Amy.

"Yeah," Amy replied.

Jill reached for a bouquet of roses that were in a blue vase. The roses had been packed in tightly in the vase, which acted as a cover to it. Jill absent-mindedly shook the vase and heard the sloshing of water from inside followed by a strange buzz.

"Hey, what is that noise coming from the vase of these dying roses?" she asked.

Lance pressed his ear against the vase to listen.

"It sounds like buzzing bugs," Lance said curiously. "Weird. Who sent these?"

"I don't know," Grace replied. "They were the first gift to arrive, but that one did not have a card saying who it was from."

Jill reached for one of the roses and tried to pull it out. The roses still had thorns on the stems that Jill had not noticed until one pricked her finger and caused her to bleed.

"Ouch!" she yelped and without thinking, she lost grip of the vase and it felt to the floor.

It appeared to have occurred in slow motion. The blue vase crashed onto the white clean hospital floor. It shattered into hundreds of pieces. The roses rolled all over the floor and the water spread to all corners of the room. Then, the source of the buzzing was revealed. Inside the vase were several bees. They flew off angrily in all directions of the hospital room. Amy, Grace, and Jill shrieked in horror at he top of their lungs and raced out of the room without a backwards glance. They kept on running down the hall in hopes of putting enough distance between the angry bees and themselves.

A few bees immediately stung Lance and Simon. The doctor and nurse quickly grabbed Simon by his arms and pulled him out of the room with Lance running behind them. Lance closed the door quickly to trap most of the bees inside the room. A few escaped into the hallway with them, but they flew off in various directions away from them.

"Oh my God!" Grace yelled while running back to her husband who was panting against a wall by his room. "What the hell was that?"

Lance looked over at Amy who also joined them and looked as if she had witnessed a murder.

"I h-h-hate bees," Amy stuttered.

Lance knew that Amy's number one phobia was her fear of bees. She was deathly afraid of them, and the color that escaped her face in horror proved that.

"I've called the police," a nurse said coming up to the doctor.

"That was intentional," Simon said. "Who would send someone a bouquet of roses with no name and several killer bees inside the vase ready to attack anyone in their way?"

"What the hell?" Amy cried. "What's going on? Who would do this to my dad?"

Lance remained quiet with his fists clenched. This incident was his last straw.

Chapter Eighteen

Officer Grant was drinking coffee in his office when Lance arrived the following morning before work. Lance barged through the door catching Grant by surprise. He spilled some of his coffee on the paperwork on his desk.

"Dammit!" he cursed. "Have you ever heard of knocking Avery?"

"My apologies," Lance told him. "They said I could let myself in."

"Right," Grant replied disgruntled. "So, we spoke briefly on the phone last night, but you wanted me to look into the situation you were last in here for?"

"Well," Lance began, "there have been a few strange incidents that have happened to me and those close to me. There was that homeless man who threw his coffee at me, my fiancé was run off the road, a cow's heart was delivered to my mom, someone broke into my apartment and left invisible writing on my walls that I was able to find because a black light was mysteriously delivered to my door. And yesterday afternoon, my fiancé's ill father, others, and myself, were attacked by bees. They were in a vase that was sent to his room. Something—no someone—is out to get me. This has gone too far. I've had a P.I. look into my ex girlfriend and there was no dirt found on her, but I'm pretty sure she's behind this. She's stalking me again and I still have a restraining order against her."

"What's her name?" Grant asked.

"Claire Carpenter," he said.

"Right," Grant replied. "I remember you gave Detective Ross and myself that name. We looked her up. She resides in Seattle and has a clean record. There's no way this person is in town to cause you trouble."

"She has to be," Lance said. He recalled the writing on his wall and how it was the best clue he had to pin the events on Claire. However, he had painted over the writing. "If she's in town, then she's working with someone."

"I can look into her records again," Grant said.

"I'm sure you won't find anything different," Lance said defeated. "What next measures can I take regarding this? Someone is definitely out to get me or someone close to me. I don't feel safe, and I have a wedding in less than four weeks."

"There's not enough evidence," Grant said, "if not I would say we could put police detail on you and your property to keep watch."

"Ok," Lance said angrily, "well, when I am in the hospital next time after nearly being killed by something, we'll talk."

Lance stormed out of the police station and muttered "useless" out loud when he passed the receptionist.

The next two weeks were abnormally quiet for Lance. Nothing out of the ordinary had occurred to him or anyone in his close circle of friends or family. His apartment community manager even reported that he had not caught any woman dressed in all black on the complex's camera system. Lance's worry was focused more on the wedding that was days away. His tuxedo had arrived one evening, and he had hung it in his closet. Gifts from the registry that Amy and him had created began to arrive at his apartment as well.

Lance was preparing to go to bed, when his doorbell rang one evening. He opened it with his glasses on as he had taken out his contacts. Dana was framed in the doorway.

"Sorry to bother you neighbor," she said.

"What's the matter?" he asked.

"I saw this newspaper on your floor and thought you forgot to pick it up," Dana said pointing at the paper on the floor, "but then I took a closer look and it's an old print."

Lance looked at the paper on his doorstep and bent over to pick it up. His jaw immediately dropped at the headline splashed across the top: "Victoria Price Set Free; No Evidence in Avery Murder Case."

"Son of a bitch," Lance muttered.

"What is it?" Dana asked curiously.

"Nothing," Lance said. "Someone left this for me. I...I need to go."

Lance bid Dana goodnight and closed his door in haste. He looked at the newspaper and walked over to his fireplace. He threw the paper on top of a log and pulled out a match. He struck the match and the orange flame glowed lazily before its embers licked the decade-old newspaper into black ash. Once the newspaper had completely turned to ash, Lance slapped his forehead in anger as he realized he could have used the newspaper as a clue to give to Officer Grant.

Lance paced his apartment for twenty minutes as his adrenaline began to flow in anger. Someone was playing a dirty game with him, and he felt powerless against this anonymous entity that was taunting him. During the entire time he was pacing, his mind kept racing back to Claire and how she became obsessed with finding out about his life the few months after their breakup.

"She knows," he said to himself. "She knows where I live. She has to. She knows about Amy. She just has to know. She's targeting those people that are close to me. She's screwing with me. But how will I catch her? I know it's her. What the hell do you want Claire?"

Lance jumped when his cellphone began to vibrate. He reached for it on his living room coffee table and answered. It was Edward.

"Have you seen the news?" he asked Lance.

"No, why?" Lance asked.

"Turn it on to channel five," Edward said. "I'll stay on the line."

Lance turned on his television and changed the channel to the one that Edward asked him to. There was a news anchor reporting from outside...

"Victoria Price's house!" Lance gasped. "What the hell?"

"She was found hanging from her closet," Edward said. "Can you believe that? She killed herself by hanging herself by the throat."

"That's crazy," Lance said with unease.

"Serves her right for killing your dad," Edward said with pride. "She should have done it sooner."

"Hey, my mom is calling," Lance interrupted. "I'll call you later—Hey mom..."

"I just heard the news about Victoria Price," Marissa panted over the phone. "Did you hear?"

"I'm watching the news coverage of it now," Lance said. "She hanged herself. Wow."

"That slut deserved it," Marissa said angrily.

"Death is not something you should wish upon someone," Lance said. "We'll never know if she really did it."

"The police will be doing a sweeping search of her home for more clues," Marissa said. "I feel like we will finally have an answer soon. The officer I spoke with said he knows you. His name is Grant."

"Oh yes," Lance said sarcastically. "What a small world this is."

Lance found himself driving to the north part of town to the rural neighborhood that Victoria lived in. He parked his car a few blocks away and slowly walked to her house. A few news vans were packing up their equipment and preparing to leave the scene. There was police caution tape roping off the house, and a few police were questioning neighbors. Lance saw the cops walk out with bags labeled "evidence" and put them in their vans. Lance felt someone tap his shoulder from behind, and it made him jump.

"Didn't mean to startle you," an old woman with a walking cane said.

She was a foot shorter than Lance and had white curly hair.

"Can I help you?" Lance asked.

"I know who you are," the woman said. "You're the son of the man Victoria allegedly killed."

"That I am," Lance said. "I came for closure."

"Do you think her death is closure for you dear boy?" she asked.

"No," Lance said. "I spoke with Victoria a couple of weeks ago. She did not look happy. She was broken, but that day I found my closure."

Lance's phone began vibrating in his hands. It was Amy trying to reach him. He ignored her call.

"How did you find closure?" she asked somberly.

"I feel in my gut that she was not my father's killer," he said.

"She wasn't," the woman said. "I got to know her a few years ago when she moved into the neighborhood. In the past years or so she stopped coming out. She became a hermit. But when I got to know her, she spoke to me in great detail about the pain she had to face because she felt she was set up."

Lance looked at the woman with peeked interest.

"Set up?" Lance said. "I was beginning to think my father's death was an accident."

The woman looked at Lance and smiled at him as if she were taunting him.

"What do you mean?" Lance insisted.

"Victoria told me her theories," the woman said. "Her theories on how your father died…well…she was too afraid to ever say them out loud. She knew the law would not believe her, and she did not have the money to afford her a powerful lawyer."

Lance looked over at Victoria's house and saw two officers running out of the house yelling "You need to see this!"

"What do you mean?" Lance asked the woman again and he gave her his full attention.

"Victoria had a visitor a few nights ago," the woman said. "I couldn't tell who it was, but I saw this person walking up from down the street. The individual was wearing black. This person was hidden in the darkness. Apparently Victoria knew who this person was and let them in. An hour later, the person fled the house in a rush without looking back. I wanted to follow this individual to see who it was, but with my old age, my legs cannot really get me far."

"Have you told this to the police?" Lance asked.

"Yes," she said. "They are keeping it quiet because they feel that Victoria's killer will become lazy and reveal him or herself by accident if everyone believes her death was a suicide. I also told the cop about how Victoria said she was set up."

"Who did Victoria think set her up?" Lance insisted.

The woman began to laugh a very menacing laugh. Lance looked at her with distrust.

"This is not a joking matter," Lance spat.

"Careful," the woman said. "Temper, temper…"

Three officers were carrying a box out of Victoria's house. One of the officers looked like he was going to throw up.

"It's disgusting," the sick officer said. "There's a cow's heart in that box. It was in her refrigerator."

Lance's heart sank.

211

"It *was* her…" he uttered into the night.

The woman was no longer smiling or laughing. She had a look of shock on her face.

"She's sick," Lance turned to woman. "My mom was sent a raw cow's heart to her home. It was Victoria!"

"I imagine they will make her look like she's insane again," the old woman said in a defeated tone. "I told her not to send that raw heart."

"You knew she sent that to my mother?" Lance asked in disgust.

"Yes," the woman said not meeting Lance's eyes. "She was going to send another one. I think your mother realized it was Victoria because she came by her house…"

"When?" Lance said in shock.

"The same day you came," the woman said. "I saw you both at Victoria's house a few weeks ago through my window…I guess I should have mentioned that earlier."

"Oh…right," Lance said. "Well, that matter was cleared. Why would Victoria want to send that raw heart to my mother when she had been in so much legal trouble in the past?"

"Do you not remember?" the old woman asked. "Your mother was the main reason Victoria was named a suspect. Your mother stopped at nothing to point a finger at her."

Lance recalled the day they were all at his father's hospital bedside and his mother was crying and blaming Victoria for what had happened.

"So Victoria wanted to send that heart as a sign or threat to my mother?" Lance asked.

"It was her way of saying 'go to hell' to your mother," the woman said.

"And now she's killed herself!" Lance spat.

"Victoria did not kill herself," the woman said. "I saw someone dressed in black coming into the house.

"Could you tell if the person was female?" Lance asked with a thought that perhaps the veiled woman in black was behind Victoria's death because earlier he had received a newspaper on his doorstep with an old headline of Victoria's freedom from jail.

"I don't know," the woman said.

Lance stood quietly in thought. The newspaper was not a coincidence. Victoria's killer had probably delivered it to his doorstep knowing that her name would become the subject of headlines the following morning.

"You said earlier," Lance began, "that you believed Victoria was set up for the murder of my father. Who did she think it was?"

"Isn't it obvious?" the old woman said. "From everything we talked about, I thought you would have made the connection. She believed your father's real killer was Marissa Avery—*your mother.*"

Chapter Nineteen

"**Y**ou're crazy!" Lance told the woman with disgust. "My mother did not kill my father. How dare you!"

"I apologize for saying such dark things," the woman said sadly. "But I'm just repeating what Victoria's beliefs were. I cannot say if it is true or not, but there is no doubt that the police will be reopening your father's case. His death might not have been accidental."

Lance was livid. He ended up at Amy's apartment after he left Victoria's neighborhood. He did not tell Amy about his encounter with the old woman. He was left with a feeling of unease. His family had worked hard to stay out of the press since his father's death had been blasted all over the news a decade ago. He cried onto Amy's shoulders because he was worried that old wounds would be reopened for the entire city to read about the following morning.

The *Wedding March* began to play on a piano. The church was decorated brilliantly with white flowers. All of the wedding guests had taken their seats at the pews and waited with bated breath for the bride to walk down the aisle. Lance was standing at the alter with Edward beside him. He looked over at his mother who was wearing a bright green dress that brought out the color of her eyes. Her makeup made her look young and rested. George was seated by her and holding her hand.

Lance looked up as the chapel doors opened and Amy appeared at the doorway. The sunlight outlined her body as if she were an angel in a magnificent white wedding gown. She walked slowly down the aisle with her father Simon holding arm in arm.

Lance felt his face flush red in excitement and nerves. All eyes were on Amy as she inched closer and closer to Lance. Edward patted Lance on the back as to signify inaudible congratulations to him. Lance turned over to Edward and smiled. His head turned quickly to Amy when a loud bang echoed in the chapel causing many men and woman in the crowd to scream and scramble.

Lance looked over at his future wife's shocked eyes. The middle of her chest began to turn red. There was a small red circle on her gown that kept growing larger and larger. Amy put her hands on it and began to cry. She gave Lance one last look before her life escaped her eyes and they glazed over into emptiness forever.

Amy's body crashed onto the floor. Her father Simon had dropped her in the sudden shock from the gunshot that had taken her life. Lance looked at a woman wearing a black hoodie at the entrance to the chapel. She had a gun pointing at him.

"Claire!" Lance gasped, but before he could duck and move, Claire had pulled the trigger and the bullet hit Lance.

"AAAARRGGGHHH!" Lance gasped waking up from his nightmare.

"Baby, are you ok?" Amy got up in shock and reached for her nightlight.

"Oh my God," Lance panted. "I just had a terrible dream. It's…it's nothing."

"What was it about?" Amy asked.

"Nothing," Lance lied. "Um…Dylan was in a car accident. That's it. It felt real."

"You must have had a very vivid dream?" Amy comforted Lance and kissed him on the cheek. "I think you've been stressed out what with your Vegas trip and now Victoria's death. Do you want to call in sick to work in the morning?"

"Yeah," Lance said. "Let's spend the day together. Can you call in sick?"

"I will," Amy said.

Lance and Amy woke up that morning to newspaper and newscaster headlines about Victoria's suicide. Stories about the Avery family had been dug up and as Lance predicted, his family was in the public eye again. Lance had tried all morning to get a hold of his mother, but George kept answering and told him that she was having a really difficult time with the news and there were reporters hanging around their condominium.

"I should probably go see my mom," Lance told Amy once he was dressed. "I'm worried about her."

"Of course babe," Amy said.

"Are you ok?" Lance asked.

"The timing of all this is crazy," Amy sighed. "With the wedding only a few days away, I don't know how any of us are going to focus. I mean, your side of the family already has a handful. Not to mention Dylan will be out of rehab in a few days too."

"Everything will work out," Lance said.

"They are reopening your dad's case," Amy said worriedly. "That's what the news has been saying. They said they received an anonymous tip that Victoria was set up and her death was not suicide."

"Wait…what?" Lance asked in surprise.

"Look!" Amy said raising the volume of her television.

"Police do not have a person of interest yet," the reporter was saying, "but police arrived at the station this morning to an anonymous letter left for them at the front desk. They are not sure if it is a hoax or not, but due to standard protocol, they have to take the tip seriously just in case. This strange mystery opens up several more doors into the mysterious death of Jeremy Avery almost sixteen years ago. Victoria Price was released from jail when there was not enough sufficient evidence to keep her incarcerated. It was ruled that Jeremy Avery's death was an accidental drowning. Sources close to the family have always said that they believed Avery's death was not an accident and that Victoria was behind it. Hold on a minute…we are getting some conflicting reports now. Police officials say they found a cow's heart in Victoria Price's refrigerator, which is adding some darkness to this woman's story. Police confirmed that Mrs. Marissa Avery, the ex wife of Jeremy Avery, had received a cow's heart in the mail a few months earlier from an anonymous person. Police are now concluding that Victoria Price sent the animal part as a malicious act, however they cannot prove she was planning to harm Mrs. Avery. This story is baffling and confusing because it leaves us wondering if Victoria Price really was Jeremy Avery's killer? Does this anonymous tip have some validity?"

"Turn it off," Lance said angrily. "The news is screwing everything up."

Lance had a new worry. There was someone who was telling the police that Victoria was innocent and set up. His first thought was it was the old woman. His next thought was fear. If the old woman had given the anonymous tip, then he wondered if that tip mentioned his mother's name. Were they covering up that piece of information from the media? His heart began to sink.

"I need to go see my mom," Lance said.

He kissed Amy goodbye, and darted out of her apartment to his car. When Lance arrived at his mother's condo, he saw a few news vans and reporters hanging right outside of the lobby entrance. He rolled his eyes and took a deep breath before walking through the madness.

"Lance! Mr. Avery!" several reporters shouted as cameras began to flash and microphones were pushed against Lance's face.

217

Lance kept his mouth shut and pushed his way through the mob of media. When he arrived at the lobby, the security guard at the front desk let him in.

"Ah, Mr. Avery," the male security guard said. "It's crazy out there."

"It is," Lance said. "Make sure they never step foot in here."

Lance gave the reporters a dirty look before retreating to the elevator. When he arrived at the penthouse, George answered and gave Lance a hug.

"I would not watch the news if I were you," George said. "They keep creating this story crazy. And this nonsense about an anonymous tip is ridiculous. Victoria Price is your dad's killer. We've always known that. It's so disgraceful that they are even considering opening the case because of some bullshit tip!"

"Yeah," Lance said automatically while looking at his mother who was seated on the couch with the television on one of her soap operas.

"She's been drinking," George whispered. "She's really stressed out about this. It's bringing up some emotions."

"Right," Lance nodded. "Hey mom…"

"Oh hello Lance," she replied. "Thank you for coming by. I'm sorry I've not been able to speak with you on the phone. All this is driving me mad."

There were tissues on the coffee table in front of Marissa and she was wearing a pink bathrobe. She had no makeup on and looked much older than Lance was used to seeing her.

"Excuse my appearance," Marissa said. "It has been a difficult day."

"The police stopped by to ask a few questions," George said angrily. "They are looking to see if their tip is legitimate."

"Do you know what the tip said?" Lance asked.

"No," George responded. "They won't tell us. But they kept asking your mother and me several questions."

"They don't think she—or any of you—have anything to do with dad or Victoria—" Lance began but Marissa cut him off while spilling some of her martini on herself.

"No Lance!" she yelled. "What would any of us have to do with that woman?"

"That officer...Grant is his name...he told me a bit about that tip," Marissa said.

"Grant was here?" Lance asked. "The weird shit that has been happening to me...well...I've told Grant about it. Maybe this will finally help lead him to finding out who is behind stalking me. I think it's related."

Lance realized he had not told George or his mother most of the details of the issues he was dealing with, but they seemed unfazed by what he had said.

"What was the tip?" Lance said after a few seconds of silence.

"The tip said that both Victoria and your father's deaths were not accidents or suicide. That's all. It was a type written note. The note also said that when the time was right, evidence was going to be sent to the station by this anonymous person," Marissa divulged and she began to cry.

"Calm down honey," George sat by Marissa to try to ease her.

"Calm down?" Marissa yelled again. "How the hell do I calm down when a crazy woman that murdered Jeremy is found dead and now the whole world is ripping off the bandages of old wounds?"

"Mom—chill," Lance said. "We're all stressed. I have a wedding in a few days and this is not what I wanted to be dealing with. The media will be bothering us for days."

"Dammit," Marissa said, and she closed her eyes and cried into a pillow.

Lance was not sure what to believe anymore. He felt violated on so many levels. He knew there was some unknown entity that was trying to ruin his life and tear his family apart. He felt anger surge when Claire's name flashed in his mind. Then he thought about that old woman and how she accused his mother of being a murderer. Lance looked at Marissa with pity. She looked worn down and old. She was crying more than he had ever seen her cry. It was as if she was finally releasing emotions she worked so hard to conceal from her family. She never wanted to be perceived as weak or as a widow. She cared too much about her image.

"Your apartment is looking nice," Lance tried to think of something to get her mind off Victoria or his dad. "Did you do something new?"

"No," Marissa pulled her face out of the pillow and looked around her penthouse.

"Are you sure?" Lance said. "The carpets look cleaner than normal. Did you get those cleaned?"

"Not since last year," Marissa replied.

"Oh," Lance said with confusion etched all over his face. "I thought Dylan told me you had your carpets cleaned recently."

"No," Marissa said suspiciously. "Why would he say that?"

"Well," Lance responded, "he said he let in a carpet cleaning team one evening when you and George had left and he stayed behind in your apartment."

"What?" Marissa said so suddenly that she spilled her martini glass on the carpet itself. "Shit!"

"Did you not have an appointment scheduled?" Lance asked curiously.

"No!" Marissa looked horrified. "Someone was in my apartment without my consent! The carpets look the same as they've looked for the past few months. Nobody cleaned them."

Marissa ran to her room and began looking through drawers.

"I'm checking if any of my most valuable hidden jewelry is missing," she shouted out to the living room where George and Lance were sitting.

"Honey," George called, "I'm sure nothing happened. Maybe it was a mistake and they realized they had the wrong unit."

"I think I'll call the police," Marissa said.

"Let's not jump into any conclusions just yet," George said. "We don't even know if anything's missing...wait a minute...you lost some book a few weeks ago. That was around the same time Dylan was last here."

Marissa walked out of her room with a scared look on her face as if that was exactly what she was looking for.

"It's the book, isn't it?" George asked. "What kind of book was it?"

"Just a book!" Marissa snapped.

George and Marissa began to bicker, and after a few tense minutes, the bickering became a much more heated verbal argument. Lance bid them farewell and excused himself as he did not want to be involved in their screaming match. When he arrived at his car after avoiding the reporters once again, he pulled out his phone to dial Rose. He had not been to a session in weeks since he had parted ways with her, but he was so overwhelmed with the recent events in his life and how much crazier things were becoming.

"Thanks for meeting me," Lance said as Rose arrived at Lance's favorite coffee shop, Beethoven's.

"Of course," Rose said sweetly. "It was really good to hear from you."

Rose was wearing a white linen dress with white sandals. Her golden locks shone in the sunlight while they sat outside on a bench.

"I'm sure you've seen the news," Lance said.

"That woman—Victoria Price—she's the one who we talked about in our session, huh?" Rose asked.

"The woman allegedly responsible for killing my father," Lance added.

"You told me that you believed she was innocent," Rose stated.

"Right," Lance responded. "However, the cops found a cow's heart in her fridge. A raw heart was sent to my mother a few months ago. It seemed like a threat. I was under the impression it was Claire, but now we know that Victoria Price sent it. The police are going to look into it, but the cops are also looking into an anonymous tip they received saying essentially that Victoria was set up with my father's death."

"It must be hard to have this opened up again," Rose said.

"You have no idea," Lance said sadly. "I thought I put all this behind me."

Rose took a sip of her coffee and put her hand on his. She looked at him intently with her eyes and smiled.

"If the threats stop," Rose began, "then you'll know it was her."

"That's what I'm hoping," Lance said. "I want this all to be over. I need my life to have some kind of normalcy. I need order."

"You'll get it," Rose said. "You need to focus on your priorities right now."

"Like my wedding?" Lance said sarcastically. "I've already screwed up. I...you...me...that day of indiscretion..."

"I've been thinking about you so much," Rose said squeezing Lance's hand. "There's something special about you. I know this sounds wrong, but I fell for you during our sessions. I really find you attractive and smart and kind. I know this is all sorts of messed up. I mean I'm—was your therapist. I'm crazy right now. I mean if you wanted to file a claim against me, I would lose my license. I do know I cannot control what the heart wants. It wants you Lance."

Lance stared at Rose in stunned silence. He had been so deeply attracted to Rose, but he did not know her well enough to say some of the things she had told him.

"I," Lance struggled for words, "don't know what to say. I mean I'm engaged to be married."

"And you hooked up with me," Rose interjected. "We shared a passionate moment together. You felt it. I saw it in your eyes. You had a look on you that read familiarity."

"You did feel great," Lance said. "I felt comfortable and at ease. You knew all my dark skeletons and you did not judge me. You made me feel normal."

"I get you," Rose said. "And not because I'm a therapist, but because you remind me of someone I used to be with. The heart yearns for that familiarity and I have that with you."

"But I'm in love with Amy," Lance retorted.

"How can you be in love with her?" Rose had tears in her eyes. "You allowed me to give myself to you. You allowed me to open up. Did you give me false hope?"

"I mean we hooked up," Lance blurted. "You can't have expected me to think of it as having more substance when my heart and mind are too full and messed up to really think clearly about my wrong-doings."

"Fine," Rose said while wiping her eyes with a napkin. "Well you're no longer my patient anymore. It probably would be best to cut off all communication."

Lance closed his eyes and flashed to a memory of him and Claire fighting outside his Seattle apartment door. Lance was pushing her out of his apartment because she was angry and becoming physical over an argument about Lance's past.

"This is done," Claire snapped. "I'm going to Portland for the weekend and I'm going to cut off all communication from you."

Claire had disappeared that weekend and made no contact with friends, family, or even Lance. She had gone radio silent in an attempt to show Lance what life would be like if she cut him off. Lance had felt so depressed that weekend that in his mind, she had instilled a fear in him of losing her.

Lance looked up at Rose and said, "Why do all women who come into my life feel the need to cut off communication with me when in our sessions you always told me that communication was key with relationships. A few days ago, Amy stopped talking to me for almost a week so she could cool down about some things that I said to upset her."

"I don't know Lance," Rose said. "I know what I say in our sessions, but I'm a human and we are not in my office and you are not sitting on my couch."

"You don't practice what you preach," Lance said bitterly.

"I live down the street," Rose said to change the subject. "Come over for one last *session*..."

Lance found himself seated on the corner of Rose's bed in her apartment. She had a one-bedroom unit decorated with a modern contemporary style. Everything was sleek and mostly in shades of gray, black, and white. The only color that stood out was a brown shag rug in the middle of her living room that was under her coffee table.

"I'm glad you came," Rose said to Lance as she began to unbutton her blouse. "I'll give you one last taste before you exchange your vows and your life changes forever."

An hour later, Lance was zipping up his pants and frantically fixing his hair with his hands in front of Rose's bathroom mirror. Rose was lying on her bed with a bathrobe on and smoking a cigarette. Lance desperately wanted to shower to rid his body of the sins and lustful act he had committed. He began to tear up and had the urge to punch the mirror. He was angry with himself for the affair in which he had partaken.

"That was fun stud," Rose said. "You're a gorgeous man. Amy is a lucky woman."

"Don't say her name!" Lance spat. "I can't believe you made me do this."

"I made you?" Rose said angrily. "It takes two to tango, honey."

Lance rolled his eyes and walked back into her bedroom. He gave her a stern look.

"We can never talk about this," he said. "And don't tell Dana either."

"Our dirty little secret," Rose teased.

Lance reached for his wallet that was on top of a small black battered book on Rose's desk.

"I got to go," Lance said.

"Good luck," Rose said with a changed expression of hurt written all over her face. "I'm sorry to have complicated things."

"Right. Farewell then," Lance walked out of her apartment in a hurry.

Chapter Twenty

The few days leading up to Lance and Amy's rehearsal dinner were grueling for Lance because of the pang of guilt he felt in his heart every moment he was with Amy. Amy was under a large amount of stress and Lance had to tread lightly as any little thing could upset her.

"White roses!" Amy snapped at a florist over the phone the morning of their rehearsal dinner during brunch. "They should be fresh and sent to 619 Lone Star Lane–St. Austin Church—no later than three o' clock tomorrow. The ceremony will begin promptly at six."

When Amy ended the call, she looked over at Lance and smiled.

"Our big day is finally almost here," Lance said automatically.

"June 17," Amy replied. "I hope everything goes well and without any issues. I'm seriously getting gray hairs out of all this planning."

"We should have hired a wedding planner do all this," Lance admitted. "You've been doing so much on your own."

"It would have been a waste of money," Amy replied. "You know I love to have my creative freedom."

"Yeah, I know," Lance said. "How's your dad doing?"

"He's fine," Amy answered. "He's recovered from the few bee stings he got—and we still don't know who sent those roses. He's also been getting a lot of rest. Mom is keeping him off his feet so that he isn't stressing himself so much. She wants him healthy for tomorrow so he can walk me down the aisle."

"Good," Lance said. "My mom has been a constant nervous wreck. I don't think it has anything to do with the wedding. She's been in a weird mood since she learned my brother let some random people into her apartment posing as carpet cleaners. I know I told you about it earlier, but I think she feels violated."

"Did she talk to the police?" Amy asked.

"Yes," Lance said. "However, the police are not the people she wants to talk to right now. That officer, who helped us out after your car accident and my coffee incident at work, has also been looking into the Victoria Price case. They think she might not have committed suicide."

"Do we need security at the wedding?" Amy asked. "I've been thinking about the strange shit that has happened lately what with the bee attack, the person who drove me off the road, your apartment break in…"

"Look," Lance said. "It very well could have been Victoria doing this to me. They did find that cow's heart in her fridge, which is very gross and messed up. So, she must have sent it to my mother. However, my mother says the police received an anonymous tip telling them that Victoria was set up. I mean you heard that news report the other day. Everyone is buzzing about the possibility of my father's case reopening."

"This timing is really poor," Amy said somberly. "I can only imagine how you must feel to have that Band-Aid ripped off you after you felt you had closure."

"You have no idea," Lance said while putting his hands on his face. "My family is a mess. Dylan was also released from rehab. He's clean again, which is great. At least that issue is no longer a problem."

"Do you all need anything else?" the female waitress that was serving them came by their table.

"Just the check please," Lance said.

"Perfect, I'll be right back," the woman replied.

Lance walked Amy to her car that was in a lot across the street from the downtown Austin restaurant where they had brunched.

"Rehearsal dinner is at seven. At Goldie's," Amy told Lance before she got into her car. "Try to arrive thirty minutes before so we can go over a few logistics."

"Right," Lance said, and he kissed Amy on the lips. "I'll be there on time."

"I'll see you tonight," Amy opened the door to her car.

"So, you're staying at your parents' cabin tonight?" Lance asked. "Alone?"

"Yeah," she responded. "I want to spend my last night alone to have *me* time. I've been around so many people all week and will be around so many people at dinner and the wedding tomorrow. I want to have time to reflect and rest."

"Sounds like a good plan," Lance agreed. "Everything will be flawless. *You* will be flawless in your dress."

"I hope so," Amy said. "See you tonight. I'm off to meet Jill to get a manipedi. Love you."

Lance watched as Amy drove off. He pulled his phone out of his pocket and saw that he had a few missed calls and text messages from Dylan.

"Hey Dylan," Lance said over the phone when he called him back. "What's up?"

"Hey," Dylan said. "Do you have a second? In private?"

"Yeah," Lance said. "I just parted ways with Amy. What's the matter?"

"I just left mom's apartment," Dylan said. "She yelled at me for letting in those fake carpet people a few weeks ago. She was ranting about that book she lost and thinks it was stolen."

"I don't know why she's still going on about that," Lance sighed. "It's only a book."

"She says it was a childhood gift from grandma," Dylan added. "It meant the world to her. She didn't tell me what kind of book it was though."

"I'm surprised they did not take any jewelry," Lance said.

"That's why this is a big mess," Dylan said. "And why I'm calling you even though mom wanted to wait to talk to you until after your wedding and honeymoon. The thing is, Officer Grant has been questioning her and George about our family history and what not. Whoever those people were, they were targeting that one specific item. You know mom has thousands of dollars worth of gold and jewelry. All of her items were in tact. I gave the cops a description of the man and woman that I let in, but my memory was so vague because I was high at the time. Anyways, there have been so many weird things that have been happening to us. The raw heart, Amy's accident, your accident, your apartment break in, and there have been weird blocked calls that I've been getting."

"I still think Claire could be behind this," Lance said.

"Grant told mom he did some digging into her," Dylan said. "They found nothing on her. She's in Seattle."

"I know," Lance said. "This is nuts. I'm going to give Grant a call."

Lance finished his conversation with Dylan and hastily looked for Grant's phone number in his recent contact list. Once he found it he initiated the call.

"Hello?" Grant answered.

"Hey—it's Lance Avery," he said.

"Hello Lance," Grant responded. "What can I help you with?"

"What's going on?" Lance said. "I have a wedding tomorrow. My mom is going crazy over the stress of Victoria's death and my father's case being reopened. What is this tip you received?"

"Why don't you come down to the station and I'll show you," Grant said. "There's a piece of the tip that has not been released to the media or your mother. It's the reason why your father's case *will* be reopened."

"I'll be there in ten minutes," Lance said. "I'm already downtown."

Lance arrived at the police station. Several of the cops sitting at their desks turned and looked at Lance. A few of them put their heads together to exchange whispers. Lance felt his face grow red with annoyance. He knew the whole station was very familiar with his family and the tragedy they had faced.

"Mr. Avery," Grant called from down the hall. "Come in."

Lance walked into Grant's office and took a seat opposite of his desk.

"What is this tip?" Lance said firstly.

"We received this type written note in an envelope. There was no name or address on it," Grant said. "It was mailed to us from here in Austin, but that is all we know. Also, this is confidential, but I'm sharing this with you because it was about your father."

"Why didn't you share the entire information with my mother?" Lance asked.

"We'll get to that shortly," Grant said with a serious look on his face.

Lance opened the envelope and pulled out the letter-sized piece of computer paper. Written in cursive type font, the letter read: "*Victoria Price's death was not suicide. Her killer was the same person who killed Jeremy Avery. Jeremy Avery's killer is still alive.*"

"This has to be a hoax," Lance said flabbergasted.

"Do you think Victoria Price killed your father?" Grant asked him.

"I...I...I don't really know anymore," Lance said. "If I'm being honest, I went to pay her a visit recently."

"I know," Grant replied.

"You know?" Lance asked feeling his heart race. "How?"

"Victoria's neighbor is an elderly woman by the name of Maggie," Grant said. "We spoke to all the neighbors. Maggie was the only one who ever spoke with Victoria. She said that Victoria insisted she was innocent and only God and your father knew the truth. She said that you stopped by her house a month or so ago and had a talk with her. Victoria then told Maggie that you had come to the conclusion that Victoria was in fact innocent and Avery's death may have actually been an accident."

"I could have sworn that lady said she no longer spoke to Victoria. Ugh! Did Maggie also tell you that Victoria sent the heart to my mother?" Lance spat. "A disgusting and smelly organ from a dead animal. Did I mention it was bloody?"

"We know Victoria sent that," Grant said, "but there's more to the story. The cow hearts were purchased from a butcher shop south of Austin. The one in Victoria's refrigerator was still wrapped in a vacuum-sealed package with the butcher's label on it. We recently paid the butcher a visit and he told us that the person who bought them was a man."

"So what are you getting at?" Lance asked with clenched fists.

"A man bought those raw hearts and gave them to Victoria," Grant said. "Maggie admitted that Victoria had confided in her that some random man wanted to help her get revenge on your mother for not going to jail in her place. He orchestrated the anonymous shipping of the dead cow's heart as a scare tactic."

"Hold on," Lance said. "Surely my mother has told you that a man and a woman came to her apartment posing as carpet cleaners. Maybe it was the same man?"

"We are looking into that as a possible lead," Grant said. "We are checking security camera footage from that day. We should have information about that within the next few hours."

"Can I ask why my mother or the media do not know about the part of the tip that says my dad's killer is still alive?" Lance asked.

"Maggie told us that Victoria believed she was framed by your mother," Grant said. "I know this is very hard to hear but—"

"NO!" Lance shouted. "You listen to me! That woman is old and does not know what she's talking about. I was fourteen. I saw my mother going through a tailspin of a depression. My childhood was screwed up beyond recognition of any kind of normalcy because of my father's death whether it was Victoria or someone else. There's no way my mother would have or could have..."

"She's a suspect Lance," Grant said with a frown. "She had a motive. Victoria Price had an affair with your father. From the old files we have on the case, your mother was the first to put the blame and accusations on Victoria. You believed Victoria was innocent the night you spoke to her about the incident. So now the only suspects we have is your mother, and this mysterious man is a person of interest."

"What about the things that have been happening to me?" Lance asked. "The break-ins and everything else? My mother did not do that to me. She did not run Amy off the road. She did not send a vase of flowers with bees hidden inside to my fiancé's father's hospital bedside. There's no way. There's some other culprit out there and I still think it's my ex girlfriend."

"The restraining order has ended," Grant said. "We can bring her in for questioning or have a phone call with her if you want."

"Um, no," Lance said taken aback. "I never want to see her again."

"Then there's no point in blaming someone who is thousands of miles away," Grant said. "And married."

"Married?" Lance said in shock. "She's married?"

"Yes," Grant said. "We spoke to your lawyer Cohen. He's the one who you had dig up information on her."

"Married to who?" Lance asked.

"A lawyer," Grant said. "And she has two step daughters. They were from the lawyer's first marriage. He's about ten years older than Claire. I think it is safe to say Claire has moved on with her life. I also looked into the restraining order you filed with your lawyer. I saw the crazy emails and texts she sent, but nothing was ever physical or life threatening. It was childish and immature. She was very bitter about your break up and infidelity."

"Well, you are the law," Lance said sarcastically. "Who do you think made that homeless guy throw hot coffee at me?"

"He may have been crazy," Grant said.

"Or the black car that ran my fiancé off the road and into a pole?" Lance retorted.

"There are a few holes in these cases," Grant said. "I admit that, but we will find answers."

"You can't arrest my mother until you have proof, right?" Lance asked.

"Right," Grant said. "And if you truly believe she had nothing to do with your father's death, then you have nothing to worry about. This tip, whether real or not, has to be taken into serious account. That being said, we have no choice but to question your mother soon and open up the case. Now, I told you this information in confidence. I know and trust you will not tell your mother because you have your wedding tomorrow, and you probably do not want to see her more frantic than I'm sure she has been lately."

"I won't tell her anything," Lance said. "I also think you should only question her if you have reasonable evidence or you will cause a hailstorm of trouble, and the last thing we need is more press."

"I am waiting for more evidence," Grant replied. "So unless we find something, there won't be any need to tell her that Victoria was under the impression that she was framed by her."

"And will you also look more into the fact that maybe Victoria really was the killer after all and she tried to set my mom up before killing herself?" Lance asked.

233

"That's a probable theory," Grant said. "Trust me when I say we are looking into that as well and analyzing her house from every nook and cranny to see if we find something that could connect Victoria to your father's death."

There was a knock at Grant's office door.

"Come in," Grant called out.

It was Detective Ross.

"Oh," he said awkwardly when he realized Lance was there, "I didn't know you had company."

"We were just talking about the case," Grant replied. "I let him in on that anonymous letter we received."

"I see," Detective Ross replied. "The video from that night was missing. Someone deleted them. The apartment complex was baffled because they archived footage on a computer hard drive and the footage of the night that the alleged carpet cleaners came to the Avery household was nowhere to be found."

"Well," Grant said. "Somebody does not want to be found."

"Someone was covering up something," Detective Ross added. "And Marissa Avery had nothing to do with it. Her apartment was vandalized."

"She said all that went missing was a book from her childhood," Grant added. "But she's apparently in shock and feels violated. Do you know anything about this book, Lance?"

"I don't," Lance said. "The only thing I do know is that it was a gift from my grandmother to her."

"Well, do we have any other leads, Ross?" Grant asked.

"You know what you can do?" Lance said to Detective Ross. "Look at the camera footage in my apartment complex. There was a strange woman who was walking the grounds wearing all black and dressed as if she were attending a funeral. The complex manger is calling her the widow. That old woman—Maggie—also said that she saw someone dressed in all black leave Victoria's house the night she allegedly hanged herself. Maggie assumed the person knew Victoria. What if it is the same person? I have also seen a strange woman in black in various other places. I got locked in the old Austin zoo a few weeks back and the strangest thing happened. There was graffiti written in lipstick and red rose petals on the ground. I saw this woman holding a red rose on two various occasions. One was at the cemetery. I'm pretty sure it is the same woman. I'd bet my gold wedding ring that this woman is the one that's doing all this. I mean, bees came out of a vase of roses that were anonymously sent to my fiancé's father! This person could even be my father's killer."

Grant and Ross looked at each other.

"I mean...a woman dressed in all black?" Ross laughed. "That sounds like something out of a horror film."

"If you don't believe me then go take a look at my apartment complex's footage," Lance suggested. "I'll give you the address."

"I guess I can look into this afternoon," Grant said.

"No, I'll go," Ross insisted. "I'm the detective on the case."

"Right," Grant said sounding annoyed. "Ok then."

"Thanks," Lance said with a feeling that this would take the pressure off their suspicion on his mother because he knew he was not crazy and there was some strange woman stalking him.

Deep down inside, he knew that it had to be Claire. The strange quotes from *The Scarlet Letter* that were written on his wall kept haunting him. The only hole in this mystery was he knew Claire would have had no part in his father's death because he did not meet her until almost sixteen years after his passing. Who was the anonymous person that said Lance's father's killer was still alive?

"Well, I have some work to do," Grant chimed in. Ross, do you mind walking Mr. Avery out? We'll talk soon Avery."

"Ok," Lance said. "Later."

Lance and Ross walked down the hall of the station towards the exit. Ross put his arm on Lance's shoulder in a very comforting manner.

"I know you must be going through so much right now," Ross said, "but put your mind to rest. You have a big wedding tomorrow. Should we find footage of some woman wandering your apartment complex, then maybe it will be the best lead we need to find out what happened and if Victoria's death was a murder or not."

"I really hope so," Lance said. "And don't worry, I'm not going to tell my mother anything. The last thing I need is for her to have a nervous breakdown."

"So if your wedding is tomorrow," Ross said, "does that mean your rehearsal dinner with your wedding party is tonight?"

"It is," Lance said. "I need to get back home to shower and change."

"Any other evening plans before the big day?" Ross asked. "Maybe a final single night out with your groomsmen?"

"We might get a drink after," Lance said. "I do have one surprise I'm working on doing."

"Oh, what's that?" Ross asked with interest.

"My girlfriend is staying alone at her parent's cabin in the hill country," Lance said. "I'm thinking of going up there to surprise her."

"How do you think she'll feel about that?" Ross asked. "Isn't it bad luck to stay with the bride the night before?"

"I've had enough bad luck in my life to last a lifetime," Lance said as they arrived at the front lobby of the station, "I think I'll risk it."

"Well then, live it up as if it is your last night," Ross said. "Well, last night as a single man is what I mean, because it really is."

"Thank you," Lance said, and he walked out of the station and into the parking lot to his car.

Lance sat in his car for a few minutes absent-mindedly twirling his iPhone in his fingers. He pulled opened his contacts menu and looked for Claire's number. He realized as he scanned the C's on his list, that he had deleted her number years ago. Lance pulled up his email on his phone and looked at his archive folder and found Claire's email chains he had never deleted. He perused the titles of them and got chills on his arms. The last emails he received from Claire were from a few days before he had served her with a restraining order. The emails were very long and detailed about how Claire had learned about his dark past because she had hacked into his email and read some of his personal files. She had written very angry words in her emails but nothing was ever threatening. The emails were written more to shame Lance or at least make him feel terrible for his infidelity.

Lance felt bothered by something else. He began to feel his pangs of guilt pulling at his heartstrings because he had cheated on Amy with Rose twice. Lance began to cry. There was no way he would be able to exchange his vows with Amy if he was living a lie.

"How do I find myself in this mess with every relationship I enter?" Lance said to himself while hitting his steering wheel in anger. "Why? Why do I screw up all the time and end up hooking up with other women on the side when I'm in a relationship? Why am I messed up? Why did I fall apart and sleep with the one woman that I was paying to help fix me. She broke me. No...I am broken. I've always been and I can't fix myself. I need a new kind of closure. I really want to be well."

Lance reached for his cellphone and took a deep breath. He found an email that had a copy of Claire's resume that she had sent to him when he was living in Seattle near her. Lance wanted to get an example of how a well-written resume looked as he was trying to find a job in Seattle, so he had Claire send him hers. He had used hers as an example to tailor his for the jobs he was applying for.

Her resume had her cell number on it. If she had not changed her number, then he would be able to call her. He felt like it was the only option.

"Face your demons," Lance said. "Maybe, if I give her closure and she's the one behind all this mess, she'll leave my family and me alone."

Lance thought about it for a long time. Then he pressed her name on his phone's touchscreen and it began to dial. Before the first ring could initiate, he ended the call.

237

"I can't do it," he told himself, and he threw his phone onto the empty passenger seat and stared at it in silence.

Lance reached back for his phone and looked back at the emails he had archived from Claire. He read the last one, which had the title "Sorry" on the subject line. Lance read the email aloud to himself.

"I want to say that I am sorry for everything, and I will no longer attempt to communicate with you or with anyone of your friends or family. I was hoping we could talk and get over the past so that we could move on, but I will no longer be a bother to you.

I am sorry. I've put all this disaster to rest and may we all move on in peace. Thank you for all the good memories that you did give me.

I think you've hurt me enough to last a lifetime, and I have hurt you so much as well. I'm setting off to somewhere new and far away from here where I can clear my head. God bless."

Lance scrolled through several more emails on his phone until he found one particular email exchange from a few springs ago. There was a time when Lance had told Claire he was going to move back to Austin because he had been offered a job that his mother had helped him secure. It would bring him back to his home because she wanted him back in Texas. Claire sent Lance a series of riddles and puzzles via email as her way of being romantic because she had a secret message she wanted to give him. He found one of the messages and read it.

"Email me a number that is special to us. It will be the hour and exact minutes of when your next email challenge will arrive at your inbox."

Lance wrote back "6:17" which signified the date they officially began a relationship: June 17. It was also the same date as his wedding happening the next day. Lance was not sure why he wanted to choose the day he became official with Claire except for the fact that in a way it set him free to live a better life and start anew. June 17 meant a fresh new start, however recent events of infidelity made him feel like he was spiraling back into the old Lance he was before he started dating Amy.

In the email chain, Claire had written back to him telling him he was correct and at "6:17pm" he received an email with a link to a YouTube video that Claire made for him with a picture slideshow of all the wonderful events and places they had visited in their relationship. Lance backtracked to the email saying he was correct in his guess about "6:17pm."

Lance read aloud: "Stand by for the message at 6:17 pm pacific time.

For now I leave you with a hint (for the future). The poem "Fill Up" in yesterday's email will be useful in the future. It has a hidden message..."

Lance suddenly remembered a very kind poem that Claire had written for Lance because she was a writer and poet outside of her marketing job. She had even published a few poems in some poetry books. It was the creative part of Claire that he greatly admired. Lance typed in "Fill Up" on his email search bar and up came that email she had sent to him. He read it:

"Last night I tossed and turned

Thinking about what I yearned

My skin was dripping wet

as it glistened with sweat

Heart beating so loud

Wishing I were on a cloud

The pangs of my humanly need

crying desperately to be freed

tortured me in my sleep

What is this you keep?

Empty is my cup

That I want you to fill up."

Lance clicked on the YouTube link and as expected, the video had been taken down and no longer existed. There was also a link to a website Claire had created as part of the email game she had sent to him. The website still existed to Lance's surprise. The

239

site looked empty for the most part except for a text box with the word "Enter" next to it that one was able to click on. The website looked distorted because he was viewing it on his smartphone's web browser. Lance remembered that he was supposed to try and figure out a password and enter it, but he would only get it from Claire if he had decided to stay in Seattle.

"Wow I forgot about this game she played with me," Lance said feeling nostalgic. "It was a cute way for her to convince me to stay. I apparently even bookmarked this website but was never actually given the password. Eventually, I made the decision to stay in Seattle for a few more months. Lance carefully read the email with clues about what the password was. A sentence in the email caught his eye: *"CAPITAL letters for each of a word's first letter is how you figure it all out..."*

"Wait a minute!" Lance had an epiphany.

He looked at the poem "Fill Up" that Claire had written and noticed that not all of the letters in the poem's first word were capitalized. Lance then typed each of the capital letters in the poem from top to bottom into the text box: "LTMHWTWET"

While the random letters did not spell a word, they did allow him access to a secret website he had never been on. This was the true hidden message that Claire had wanted to give him during the time when he was in limbo and thought he would be moving back to Austin for a job more than three years ago.

Lance's heart began to beat fast. He could not believe how ignorant he was. The answer was in the email and right in front of him. He had forgotten that there was a code to break when he and Claire rekindled their relationship upon his decision to stay in Seattle. Now, three years later, he was finally about to see the real *hidden message*.

The website had a plain black background and a YouTube video window in the middle. The word "PLAY" was written below it in red text. Lance pushed play and could feel his fingers shake with nerves as the video expanded into a full screen mode on his iPhone.

"Hey baby," Claire's recorded self and voice was saying to a camera, "If you are watching this it is because you decided to stay in

Seattle and I've given you the password or you figured out the password was hidden in that poem. I wanted to do something very different and non traditional. First off, I love you more than anything. I trust you. You're my rock. You're my better half and my everything. I want you here in Seattle with me. I want to start a new chapter. I know we are still young and you need to establish yourself with a job like you keep telling me, but we are in love. I know you are the one I want to spend the rest of my life with. Woman do not traditionally ask this, but I thought by creating this fun riddle, it would make it romantic. And if you figured it out, it is because you really care about me and want to find my hidden message. Lance Avery, I Claire Carpenter, would like to have the honor to be your wife one day. Will you marry me? I will anxiously await your response in person when I see you next."

Lance stared at his phone with his mouth open wide. Claire's secret message was a wedding proposal that had never been viewed because he never unraveled the clues and located the password. Lance took a deep breath because there it was before him, haunting him like a ghost from his past.

Chapter Twenty-One

The rehearsal dinner was held in an outside garden patio at a trendy South Congress restaurant named Goldie's. Lance arrived wearing a white suit and black bow tie. He walked into the garden patio hand in hand with Amy who was wearing a stunning white summer dress.

"I'm glad you listened to me and match me in white," Amy whispered to Lance as they waved and greeted their wedding party who were all seated at the table. Edward and Jill were on either side of Amy and Lance. Marissa, George, and Dylan were all seated by each other. Lance's groomsmen Wes, Brad, and Patrick were to the left of Dylan. Amy's parents, Simon and Grace were busy talking to the wait staff as they were hosting the party for the couple. Amy's four other bridesmaids were the last to arrive to the party. They had arrived at the same time and took their seats in the last remaining chairs. The four girls were childhood best friends of Amy's. Once everyone had arrived and taken their seats, the waiters began to serve champagne, appetizers, and salads.

Two hours before they arrived at the restaurant, the entire wedding party practiced the procession and had a meeting about all the logistics for the wedding at the church it was to be held at. George and Marissa had been bickering in a corner after they had finished. Lance was really hoping that between then and the start of the ceremony, Detective Ross would not have a reason to question his mother because her anxiety and stress levels were at an all time high, and she looked like she was close to having a nervous breakdown. Lance was happy to see that Dylan was staying sober and looked well rested and healthy. He looked at the church before him and tried to smile. He wanted to feel happy, but there was so much darkness and guilt in his heart, that he felt ashamed about walking down that very aisle in twenty-four hours.

"Something the matter honey?" Amy asked Lance.

"Just lost in thought," Lance replied with a forced smile. "June 17 is tomorrow. Can I...tell you something?"

"Yes," Amy said.

"I was not completely honest," Lance began, "when I told you about June 17 being special to me because it was the month we briefly dated the very first time. I left out some minor details."

"Oh really?" Amy sounded puzzled.

"The truth is," he shuffled his feet and stared at the ground, "it was the day Claire and I became official."

"Excuse me?" Amy looked shocked.

"I know this will sound weird," he said. "But there was one point in my life where I truly believed Claire and I would marry. That day is special to me because Claire taught me that I could love and feel loved. I was a broken person back then. After dealing with the shock and stress she caused me post breakup, I grew as a person and became stronger. I was able to allow myself to reach back out to you and rekindle the fling we had a few summers before. June 17 taught me a lot, and led me on a journey to find you."

Amy started off with an appalled look, but then she smiled.

"I was about to kill you," Amy laughed. "But in a weird way, that was a really sweet thing for you to say. However, I am slightly irked that we will share that same anniversary."

"Thanks for understanding," Lance said. "I did a lot of bad things in the past, but I am changing. I am stronger, and I will be devoted to you. The past is the past."

"I love you," Amy responded.

Lance reached for the knife on the table. He pulled it up to his face and looked at himself in the reflection. Carefully he placed the blades on top of his filet mignon and sliced it into several pieces. He picked up one of the pieces with his fork and put it into his mouth.

"How's your steak?" Edward asked. "Mine is dry."

"It's fine," Lance said snapping back to reality.

"Who chose this restaurant for the rehearsal dinner?" Jill asked Amy.

"My mom," she replied. "We love this place."

Lance left the table halfway through his meal to use the restroom. He walked by the bar and saw a familiar face sitting at the bar and stirring a glass of whiskey with a straw. It was Detective Ross. He was wearing a cowboy hat. He locked eyes with Lance and picked up his glass into the air as if toasting to him. Detective Ross then drank his whiskey in one huge gulp. His face showed no signs of the alcohol burning down his throat. He nodded at Lance and tipped his hat, then turned away and walked out of the restaurant. Lance stared at him in shock.

Was he spying on my family? He thought.

When Lance returned to the table, Edward tapped his wine glass with his spoon.

"Ahem," he cleared his throat. "And now a toast to the bride and groom. The future Mr. and Mrs. Lance Avery."

"Here, here!" Wes replied while the entire dinner party followed suit and raised their glasses as well.

"I saw Detective Ross," Lance whispered to Amy. "That is seriously out of line."

"He's just doing his job," Amy said. "He has nothing on your mother."

"I know," Lance said, "but he believes Victoria Price was murdered. This is insane."

"The timing is not great, but we'll get through this. Let's think happy thoughts because tomorrow is the big day."

"Right," Lance smiled. "And then we are off to the Virgin Islands for our honeymoon."

After everyone had devoured their desserts, Simon paid the bill and thanked the guests for attending. Marissa did her best to force a happy smile and appear as if nothing was bothering her during Simon's speech. Everyone applauded for the couple-to-be.

"Make sure you are all rested up, and we will see you at four o' clock at St. Austin tomorrow," Marissa decided to chime in.

"Want to grab some drinks at the bar down the street?" Edward asked Lance. "Just us and the groomsmen."

"Sounds good," Lance replied. "Honey, you'll be at the cabin tonight, right?"

"Yeah," Amy said. "I need some peace and quiet before the big day."

"Ok," Lance said. "Jill is dropping you off at home first, correct?"

"Yes," she answered.

"Ok then. Well, I'll grab some beers with the boys," Lance said.

"Don't drink too much," she warned. "You don't want to be hung over for our wedding."

"Nah," Lance replied. "I'll be calling it an early night."

Lance, Edward, Dylan, Wes, Brad, and Patrick arrived at the neighboring bar called The Hangar. It was modeled after an airport hanger and had an aviation theme throughout the venue.

"First round is on me boys," Brad said while pulling out his credit card. "Can't believe our little Lance is going to be a husband in less than twenty four hours."

"It's crazy to think that you ended up with Amy in the long run," Edward said. "You dated briefly one summer and then after you and Claire broke up, you were back in Amy's heart. I think you should have been with Amy the whole time."

"No kidding," Lance said after taking a swig of the beer that Brad purchased for him.

"And your vacation starts right after," Dylan said. "The bank will miss you. Ha!"

"I'm sure it will," Lance replied. "Let's check out the rooftop bar."

The summer night in Austin was muggy. It had been warm earlier in the day, and even though the sun had set a few hours ago, its heat lingered in the still air of the thriving downtown Austin. The rooftop offered spectacular views of the high-rise condos and buildings in the city. In a distance, Lance could make out the capital building and beyond that he could see the bell tower that belonged to the University of Texas.

"Excuse me," a waitress came over to tap Patrick on his shoulder. "Is one of y'all named Lance?"

"I am," Lance said.

"Someone bought you a drink," she handed him over a cranberry vodka drink with a cherry garnish on the rim.

"Who?" he asked.

"Some lady. It appears as though she's gone," the waitress replied. "She looked like she dressed up nice for something."

Lance glanced at the glass and saw that there was a red lipstick stain on it as if someone had deliberately kissed the side of the glass. There was a note on a napkin on which the drink was served with that read "midnight" in ink.

"That's strange," Dylan whispered to Lance. "What does that mean?"

"I don't know, but I'm not drinking this," Lance said with unease.

"I'll have it," Patrick said.

Lance emptied the drink into a nearby trashcan then set the glass down on the table.

"Never take drinks from strangers," Lance said. "Remember what happened to me in Vegas?"

"Hmm," Edward said. "A little overly cautious now are we?"

"Yeah, a little," Lance admitted, but the note kept burning in the back of his mind as he tried to decipher what the message meant.

Something is going to happen at midnight, he thought.

"Let's just have one more drink," Lance said to his friends. "Then I need to head off to bed."

An hour later, Lance found himself driving to the outskirts of north Austin to surprise Amy at her cabin. The ride was anything but therapeutic. He could not help think that something would happen at his wedding, and someone was planning to sabotage it. He decided to distract his mind by going over his vows aloud in the car and trying not to think about how many lies were in them.

"Amy, I want to honor and love you till the day I die. Forever. For always. You are my soul mate and best friend. We've been through good and bad times, but at the end of the day God brought us together to be one in holy matrimony. I promise to always be there for you and be the best husband I can possibly be. There is no other woman in the world whom I could love because my heart belongs to you. Today I am giving you my heart. Today I am giving you my all. Today I am giving you my life. You will join my life and I will join yours and we will create a new chapter. I love you Amy Aberdeen."

Lance wiped a tear out of his eye. He knew that he really loved Amy, but deep down inside he was conflicted with the affair he had with Rose and how it made him feel alive.

Lance parked his car a mile away from the cabin so that the darkness of the night would conceal him and his surprise appearance act at Amy's side.

The walk felt like the miles. He loosened some of the top buttons of his dress shirt, as the air was sticky and warm. He then put on a black hoodie, which was in his trunk, and put the hood over his head. It was uncomfortable because it was not cold, but he figured it would help conceal him in the shadows. Aside from the sounds of wildlife in the woods on his left and right, the only other sound echoing into the night was the sound of his dress shoes clicking on the pavement of the road.

When he arrived at Amy's parent's cabin, he saw that the light in the upstairs bedroom was on. He could make out Amy's silhouette through the window. He smiled and his nerves began to get the best of him. He pulled out a brass key from his pocket and walked up the steps of the cabin. He inserted the key into the door and opened it quietly, then shut it closed as softly as possible once he was inside.

After a few minutes of eavesdropping, Lance hid behind a couch as Amy made her way down to the kitchen. She was on the phone with Jill. Amy made a sudden yell and dropped a glass that shattered on the floor, which then caused Lance to jump up from behind the couch. Amy confirmed to Jill on the phone that she saw something outside, but it had only been a shadow. Lance eyed the piano in the living room and walked over to it and began to play the *Wedding March*; there was sheet music for it propped on the piano.

Amy turned around quickly in shock and saw Lance in a black hood. Lance lowered the hood and smiled.

"LANCE!" she yelled. "What the hell are you doing here?"

"Hi Amy," Lance said. "I'm sorry for the surprise sweetie."

"You can't see me the night before!" Amy snapped. "It's bad luck! You're not supposed to see me until I walk down the aisle tomorrow."

Lance ignored her and kept playing the song. He then turned to her and winked.

"Walk down to me now honey," he said. "And feel free to take off your bath robe."

"You're so stupid," Amy said and her look of anger turned into a happy smile.

"You know you want to laugh," Lance teased.

"I'm mad at you," Amy said, but she began to laugh. "You scared the shit out of me."

"I love you," Lance said.

"Stop playing the *Wedding March* silly," Amy said, and she walked over to Lance and sat next to him and pushed his hands off. "Save that for tomorrow."

They exchanged a long passionate kiss. Lance put his hands on the ties of her robe, but Amy slapped them off.

"You should go," Amy said. "We're getting married tomorrow. This can wait until tomorrow night."

"You have me all hot and bothered," Lance said.

"That's your fault for coming here unannounced and scaring the crap out of me," Amy said.

"Looks like you did not need me to scare you," Lance said pointing at the broken pieces of glass on the floor.

"I imagined something in the bushes, and it scared me," Amy admitted.

"I can see that," Lance teased.

"Promise me you won't see me until I walk down the aisle?" Amy insisted. "You need to leave now, and I don't want to see you until then. Is that ok?"

"Fine," Lance said, and he kissed Amy on the lips. "I love you. I'm the luckiest guy in the world. I can't wait to marry you."

"Me too," Amy said. "Now get the hell out of my parents' cabin and let me have my last night alone."

"Ok," Lance sighed and he put his copy of the cabin key on the kitchen table. "See you tomorrow."

"Bye," Amy smiled.

Lance walked out of the country cabin and back into the darkness of the night, which was still silent except for the chirping of crickets and an occasional hoot from an owl. The air was still and humid. Lance looked up at the full moon in the cloudless sky and smiled.

249

I'll be a married man tomorrow, he thought.

Lance had to walk a mile down the road to where he had parked his car. The only light was from the full moon in the sky. There were no streetlights for miles.

Lance stopped dead in his tracks when he heard the snapping of branches and leaves brushing against something. Suddenly, he heard hurried footsteps hit the pavement of the road. Lance fell over backwards in shock and fell onto a bush. When he got up he saw the silhouette of an animal running across the road and into the woods.

"Crap," Lance cursed. "It was only a deer."

Lance brushed off dirt and leaves off his shirt and continued his walk in a faster pace to his car. Once he could see the shape of his car looming in the darkness, he began to jog faster to get to it. He pulled out his keys and clicked the remote to unlock it. The headlights blinked on and Lance shielded his eyes as the sudden appearance of light blinded him. Once his eyes adjusted to the light, he picked up his pace again and arrived at the door to his car. He reached for the door handle and instantly looked on the roof his vehicle. There was a single red rose that had been placed there.

"What the hell?" Lance whispered into the night and chills ran up his arms.

Lance pulled out his cell phone to call Amy, but before he did, he realized that Amy would not have been the one to leave a rose on his hood. Lance looked around with an eerie sense of foreboding. He could not see anything else in the vicinity that looked out of place.

Suddenly, the crickets stopped chirping as if they had been disturbed or scared by something. It was extremely silent, and not a single tree swayed as the air was still. Lance took a deep breath and decided to get into his car. He closed his door shut and hit the lock button. He put the keys into his ignition and turned the car on. The radio came on instantly and so did his headlights, which sent its high beams down the deserted road. The digital clock in his car read "11:59 PM."

Lance jumped at the sound of an animal crying in the distance. He heard hooves hitting the pavement. A fluffy, black and plump sheep ran across the road and into the woods. It's cries faded away just as it disappeared into the darkness.

What the...he thought.

Lance's heart began to race when he saw a person walk onto the road directly in front of him from the same direction that the black sheep had materialized from. It was a woman dressed in all black with a veil over her face.

Chapter Twenty-Two

"The widow..." Lance gasped with fear overcoming his emotions. "This can't be...a ghost?"

Lance put his car on reverse, and it made a strange noise as he backed up. He then put the car on drive and drove onto the road. He decided to drive in the opposite direction as the woman. He hit the gas pedal and started to speed, but there was a strange screech under his car. The smell of burnt rubber permeated the air. Lance looked at his rearview mirror and could no longer see the woman. He quickly opened his passenger door and looked under his car.

"Dammit!" Lance cursed when he realized his tires were flat.

He got out of the car and looked nervously around the vicinity before he assessed the damage to his tires.

"What the hell?" Lance uttered.

It turned out that all four of his tires had been slashed. His car was not drivable. He was startled by the sound of a bird chirping in the distance. Then a couple of birds flew out of a tree as if something had frightened them to take flight.

Lance reached for his phone to call for help, but he had no signal. He quickly got back into his car and locked all four doors. His mind began to race, but he was finally able to make sense of his situation. Someone deliberately did not want him to leave. Lance looked at his watch. It was midnight on the dot.

To Lance's relief, he saw a pair of headlights coming in his direction. Lance flashed his beams then turned on his hazards. The truck in the distance flashed its headlights too. When the truck was a few feet away from Lance's car, he realized it was a tow truck.

"What are the odds," Lance sighed with relief.

The truck made a U-turn and positioned itself in front of Lance's car. The driver walked out of the door and gave Lance a thumbs up.

"Oh my goodness, thank you so much!" Lance said when he stepped out of the car.

The driver was a woman who was wearing a baseball cap and a rain jacket that looked too big and too warm for her to wear during the summer night. The light was so bright that Lance had to get closer to make out the woman's face.

Lance's jaw dropped in surprise when he recognized who the woman was.

"Dana?!" Lance said in shock to his next-door neighbor.

"Lance," Dana said in a strange and uncertain voice.

She appeared to look nervous. Her fingers were fidgeting with her cellphone.

"What are you doing out here and why are you driving a tow truck?" Lance asked.

"Lance..." Dana was searching for words. "I, um. I'm sorry. I just. I was hired. Needed money."

Dana was uttering a bunch of words that were not really sentences. Lance was trying to understand.

"Do you have a second job working for a towing company?" Lance asked. "No need to feel shy or embarrassed about it."

"Right," Dana said sounding like she was not being honest.

Dana's eyes flickered to something behind Lance. Lance took notice immediately when her nervous glance unlocked with his eyes. Lance turned around and backed away closer to Dana suddenly.

Standing before him was the woman in the veil staring silently at Lance.

"Oh my God!" Lance gasped. "Dana, we need to run, I think that is the person that broke into my apartment! I have reason to believe—"

Lance stopped mid-sentence because the woman in the veil started laughing. Dana began to breathe heavily and looked as though she was going to be sick.

"What do you believe?" the woman in the black dress asked in a whisper.

"Who are you?" Lance asked, but his voice cracked with anxiety. "Are you the person who has been causing me trouble?"

The woman cackled and this time her laughter sounded menacing and evil. She reached for the veil over her face with her long black-gloved hands. She pulled the veil of her pillbox hat back to reveal her face.

"ROSE!" Lance yelled in shock, and then he moved away from Dana immediately because he knew they were friends.

"My name is not Rose," she said in a taunting voice that sounded as if she was enjoying Lance's shock.

"Who are you?" Lance asked with confusion, even though her voice sounded different, yet familiar.

The woman put her hands over her blonde hair and pulled it off. It was a wig. The woman's real hair was reddish-brown. The woman then began to pull pieces of her face off. It was as if her skin was being torn off, but Lance realized it was prosthetic make-up. The woman had finally pulled off her entire face and threw the pieces onto the road.

"Movie make-up is quite amazing. You can literally change your face and identity. Dana is quite an amazing artist," the woman said, and Lance reached for his chest in shock when he realized that the woman before him was his ex-girlfriend...

"*Claire...*" Lance gasped, and his heart began to beat faster. "It *was* you!"

"The restraining order is no longer in effect," Claire said. "I've been waiting a long time for the day you and I would reunite. And how perfect and ironic that it is on June 17. *Our* anniversary."

"But you've been stalking and harassing me," Lance said. "Even when the restraining order was in effect."

"I don't play by the rules," Claire said. "I've been watching you for a long, long time. I've even found my way back into your life."

"All those sessions...that moment we shared," Lance began to cry. "It was you? All-this-time? You tapped into my mind. I spilled out all my secrets."

"It was all part of my master plan," Claire said seriously, and she sounded very angry. "You screwed me up so much when you cut me out of your life because *you* cheated on me, and I found out! I was the one who was supposed to be walking down that aisle with you later today. It was supposed to be me. Not that bitch, Amy. She's pretty. I saw her through her cabin window a while ago. I really wished she would have died when I ran her off the road a few months back."

"You're beyond insane!" Lance said with anger. "Bat shit crazy!"

"I was crazy in love with you..." Claire said.

"And you were a part of this?" Lance turned to Dana.

"I hired her to work for me," Claire spoke on behalf of Dana who looked too scared to speak judging by the loss of color on her face.

"When we are done with you, she'll be rewarded and can go about her life as if nothing happened."

"What do you mean 'done' with me?" Lance asked nervously, and before Claire could answer, the sound of metal hitting his skull made a loud thud that echoed into the night.

"Well done Dana," Claire said. "You finally got the nerve to knock him out cold for me."

Lance was passed out on the ground. Both Claire and Dana began to tie up his arms and legs with rope. Claire pulled out a roll of duct tape and taped his mouth shut. She then pulled out a black bandana and used it as a blind fold to tie over his eyes.

"Ok, you're going to take his car and dump it into the river," Claire told Dana. "I don't care if it gets discovered later. I just don't want it to be found until after the wedding start time. My car is parked in the woods. Stay here with him for a bit. I'll go get my car and then you can help me lift him into the trunk. I will then take him to my home and will commence with my *closure*."

"Y-y-yes," Dana mumbled nervously.

When Claire returned to where Dana was with her own car, she saw that Lance's car had already been tied onto the tow truck. Claire got out of her car and gestured for Dana to help her lift Lance. Together they were able to carry him into the trunk of Claire's car. She closed it shut and turned to Dana.

"I'll be wiring you the money from a private account under someone else's name," Claire told Dana. "Fifty thousand dollars will be in your bank after tomorrow night. I think we should part ways now. You are welcome to continue your life here in Austin or move back to L.A. where you are really from. You have an amazing talent with make-up and Hollywood will probably want you back."

"I have your word that I will not ever be connected to this crime?" Dana demanded.

"You do," Claire replied. "I've waited nearly three years for this. I've carefully and artfully planned out this execution. Rose Finley does not exist. My office will be completely burned down tonight. It's the perfect murder, and there will be no proof that Claire Carpenter was ever here. I will make the murder look like Rose did it. People will search for her, but she will have vanished mysteriously. In time, they will learn that Lance had an affair with Rose and that will give them a suspect and motive."

"You're crazy, you know that?" Dana said nervously. "I mean to scheme this entire thing."

"Love makes us crazy," Claire said. "To be loved is something money cannot buy. Real emotions and a connection between two people is so rare and sometimes fated. Lance gave me my first love experience. And then he pulled it away and ripped my heart out. It made me very sick. Tonight, I take my revenge. Tonight I will win. Tonight I stand tall for every woman who has been disrespected, cheated, and lied to."

"Very well," Dana said. "It was *interesting* to work with you. Let's never contact each other again after this."

"Will do," Claire smiled, and she shook Dana's hand.

Lance's head felt as if it were about to explode. He wanted to put his hands over what he assumed was a bump on the back of his head, but his hands were tethered to what he assumed were bedposts. A bandana was tied over his eyes, and the knot on the back of his head was right over where he had been hit. He tried to shake his legs, but they were also tethered. He was spread eagle, and his skin felt very cold. He had apparently been stripped down to his boxer briefs. He felt a pair of hands rip off the duct tape that had sealed his mouth shut.

"Where am I?" Lance mumbled.

His heart began to race hard against his ribcage at the realization that he had been kidnapped by his ex girlfriend who had been posing as his therapist for months.

"I was right," Lance groaned. "I knew it was you doing all those crazy things. I saw you at the cemetery and you were caught on video walking around my apartment complex. What is wrong with you?"

There was no answer, but he could hear calm breathing coming from a corner of the room he was in. He knew she was standing by him.

"Claire, this is kidnapping," Lance panted. "Let me go!"

There was silence yet again. It hurt Lance's lips to talk as the tape that was previously on them, left them sore.

"Help!" Lance shouted. "HELP!"

"That's not necessary," Claire's voice chimed in. "Nobody will hear you tonight."

"Where am I?" Lance asked.

"The same bed we had sex on last week," Claire said in a very seductive whisper.

Lance shivered when he felt her cold fingers brush up and down his bare chest.

"You're still as sexy as the day we met at the sheep's meadow," she said. "It would be nice to go back to that ranch and have my way with you there, but the memory would bring me great pain. Did you see that beautiful black sheep I released into the wild earlier?"

"Nuts...you are nuts! You need to untie me," Lance demanded. "Now!"

Claire reached for the back of his head and untied the knot of the bandana so that he could see. He took in the room and saw her familiar decor; only he thought it belonged to a Rose Finley last time he was there. Claire was wearing a red silk bathrobe and staring at Lance as if he were her toy.

"I could take advantage of you," Claire said. "It wouldn't be the first time I used you without your consent."

"Huh?" Lance said sternly.

"In Vegas," Claire said. "I had my way with you in your hotel. I drugged your drink. You must have imagined it to be dream. I took you to your room from that strip club."

Lance's heart sank, and his mind raced to the memory of that bizarre evening.

"It was you!" Lance yelled. "I wasn't dreaming. You were really there! You...you raped me."

"Rape is such a negative word," she teased. "I took back memories from you that night. Or maybe I gave them back to you. It was I who orchestrated your brother's arrest. I posed as that woman on the plane that lost her chips. It was so much fun to ruin your bachelor party and to cause your brother to fall into a downward spiral to attend rehab. It was I who supplied his drugs.

I posed as his dealer. I made him get back into his drug habits and harassed him with blocked phone calls to scare him. It even affected you."

"You're sick," Lance spat.

"I'm not," Claire stated. "Oh, and paying that crazy homeless man to throw coffee at your face was so fun."

"You've been tormenting me all this time. I can't believe this," Lance cried.

"You can't?" Claire laughed. "You put a restraining order on me because I stalked and tormented you. You told the police and your lawyer about me. They investigated my life. I was smart and made sure they could find nothing."

"And you tried to run Amy off the road," Lance yelled. "You will go to jail."

"Like Victoria Price did?" Claire taunted. "She was innocent. Of course, she also became a hermit and strange as she aged. I coerced her to send your mom that bloody cow heart. I thought it would be fun to use her to take the pressure off accusations towards me. She agreed to it because I told her I'd get revenge and help put the real person that killed your father in jail. I know who it was."

"What?" Lance said in shock.

"I convinced Victoria Price to die. I tied the noose for her and staged her suicide," Claire said. "But in the end, her blood is on my hands. I made her die. She wanted to die, however. Your father's killer ruined her life forever and pointed the finger at her and threw her under the bus. Poor Victoria Price—she paid the price just like those newspaper headlines read, which I left at your doorstep."

"You're crazy," Lance said.

Claire walked over to her desk and picked up a tattered old book. Lance recognized it because he had set his car keys on that very same book when he had his sexual encounter with her the previous week.

"See this book?" Claire held it up before him. "It's a journal. Look at the name that is engraved on it, and read it out loud."

Lance looked at the small book. He felt like his heart was stuck in his throat. He could barely speak out the words written on the bottom right hand corner of it.

"Marissa Rebecca Avery."

"Your mom," Claire said. "She kept this journal that she started writing around the time she and your father were having a rough time. It was her way of venting, apparently. It's quite an interesting read. I'm so glad I walked into her apartment posing as a carpet cleaner and found it. It was like gold. She hid it very well. But as I watched your family and you for over the past couple of months, I realized that I could see what no one else could. She had a look about her as if she was hiding a deep, dark secret. I've bookmarked the entry that will explain everything. You'll never think of Marissa the same."

Claire opened the book to a page that she wanted Lance to read and held it a few inches away from his face. It was written in his mother's handwriting.

It had to be done. He was with that wench. They were fornicating. She's a dirty money-hungry skank. She ruined my marriage and took the love of my life away. She will pay for this. I still cannot believe I did it. It was so easy to make it look like an accident.

I arrived at the open house we were prepping to show. He was drinking whiskey out of the bottle. That drunk. He greeted me with his obnoxious and fake smile. He tried to hug me, but I backed away. When he turned around, I pushed him right into the pool. He yelled and cursed at me. He probably cared more about his expensive suit than me in that instant. I don't know what came over me. He tried to come up for air, but I pushed his head under the water. It was in the deep end of the pool. He was so belligerent that he could not fight me off as I kept his head submerged. I wanted to stop. I never meant to do it, but I couldn't. I don't know what came over me, but I let the seconds pass as he struggled for life and fresh air.

Then the water was still. He stopped splashing and gurgling. He was gone. Just like that. I was so scared after the moment it happened. I began to panic. I knew Victoria Price would be coming to see him that night. I wanted her to find his body. I would pin the death on her. She would face the consequences. Both of them would be out of my life forever. I would keep this secret with me. Forever.

Lance was horrified. His mom really did it. Detective Ross' intentions of questioning her were solidified. Then anger began to course through his veins and tears began to flood out of his eyes. His mother was a cold-blooded killer. She blamed it on a woman whose life became ruined and ended in a staged death. His mother had been a liar this whole time.

"Hurts doesn't it?" Claire teased. "I knew your family had a whole lot of crazy, but this just takes the cake. If you weren't messed up before, you are now."

Claire walked over to her vanity and pulled a red rose from a vase.

"I love roses. He loves me, he loves me not..." she said playfully as she began to pluck out the rose petals and threw them on top of Lance's body. "It was exhilarating to lock you and Edward in that old abandoned zoo with a lion. You saw me there too. I left red lipstick messages on the wall. Oh, and speaking of messages, I'm sure you saw the invisible ink ones on your apartment wall. The quotes were from *The Scarlet Letter*."

Claire reached for another book on her desk that had red letter A's on the cover. It was a copy of *The Scarlet Letter.*

She continued, "And the bees in Amy's father's bouquet of roses, was a little extra nudge to knock you over the edge. I even sent an email to Jill anonymously to attempt to stop you from marrying Amy—the engagement was mistake. It should have been me."

"You're insane," Lance said. "You even compared me to my father when you wrote 'Like father, like son.' How insensitive of you."

"Your father died because he was an adulterer," Claire teased. "And his dirty slut of a son will do the same. I mean, I made you fall for me again when you thought I was Rose Finley.

261

You cheated on your wife-to-be. You are not honest, and you do not deserve to have anything."

"So you're going to kill me?" Lance asked. "As if that will solve anything. You'll never have me. So what's the point?"

"Revenge, asshole," Claire cursed.

"I'm sorry I'm a horrible person," Lance broke down. "I don't even deserve Amy. I'm a bad person."

"Why couldn't you have just called me back, replied to my emails, or texts?" Claire asked. "You cut me off high and dry and moved out of Seattle."

"I was afraid of you," Lance cried. "You yelled at me and—"

"Shut up!" she cut in. "You deserved those harsh words for sexting some woman you used to date while you and I were together. And that was not the first time you cheated on me. I had transcripts of your text message history. You were lying to me so much. I trusted you. I gave you my heart and put down my wall. You couldn't be there for me, and you went to seek sexual arousal from some stupid hoe in another state over Facebook."

"This is why I was afraid of you," Lance gushed. "You are crazy. You've kidnaped and restrained me to a bed. You've raped me. You've stalked me, my girlfriend, my brother, and my mother."

"You abandoned me," Claire stammered. "I catered my life around you. I made you feel at home. We traveled places together. We could have been engaged or married by now. This day could have been our fifth year anniversary. We could have had a home. We could have had a dog. You were my everything. You lied and disgraced me behind my back. Lance Avery, you are dead to me. You are rotten. You are putrid."

Lance could not stop himself from crying. He knew that he was unkind to Claire and that he had failed her in their relationship. He knew that one day all the dark skeletons and his childhood tragedies would catch up to him. He looked at Claire and wondered if he had been a good boyfriend, would she have gone crazy. He knew there were parts of her that were not normal. She had a temper when she was drunk. Lance felt comforted knowing that in the end of the day, they would never have lasted forever because she was unhinged and abnormal…and so was he.

Claire walked out of the room and returned a few minutes later with a large kitchen knife. When Lance saw the knife, his eyes widened in shock. He began to fight his restraints in hopes that he could free himself. He did this to no avail. The ropes were tied very well.

"Imagine how embarrassing it was to be served with a restraining order outside my workplace?" Claire taunted. "It was the ultimate bitch slap to me. You undermined our relationship and threw away anything I meant to you all because you could not deal with your guilt. You made yourself a victim by restraining me from ever contacting you. I was the victim. Not you."

"I'm a broken man," Lance mustered the courage to speak. "I know that. I tried hard to change. I'm sorry I could not be the man of your dreams. I'm sorry that I failed you. I know that you have had to live with anger and embarrassment. I know I abandoned you. I take full responsibility. But I beg of you to show mercy."

"There's no way the both of us are walking out of this apartment," Claire spat. "You know too much. And why would you want to go back into the real world? Your mother will be in cuffs after today. I'm going to drop off this lovely journal at the police station."

"They'll find out it was you," Lance said. "I've had an officer by the name of Grant and a detective named Ross in on my suspicions that you were possibly harassing me for the last half a year—but you already know that."

Claire started laughing. She sat on the corner of the bed and gently stroked Lance's leg.

"What's so funny?" Lance snapped.

"Aren't you aware that a man and woman entered your mother's apartment and posed as carpet cleaners?" Claire asked. "It was myself, and the man was Detective Ross."

"What?" Lance struggled against his restraints, but failed.

"Detective Ross will be getting a very nice payday and an amazing promotion for finally solving the murder of your father. I will also pin Victoria's death on your mother. He'll have both cases closed and be the town hero. And Rose Finley will have disappeared, and he will work on trying to find her—but he won't. And he knows that since he's been working for me. See, Lance, it has been a perfect plan all along. I've had people working for me on the inside. It's the perfect crime. I will never be caught. Nobody will ever know the truth or be able to find Rose. I will get away and live happily ever after—with my husband."

"That's right, you're married!" Lance spat. "And you're sick."

"And I have two young stepchildren from my husband's first marriage," Claire teased. "My life is pretty normal and safe."

"You're sick. Ross is sick. Dana is sick. This is all messed up," Lance cried.

"Your mother is sick too," Claire added. "I learned all your dirty secrets and then learned a few more things along the way. It has been one hell of a journey, and my time spent between Austin and Seattle the last few months have been exhausting. I wasn't traveling to Dallas on weekends. My husband thinks I've been traveling for work during my Monday through Thursdays and an occasional weekend here or there. He's a wonderful man and very wealthy. He'll never know I've taken a couple hundred thousand dollars to pay off my accomplices. Life will be picture perfect from here on out, now that my plan for revenge has come full circle."

Claire left the bed and reached for the kitchen knife she had been holding earlier. She brandished it with her fingers and looked at her reflection in it.

"So strange to be myself again," Claire said. "I can't tell you how strange it is to be two different women every week and have that make-up put on. It stayed on well. Even when you and I were intimate, my wig or prosthetics never came off. Dana did well."

Claire walked over to the right side of the bed and put the knife on the nightstand. She reached for a roll of duct tape that was in the nightstand's drawer and tore a piece off.

"Any last words?" Claire asked. "Let's make this quick. I need your blood."

"Go to hell," Lance yelled. "AAARGHH—"

Lance began to yell at the top of his lungs, but Claire slapped on the duct tape to quiet him. He moaned and attempted to yell, but he was barely audible.

"Your bride will get to see you," Claire said. "I have the most poetic plan for you. She'll find a casket where you both should have been standing at the alter hand in hand. Lance Avery, today I take your life away from you as you took my heart and ruined it."

Tears began to flow out of Lance's eyes. He moaned an inaudible plea for forgiveness that could not be heard. He began to shift and struggle frantically, but he was tethered very well. Claire began to cry as she watched him struggle for freedom on the bed.

"Love is beautiful. Love is ugly. When our hearts break, so does our mind, and we do crazy things for love. This breaks my heart baby," she said softly. "We *will* have a future together."

Claire raised the knife up over her head with two hands and held it over Lance's heart. She took a deep breath before continuing with her plan.

Chapter Twenty-Three

Marissa Avery and Grace Aberdeen were walking out of the hallway of the chapel in rushed footsteps. Their heels echoed down the hallway, which led to the chapel where hundreds of guests were waiting anxiously for the ceremony to begin. Marissa felt her phone vibrate in her purse. She pulled out her phone and read a text message that came from a blocked ID. The message read, "I know you killed Jeremy Avery."

Marissa's nerves got the best of her, and she began to shake with fear.

"What are we going to say to the guests?" Grace asked.

"I suppose we should say that the wedding is going to be postponed," Marissa said shakily. "I think it would best to call it off right now."

"But so many people traveled to be here today," Grace pleaded. "Where the hell is your son?"

"I do not know, Grace!" Marissa snapped.

Marissa began to fear that the reason Lance was missing was because he may have learned about her secret. Someone had anonymously harassed her in a text. She knew that someone had been sending the police information that Victoria Price was not her late husband's killer.

"Why don't you address the guests?" Marissa suggested. "I'm going to step outside to try and call my son."

"Ok," Grace obliged.

Marissa stepped outside of the church and wandered into a garden courtyard that was located on the side of the building. She attempted to call Lance a few times, but it went to voicemail after a few rings.

"Where are you?" she said to herself.

Marissa looked at the other end of the courtyard and realized she was not alone. There was a woman dressed in all black wearing a pillbox hat and a veil. Marissa thought it was a strange thing to wear to a wedding, but then she figured this woman was not a guest.

"Are you attending a funeral?" Marissa awkwardly asked the woman. "Because I believe you're at the wrong church."

The woman did not speak. She stood up from a bench she was sitting on and walked away to the back of the church. Marissa was curious to follow her, but a sudden rush of wedding guests exiting the church distracted her. There were angry and confused murmurs coming from the crowd.

"Mrs. Avery?" Brad said when he saw that she was alone. "What's going on? I heard nobody can locate Lance."

"I don't know," Marissa began to cry.

"Should I call the cops?" Brad asked.

"No, that won't be necessary," she said. "I have dealt with enough cop visits ever since the death of Victoria Price."

"Honey!" George also appeared at the courtyard after leaving the queue of frustrated wedding guests.

"I was looking for you," he said. "Any luck?"

"None," she replied.

"Mom!" Dylan had also joined them. "This isn't like Lance. Maybe something happened to him?"

"They're clearing out the decorations," George said. "They are wasting no time. It's almost as if this wedding was never planned. They have an early service tomorrow, so they wanted to make sure that everything was picked up and taken care of."

"Hey, what's going on?" Brad asked, and he pointed at two police cars that pulled up in the driveway of the church.

A few lingering wedding guests stuck around out of curiosity to see why the police had shown up. Grace came running out of the church and called to the cops.

"Did somebody tell you that we might have a missing person?" Grace asked. "The groom did not show up, and we can't seem to locate him."

Officer Grant and Detective Ross came out of their cars. Detective Ross spoke first.

"Actually, we are here on official police business," Ross said, and he caught Marissa's eye.

Marissa began to breathe hard.

"Are you ok?" George asked.

"What's the matter mom?" Dylan asked with a startled look on his face.

Detective Ross and Officer Grant walked up to courtyard. Grace and a few wedding guests trailed behind them.

"Marissa Avery," Officer Grant said. "You are under arrest for the murders of Victoria Price and Jeremy Avery."

"What?" George said in outrage.

"Excuse me?" Dylan's face contorted with rage as if he had just been slapped.

Detective Ross pulled out Marissa's journal and showed it to her.

"This was sent to our office," Detective Ross said. "I'm sure you are aware of what its contents hold?"

Marissa began to cry.

"I did not kill Victoria!" she bawled.

Officer Grant continued, "You have the right to remain silent. Anything you say can and will be used against you in a court of law. You have the right to an attorney, and if you cannot afford an attorney, one will be appointed to represent you. You can choose to exercise these rights at anytime."

"This must be some kind of sick joke," George gasped.

Grant began to handcuff Marissa.

"That's my wife!" George spat. "Get your hands off her. She is not a murderer. Victoria Price killed my brother!"

"Victoria Price was framed by Marissa," Detective Ross said. "We have proof. There is a journal entry in this book of hers that explains in black and white what she did. She drowned Jeremy Avery and we have reason to believe that she may have recently silenced Victoria Price and made it look like a suicide."

"But that book was stolen from her apartment!" Dylan snapped. "Wait a minute! It was you!"

"Excuse me?" Detective Ross said taken aback.

"I thought you looked familiar," Dylan said. "You and some woman posed as carpet cleaners, and you must have stolen this book when you entered. That's illegal. You had no warrant."

"Mr. Avery," Detective Ross said sternly to Dylan, "I would keep your mouth shut if I were you. An accusation like that will land you in jail for the night. Grant—let's take her to get booked."

George was in shock. He read the entry that was in Marissa's journal when Detective Ross handed it to him. He dropped the book on the ground in shock and fell to his knees. He gave Marissa a look of pure hatred. Dylan then picked up the book as well and began to cry with every sentence he read. Grace was crying silently on Brad's shoulder, but was soon comforted by her husband Simon who had come out of the church looking flustered and angry. His anger dissipated at the site of Marissa being taken into a police car.

Detective Ross and Marissa were alone in his car as he drove it to the downtown station. Marissa stopped crying. She was staring blankly at the sky out of her window in the backseat. She finally made eye contact with Detective Ross through the rearview mirror and spoke.

269

"Someone tipped you," Marissa said. "It wasn't anonymous. I know that you know who told you. And if my son was telling the truth, and it was you and some woman that came into my house to find this journal, then you've been a shady law detective."

"You have no room to speak Marissa," Detective Ross said. "It's over. You have no proof and nobody will ever believe you because she made sure that the plan would be full proof."

"Who is *she*?" Marissa asked through gritted teeth.

"The woman that texted you earlier," Detective Ross said. "She's everywhere and nowhere at the same time. She's all knowing. She's the one who finished off Victoria, but it was all so that you could get a taste of your own medicine. Now you'll see how it feels to be framed for a murder you did not commit. However, you did kill your ex husband and that blood is on your hands forever."

"If you know someone killed Victoria," Marissa said sternly, "then why would you let that person run loose."

"That person has given me a valuable reward, and now I'm going to be a hero and finally solve the murder of Jeremy Avery after so many years of setbacks and misleading information," he taunted.

"You're a crooked cop," Marissa spat.

"I'm a detective," he corrected her. "And you're an evil woman. There won't be any fancy clothes and parties inside the confines of jail."

"My son Lance is missing too," Marissa began to cry again. "He needs to be found."

Amy, Jill, and Edward returned to the church after they realized that Lance's phone GPS, which they had tracked by using his computer at his apartment, pinpointed that his phone was at the place he should have originally been at.

They walked into the church and entered the chapel. The soft orange glow from the setting sun was the only light source inside the empty chapel.

"What the hell?" Edward said when he spotted an out of place object down the aisle at the alter.

"Is that a coffin?" Amy asked in shock.

"Are they planning a funeral tonight in lieu of the canceled wedding?" Jill added in disgust.

"This is some kind of joke right?" Amy said, and she began to cry. "My parents keep calling me, but I'm too distraught to talk to them right now."

"I'm going to try Lance again," Edward said while reaching for his phone.

There was a muffled ringtone coming from the direction of the coffin. Edward ended the call, and the ringtone stopped simultaneously. Amy, Jill, and Edward shared a look of concern. Without another word, they made their way down the aisle.

"There's something on top of the coffin," Jill whispered. "A rose."

When they were ten feet away from the coffin, they saw the rose. It was on top of a music sheet. Amy recognized the music on the sheet as the *Wedding March*.

"What the hell?" Edward gasped.

Amy continued to cry. Her heart was racing with what she felt she was about to discover. Amy pushed the rose and music sheet off the coffin. It fell onto the white carpet below. Amy sobbed and opened the coffin.

Amy, Jill, and Edward all gasped in unison. Lance's clothes that he wore the previous evening at the wedding rehearsal were neatly folded in the coffin along with his cell phone. There were bloodstains on his clothes and on the cushions of the casket. The cell phone went off again. Edward instinctively reached for it and saw the screen. "Dylan" was calling.

Amy collapsed and fell to the ground.

Edward answered the cell phone, "Hello?"

"Lance?" came the rushed voice of Dylan. "Wait, who is this?"

"Edward," he replied with a hoarse voice as he was holding back the urge to breakdown and cry. "We think Lance was murdered, but there is no body. Just his blood-stained clothes and his cell phone."

A woman wearing a red dress that clashed brilliantly with her red hair, found herself walking down a sidewalk with two pieces of luggage in tow. A taxi had dropped her off after a long trip from the airport. She wheeled the luggage up a driveway to a beautifully well kept two-story home in a very wealthy neighborhood. She rang the doorbell and heard a dog bark from inside. A man opened the door and flashed a huge smile at her. A dog ran out and started licking the woman's heels.

"Claire," he said. "Welcome home babe."

"Hi honey," she said and gave him a kiss. "This will be the last time I travel for work. Work has been murder. I need to spend more time with the kids."

"Let's go out for dinner tonight. Just you and me," Claire's husband suggested. We'll get a babysitter to take care of the girls."

"That sounds great, but I have a quick errand to run before. When I'm done, let's go enjoy ourselves at a nice dinner out," she said. "It's going to be nice to have things feel normal again. It's so good to be back in Seattle."

The next few months were very difficult for everyone that was involved with the Avery's. Marissa pleaded guilty and was sentenced to life in prison on several charges. George Avery was so ashamed that he had been living with a murderer all this time that he decided to become a recluse and kept to himself at the penthouse he once shared with Marissa. Marissa was so overwhelmed with depression in jail and for the loss of her son that she stopped talking to anyone, even her cellmates.

Amy began counseling and therapy sessions shortly after Lance's disappearance. Detective Ross had informed her that they suspected his therapist Rose Finley had killed him. On the same day of his disappearance, her apartment room was torched and burned. Her office was also the victim of arson. There were not many clues left about the life of Rose Finley, but some neighbors had confirmed that Lance had visited her apartment in recent weeks. Lance's cellphone records were used to determine that they had had an affair because of several calls he had made to her outside of office hours. Lance's body had never been recovered, but the fact that his clothes and phone were found in a coffin, made it evident that his killer left a clear message for his family. The blood stains on his clothing were tested and matched his DNA. It was presumed his body might have been burned to ash in Rose's office fire. Days after the incident, Lance's car was found sunken at the bottom of Lake Austin.

The news of Lance's infidelity struck a blow in Amy's heart. She was angry yet conflicted about the mourning of her deceased fiancé. Edward and Jill played a role in keeping her comforted so that she would not become too depressed, but even they were having a hard time coping.

Dylan began to use drugs again out of stress from his mother's arrest and his brother's murder. He was so angry at Marissa that he vowed to never visit her in jail or talk to her again. George had made the same vow.

Days became weeks, weeks became months, and months became a year. Nobody had ever heard from or seen Rose Finley. It was as if she did not exist.

Claire bid farewell to her husband and stepdaughters as they set off on an annual road trip to the Grand Canyon. Claire made an excuse that she had a presentation to work on for her job, and that she needed the time alone to focus on it. Once her family had left, she began to pack all of her belongings into her car. She filled several purses with cash and put two passports in her pocket. She pulled out a book on hypnotherapy as well as a blank CD that was labeled "Hypnosis" from her underwear drawer and placed it in her luggage. Once all of her clothes and items that she deemed necessary to take with her were packed into her SUV, she locked the door of her home she had been living in for three years.

"It was a nice life for a while," Claire sighed. "But it's not the life for me."

Claire got into her SUV and drove out of her home's gated community without a glance back. She drove up the coast to a house that her husband owned near the Puget Sound. She parked her car and looked around. The neighboring homes were vacant, which was normal as most of the homes near the water were vacation or weekend homes. Claire unlocked the door and entered the home. It was quiet upon her arrival. She pulled out another set of keys to unlock a door that was double bolted in the kitchen. After she unlocked it, she walked into the room and down a set of stairs to a basement. There was a TV on and a bed directly across from it. There was a man with shoulder length black hair lying on the bed staring at the TV as if he were entranced by it.

"Ahem," Claire cleared her throat.

The man turned over and looked at Claire with a glazed look in his eye.

"Did you take your *special* medication Lance?" she asked sweetly.

"I did honey," Lance replied, and he sounded hoarse.

"Good boy," Claire said. "I think you've been cooped up down here for far too long. It's time we get you some fresh air. It has been months since you've been out.

Lance responded, "I'm hungry."

"We can get some burgers on the way to Canada," Claire said.

"I have the car packed and a fake passport for you," Claire said lovingly. "We can finally be together *forever.*"

"I am glad I can finally make you happy," Lance said. "I love you very much."

"Good," Claire replied. "That is exactly what I wanted to hear."

Claire reached over to kiss Lance passionately. He kissed her back with a feverish hunger and put his arms around her. Then, they made their way out of the house and to the driveway. Claire opened the car door for Lance, and he entered and buckled himself into his seat. He gave her a smile that she returned. Claire entered the car on the driver's side and began their journey to Canada. She reached for her CD labeled "Hypnosis" and put it in the disc drive of her car. Before she pressed play, she turned to Lance and said a few words.

"You and I will always be the black sheep in this world," Claire said while placing one hand on his lap. "But we are going to run away and be free to graze in our own meadow. We will live happily ever after. The end."

About the Author

Photo: Dexter Brown

A.J. was born in Laredo, TX. At age 6, he began writing his own imaginative stories in notepads while in the first grade. As a teenager, he became interested in telling his stories on film. He began shooting his own mini-movies on his father's camera. His next dream was to work with movies in Hollywood. Living in the small city where he grew up, he believed the road ahead of him to lead him to those dreams would be difficult. After graduation from high school, he attended the University of Texas at Austin where he was accepted into the film program.

College came and went. They were the best years of his life. Now, it was time to face reality: the real world. Two weeks after graduation, A.J. was living in Los Angeles, CA and looking to break into the entertainment industry. He had many internships in college that were vital in helping set in motion his career. He landed his first job working for MTV. A.J. is currently working in the film industry at Paramount Pictures.

www.aj-mayers.com

@aj_mayers

@ajmayers

Made in the USA
Lexington, KY
12 November 2016